What the Shadows Say

Fred Melden

What the Shadows Say

What the Shadows Say

No portion of this book may be reproduced or used in any manner whatsoever without the express written consent of the author, except for brief quotations used in book reviews.

This is a work of fiction. All events, people, businesses and events mentioned in this book are fictitious. Any resemblance to actual events, businesses or people, living or dead, is purely coincidental

ACKNOWLEDGMENTS

Any writing of substantial length is the product of contributions from multiple individuals. First, I'd like to thank the observations and suggestions of the members of the Portland Writers Workshop. Their collective talents and experience, as well as their generosity and conscientiousness, have improved the quality of both the material and its arrangement within this book. I'd also like to thank the several writers of the Knowland Write-In collective, whose many suggestions and observations were of inestimable value in providing new insights. And last, but certainly not least, thank you Marla Perry for your time and assistance in improving this collection.

Contents

Success

Dr. Stenwick's confident smile should have reminded them of a used car salesman, but neither of them could see it. For one thing, Kirk Walters was himself a salesman, which paradoxically made him more susceptible to the incantations of salesmanship. And for another, Trisha Walters was a technician in a chemical laboratory, for which she was perfectly suited. Her forte was formulas and numbers, not reading people.

But all things considered, it would not have affected their decision. They wanted to believe. And they certainly weren't going to deny their son every advantage for his future.

"Will it increase Lenny's IQ?" she asked.

The doctor leaned back, as if dispensing his expertise to a congregation. "IQ is a contentious category. There are actually different kinds of intelligence. It's been shown that a high standard IQ does not guarantee success in climbing the ladder of life. A person needs something more. Political skills, well-to-do parents, even good looks improve a person's chances in life. But the biggest factor for attaining the American dream is competitiveness, that inner drive, the insistence on not accepting second place."

Kirk nodded. "That's exactly what our sales manager told us at our last meeting."

"Does it leave a scar?" she asked.

"Only a tiny one," the doctor replied. "Age four is the optimum time in a child's life, both psychologically and physically. It's the time he'll begin to learn about social interaction, and when the skin still rejuvenates well. The hole in the skull will be a mere quarter inch, and after implantation, we fill it in with powdered bone material. We only need to make a small incision in the scalp. Once the skin grows together, it's almost impossible to see."

The Walters were following the path of many affluent couples who took advantage of brain implants. It was their parental obligation to prepare their children for successful careers with all the associated perks. College? That was just a start, all about the diploma – a kind of career visa that allowed workers to pretend they weren't migrant workers picking paychecks in some absentee landlord's fields. However, the overseers in the upstairs offices looked for something more, that suit-and-tie aggressiveness that distinguished their best from the rest of the herd.

"What is the lifetime of the chip?" Kirk asked.

"They last at least 20 years, but the chip only directs the growth of neuronal connections. Once those structures are established – about age 18 – the chip itself is no longer needed."

"One more question. Why this particular model? I've heard some good things about the Juggernaut 7 and the Einstein 4F."

Dr. Stenwick's smile broadened as he leaned forward. "The Einstein 4F is an older design, focused purely on abstract intelligence. Children who were implanted with it are now starting their careers. They've all chosen nerdy professions." He instantly regretted his word choice. He looked directly at Trisha. "Forgive the term, but I'm sure you want what every parent wants – to have your children do better than yourselves."

She paused, before snapping, "Of course."

Stenwick continued. "To answer your question, Mr. Walters, the lifetime earnings of children implanted with the Einstein 4F will be very decent, but hardly spectacular. And given the price of the procedure, I'm sure you want to weigh the return on your investment."

"Exactly what I tell my own clients," Kirk replied.

"The Juggernaut 7 is a good product, but in my estimation, does not quite equal the Viper 3000. For one thing, it's level of aggressiveness is 12 percent less than the Viper. And the Viper 3000 is the only brain implant endorsed by the American Wrestling Foundation. Given the cost of the medical procedure and hospitalization, and the fact that insurance companies won't cover it, you might as well spend a little more to get the best."

"Well, that makes sense." Kirk looked at his wife. "You want to discuss it at home?"

"I don't think that's necessary." Her voice still had an edge.

Dr. Stenwick smiled, relaxed as a gambler whose horse just crossed the finish line. "You won't regret it. One more thing. I suggest you start calling him *Leonard*, rather than *Lenny*. It will improve his self-image. Now let's see when we can schedule this..."

***

Some 20 years later, Leonard Walters joined Valhalla Yacht Corporation. Of course, his co-workers also had implants, most of them the identical Viper 3000 model. Like the *de rigeur* $4000 suit and the $800 briefcase, it both identified the upcoming sales champions, and evened the odds between them.

As with all the other Viper 3000 alumni, the spouse had to be carefully evaluated. Leonard didn't bother with dating coaches, but instead utilized the services of

Sandra Knowles, a career consultant. "Another Viper 3000 would not be a good fit. Think of it as a musical chord. The notes are in harmony, but different. Besides, today's corporate managers are accustomed to subordinates' aggressive spouses. They automatically discount their flattery and supposed fealty to the company. If you want a spouse who stands out, I suggest aiming for someone who projects friendliness, who appears welcoming, rather than tactical or conniving. My advice is to seek a spouse with either a DoorKey-R or GladHand 4.3 implant."

"What do they do?"

"The DoorKey increases the impulse to form mutual alliances with others. It was derived from the Accomplice 1.0, which was discontinued because it created a tendency to join in criminal conspiracies. The GladHand provides its owner with the skills and inclination to be pleasant, and put others at ease, even in the most strained social circumstances."

Leonard's search on the LadderClimbers dating site netted three potential candidates. He dated them all over a period of two months, but none of them seemed suitable. One needed plastic surgery to match the photoshopping of her online image, and the others did not appeal to him personally.

Then Sandra Knowles called. "This morning, I met with a couple who want their daughter to marry into money. She's well-schooled and totally charming. And one more thing. She has a GladHand implant."

And that's how Leonard met and married Cecilia Vandershan. She had been raised for the upper crust via private schools, tutors and Vassar College. Though reasonably attractive, her frame was a bit too short and muscular to qualify for trophy-wife status. However, her face was lovely and always displayed a smile, her side-swept hair was elegant, and she had an ability to seamlessly dovetail her interests into his.

There was one hiccup at the beginning of their marriage, some discord over their new home. Narrowly focused, he had worked with the architect without consulting her.

"Really? You want our house to look like a boat?" Her hands were on her hips, for her an unusually inelegant posture.

"Not just a boat. A yacht. It will be a great marketing tool. Everyone will ask about it. Neighbors and visitors will consider buying boats. It's the perfect advertisement."

"You want to ruin the design for a few sales?"

"You don't understand how success works. It will be a good conversation starter. More important, it will impress the boss."

She eventually calmed down, her habitual smile returned, and she gracefully acquiesced, though she did draw the line at putting the company logo on the front door.

He did have to coach her a bit on impressing his boss, Benton Collier. For instance, at parties, she was something of a queen bee. By default, that role should have gone to Benton's wife, Kyrie. But Kyrie's assertive interruptions – always with a stick-on smile – could only temporarily disperse the crowd surrounding Cecilia.

Leonard finally had to say something. "Honey, you need to avoid drawing too much attention to yourself."

"Drawing attention? I'm only being a good host."

"You do the same at others' houses. It's irritating to Kyrie."

"Kyrie is just jealous. She's also...I hate to say it, but she bores people. That's why people talk with me. Why does it matter?"

"Remember, she massages Benton's balls, and he's holding mine."

She winced at his crude metaphor, then immediately smiled. "I understand, but dear, I can't tell people not to talk with me. It would be rude. I certainly never try to exclude her. She's just... boring."

"Then keep close to her."

"Close? Like, snuggling up to an iceberg?"

"That iceberg can sink our ship. Don't forget that. We can't afford her resentment. Share the center with her."

"Very well." She paused for several seconds. "You know, Leonard, your friends are probably saying the same thing to *their* spouses. 'Don't hang around Cecilia. You need to pretend you're interested in Kyrie.'"

"Not *probably* – absolutely certain. And they're not my friends."

"Sorry. Your coworkers."

"No. My rivals. Remember – every month our sales get compared. Even coming in second turns into a slap across the face. And third and below? A kick in the butt."

"What about the lowest?"

"Oh, they get fired, of course."

She opened her mouth, but was silent for several seconds. "Fired? Really? Good God, Leonard. What kind of a company does that?"

"A profitable one. And, I might mention, a high-paying one."

"Leonard, that's a horrible way to live. I don't understand how you can spend day after day holding those kinds of feelings inside."

"I could go to work for a less dynamic company, but my earnings would drop. And frankly, I enjoy the competition, the kick-ass pressure. Keeps me on my toes. Besides, I'm in line to replace Benton when he moves up."

More than Leonard realized, more than Cecilia would admit, she was unnerved by his comment about earnings. Her parents had drained most of their inheritance cultivating her like a bonsai, shaping her for the upper crust. Despite her conscious evasions, her stomach tightened at any reminder of her life's dependence on wealth. No – not exactly her life; her lifestyle, which had swallowed her identity. She was gracious, smoothly pleasant, welcoming even to boors – not only an effect of her implant, but also because of her station in life, equally implanted by years of habituation. And despite the trite narratives of both rich and poor, deep within, she knew the truth. Her and her husband's circle, even her sense of self, was a sandstone arch held aloft by tall green columns. Without that, who would she be?

***

A week later, Leonard sat in Benton Collier's office, pretending to listen to the boss reciting the previous month's sales figures. He wondered if he had miscalculated. *'Perhaps not a Viper 3000. He's too easygoing. Or perhaps he's just good at faking it. The Pacino 9?'*

Benton finished reading the figures and dismissively tossed the papers on his cluttered desk. "I'm disappointed, Leonard. You dropped from first to third in one month, behind both Laura and David. Can you explain it?"

Leonard had prepared himself for the reprimand. "No, I cannot. And you should not want me to."

Benton leaned his chair back, a smile barely visible. "And why is that?"

"Because it would sound too much like an excuse. I don't make excuses. The truth is, I've examined every encounter that did not turn into a sale – at least, not yet – and I've asked myself what I might have done with each to improve the chances of bringing it to home plate."

"And your conclusion?"

"As you know, Benton, I've been in this business for years. I know what mistakes to avoid. In these self-reviews, I found not a single flaw in my approaches, my presentations, or my closing scripts. I've decided that I have to push on the price more intensively."

"Such as?"

"The next time a sale seems in peril, I'd like to offer an extra discount, and take half of it out of my commission."

"An admirable sacrifice, Leonard, but where would we get the other half?"

Leonard attempted to make his smile appear sincere. "The company will make a profit on the sale. It seems only fair that we each share the burden equally."

Benton didn't bother appearing sincere. With a reptilian smile, he said, "Laura and David didn't require any sacrifice from the company."

"So, you're suggesting the entire discount should come out of my commission?"

"I'm not suggesting anything, Leonard. You were suggesting. Any side deal you work out with our clients is entirely between you and them. You just need to get your numbers up."

"Okay, Benton. Will do."

After Leonard had departed, Benton considered their interchange. If Leonard regained first place in sales, Benton could pressure others to copy him, kicking back part of their commissions. Sales would increase without cost to the company. In effect, it would be the same as lowering commissions, but he could still attract replacement salespeople with the official commission rate. Benton's reptilian smile widened.

Though Leonard lacked insight into such subtleties, he realized he'd been rolled. But how? *'Maybe I should have signed up for that college night course. What was it? Oh yeah – Office Acting 207.'* He speculated about Benton, *'No, not a Pacino 9. More likely an Alpha Z3.'*

However, he was wrong. Benton had a Viper 3000, just like Leonard. However, he had taken a course in MacroGolem's executive training program, Outthink 7. Outthink used shock therapy to train inductees to be cool under pressure, and to think several moves ahead in any negotiation. As his instructor had said, "Life is always about negotiation. Even love and romance are negotiations."

***

It took a lot of effort, but within two months, Leonard was once again king of the hill.

"You seem to be in a good mood," Cecilia observed during dinner.

"Made top salesman for the month."

"That's wonderful."

Yep. The $10,000 bonus will come in handy. And I'm sure the Garth sale will probably close next week."

"That should be a feather in your cap."

"You should have seen his face when I told him Langston Parson had bought the same model. Garth practically drooled."

"Parson? The billionaire?"

"Yeah. My background psych research indicated that Garth was the perfect target for keeping up with the Joneses. I'm sure it's straining his finances, the reason he's not going for the hyperturbo. That would have been an extra five grand commission. But then, when I told him..."

Cecilia's GladHand 4.3 allowed her to listen with perfect equanimity to another insufferable dinnertime conversation – a victorious sale; an ardent hope for a deal; the background research and psychological profile of this or that client. At company parties, the conversation between the Valhalla people was similar. Like Knights of the Round Table, they recounted adventures in heroic salesmanship, both their recent and past glories jousting with clients. Crystal glasses replaced tankards, and martinis replaced mead, but the epic tales suffused the air with the same vapor of heroism, the same existential validations as a medieval epic. She found it unsurprising that in a roomful of boring braggers, men and women gravitated to her. It was more than her pleasant smile, always welcoming, or her soothing voice. She understood what they did not – they were bored with themselves, with their narrow reality that carried outward marks of success, marks that masked for them the transience of their existence. She was the tranquil port in the storm, the one place of solace in the room, the one dependable smile, the one visage that held the most convincing appearance of sincerity.

But was it sincere? From time to time, she pondered the question. She made no effort to smile, to appear sympathetic. Didn't that make it sincere? On the other hand, that curve of the mouth, that warm twinkle in her eye did not reflect her feelings. They were merely the autonomic artfulness wired within by the GladHand 4.3.

Social graces made their wives more tolerable. It took longer for Cecilia to realize they too were medieval, though in a different way. Their shields were custom clothes by some exclusive design house, and their squires were a multitude of valets, clothing fitters, and restaurant servers. Squires and ladies all performed their minuet.

"By the way, you all missed a fantastic poetry reading last Saturday," Gwyneth said, as she took another bite of her salad.

"Don't tell me you got tickets to the Beau Zorchinsky reading?" Francine said.

"I did. Frank knows somebody who knows somebody. Zorchinsky has such a way of enchanting his audience."

"Oh, I know," Moira Linnon said. "I met him at one of his early readings, before he was famous."

Gwyneth put her fork down. "He comes on stage and just stands there until the applause tapers off. Then he pulls the mike close, and in a deep voice he slowly says – get this..." At this point she lowered her voice and leaned in. "...'Fuuuck Youuu.'"

"Oh my gosh!" Moira said with delight.

"And the whole place goes wild. Everyone's cheering. Well, everyone except a couple of people who walked out."

"Philistines," Patricia Taylor remarked. "They don't understand the first thing about art. Always hanging around. If they don't like his poetry, why do they go?"

"By the way, this fourchu lobster is delicious," declared Moira. "It's a perfect match to the prawn curry sauce."

"Everything here is delicious, though the sommelier at Kori's is better," remarked Patricia. "He knows my palate. I have lunch there often. It's just down the block from Merci's."

Alisa nodded. "Yes, Merci's. I go there a few times a year. Their pantsuits are fabulous. But I prefer Forenci's for shoes. They have the best selection in Italian wear."

"That reminds me," Gwyneth said. "I'll need a new pair for the Habitat For Humanity charity event."

"I've never been to that one. Maybe I should go. When is it?"

"The 26th of next month. I could introduce you to Willard Yolter, their president. He's a personal friend."

They all had special personal friends, along with personal nutritionists, personal auto repairmen, and a zoo-full of personal trainers for yoga and swimming and painting and the rest of their vanity list. And Cecilia was part of that existence too. What else was there to do with one's life?

However, one day a stray notion floated into her mind. Years later, she would ponder its source. Had someone's passing remark planted a seed that finally flowered into consciousness? Had the voice of a spirit guide spoken, or an inner anguish broken through? Her only certitude was that the source was not her implant. Instead of money, she would give her time to various community service organizations. It was at one of the Children's Tutoring Network events that she met Congresswoman Nancy Johanson. They immediately became friends.

Three days later, Cecilia received a call. "I'm going to be in the district Tuesday. Can we do lunch?"

"I'd love to, Nancy. Why don't you come to my place?"

"Oh, I wouldn't want to impose..."

"No imposition. I like to cook. It breaks up the day. Here's the address..."

On the following Tuesday, about a half-hour into the meal, Nancy said, "The reason I wanted to meet is to ask a favor. I need a business liaison in the district – someone to handle constituent's problems and complaints."

"But don't you already have a local office with a staff?"

"A couple of part-time volunteers, who are dedicated and friendly, but don't have the political or organizational skills. Mary Stettler is the full timer, and she's very good for constituents' personal needs – food stamps, VA benefits, and so forth. And I have a staff in my DC offices to schedule events and handle fund-raising. What I need is someone at the middle level, someone who can take care of the needs of small businesses. You would smooth their path for things like permits and small business loans. You have the social skills and seem to be business savvy. What do you say?"

"Actually, I'd like something like that. Housewife-plus-maid is not an exciting life. And lunches with other company wives is a chore. So yes, I think I'd enjoy the work, but it would have to be part-time. My husband's social and company events have to take precedence. He's the breadwinner."

"Of course. Your schedule will be flexible, and it would be a paying position. We have money in our staff budget.

"Then it's a definite *yes*."

Nancy's eyes seemed distant for a few seconds. "You'd be the...how about Local Business Consultant?" She looked at Cecilia. "LBC. Government people love their acronyms. Learning them would be your very first assignment."

Cecilia nodded. "Like returning to childhood, learning my ABCs again."

***

Leonard held up his fingers. "Not one, but three — count them — three yachts. And not the bottom lines either. Two Bluejacks and one Xanadu." Between bites of his dinner, he described in agonizing detail his manipulation of each customer, how he had led them to spend more than they had intended. "I'll tell you, Benton will be impressed. When I called in, I didn't give him the full picture. I want to see his face when I hand him the orders. And here's the thing. Not only am I certain to tag another top-salesman bonus for the month, but I'm sure Benton will recommend me to take his place when he moves up to corporate next year."

"That's incredible," Cecilia said. "How was Barbados? I've heard the shoreline is magnificent."

"Yeah. It's nice enough, but I didn't spend my time just lounging around. The thing is, before boarding, I bought this book in the airport, *Ripping Them Off*, by Lance Daly. It was a how-to book, and I was able to apply two of the techniques by the time I'd landed."

She smiled. "You always were a quick study."

"Daly's got some other books out. I plan to get every one of them."

"Sounds like you have a lot of homework to do. More pie?"

"Nope. It's delicious, but keeping a trim waistline is important. Image and all that."

"You have wonderful discipline."

"So, what did you do this week?"

"Well, I met Congresswoman Nancy Johanson at the tutoring school. She offered me a job."

Leonard took a sip of wine. "Oh? Doing what?"

"I'll be the LBC – Local Business Consultant. I'll be helping small businesses navigate the bureaucracy."

"That's good. Probably doesn't pay much, but maybe some of them will want a yacht? I'll give you some cards to pass around. Maybe some brochures, too."

"Actually, I think that might not be legal."

"Hmm. Maybe not, but you could have them just sitting on your desk. You wouldn't have to actually hand them out. Besides, who would complain?"

She smiled, imagining herself trashing them. Years earlier, she had learned how to circumvent his arm-twisting salesmanship.

***

As LBC, Cecilia's first clients were Renee Unger and Lois Breem.

"Lorca Placement Services?" Cecilia said with raised eyebrows. "Named after the poet?"

Lois nodded. "Yes. It was intended to convey a sense of art, but few of our clients ever heard of him."

They needed a small business loan for expansion. Cecilia, who had been the LBC for all of three hours, assured them she would look into the matter. After they had left, she quickly researched the small-business loan process. Then she called Nancy.

"Anything else I should look into?"

"You know, Cecilia, the state legislature passed a bill a month or two ago. What was it...? Oh yes, something about matching federal loans. Google that, and if that doesn't work, you can always search for state Senator Dershon plus business loans."

"I'm sorry to trouble you, Nancy, but I'm so unfamiliar with all this."

"Of course you are. It's to be expected. But you'll learn, and you're saving my staff the time of doing the actual web searches and meeting the constituents. Don't hesitate to call anytime you run into a roadblock. You're doing fine."

Two days later, Cecilia visited Lorca and presented the women with the information and forms as well as directions for applying for the loans.

They insisted on taking her to lunch. It was lively conversation. They spent little time discussing business, but a lot talking about their kids, about local playhouses, about the different experience of live plays compared to movies. They ended with a date to see a local stage production in a theater of modest size.

Driving home that evening, Cecilia pondered her encounter with the two women. For some reason, she remembered a scene from her childhood. As her mother was driving her to school, she noticed a stream of kids entering a schoolyard. Unlike her, they were all dressed in different kinds of clothes. None of them wore a uniform.

"Mommy, what kind of school is this?"

"That's a public school, dear." She paused. "It's not as good as your school."

Cecilia realized that Renee and Lois probably went to similar schools. Perhaps one of them was among the crowd of children she had seen that day.

The following week, she met Martin Carnahan, whose business involved creating and maintaining interiorscapes – the plants and fountains inside large business buildings. She researched the requirements and made a few calls to expedite his path through the bureaucracy at the EPA. A week later, he picked up the form and information packet. As a thank you, he treated her to lunch. Their conversation sparkled. He talked about his interest in photography, which led to her first insights into the art of Bresson and Weston. She asked about the buildings his business serviced, and he offered her a tour of some of his interiorscapes for the following week. This time, she treated him to lunch. A couple of weeks later, he invited her to a special exhibition at the local museum. It displayed old photographs of their city. He described several of the buildings, criticizing the architecture of some and praising others. She was not familiar with any of them.

"Would you like to see my house? I'm certain you will find it unusual." She was surprised by her own impulse.

As he followed her in his car, her recklessness became clearer. He seemed decent, very responsible, but what had she been thinking? How would he take the invitation? How had she intended it?

They arrived while it was still light. Martin paused for a few seconds before walking around to the side of the house. "Huh. Interesting." He nodded. "Unusual."

She led him inside, then gradually, from room to room. "Well, what do you think?"

"The furnishings are lovely. You have great taste."

"And the house?"

"It's certainly unusual. I've never seen anything quite like it."

She spoke more slowly. "Martin, what do you think of it as architecture? And please be honest."

He looked at her, considering his response. "Okay. It, uh, seems a bit too literal."

She had to ponder his meaning. She often had to ponder his meanings, one of the things that made him interesting. "Too literal?"

"The museum at Bilbao is designed to remind us of a ship. But it isn't a model of a ship, just reminiscent of one. There are aspects of it that I think are overdone, but what separates good art from bad is whether it can evoke a sense of something, without reproducing it." He paused, looking around. "Not actually bad, but not terribly artful."

"I don't know about this Bilbao, but I agree with you. You must have an artist chip." To his confused expression, she elaborated, "Your implant?"

"Me? No, no. My parents could never afford an implant."

"Oh, sorry. I had no idea. I just assumed everyone had one." After a few seconds, she remarked, "That's a shame."

"I don't think so. You have one, and you're not happy."

The statement caught her off guard. She recovered her smile. "Why...why would you say that?"

"I'm not psychic. It's just that during lunch, your smile was different, and also, today in the museum. From the moment we entered your home, your smile has been merely pleasant. And also, you said your husband sells boats, so the exterior had to be his idea, but the furnishings are Queen Anne, and the wall paper themes are nature. It's a very different esthetic, so I figured those were your own choices." He paused before adding, "And frankly, Cecilia, the two don't go together."

It took several seconds for her smile to reappear.

"I've made you sad," he said. "I'm sorry."

"That's okay. I'm just tired from a long day. I want to thank you for being my museum guide. I've enjoyed the day immensely."

"And I've enjoyed it too." He looked at her directly. "I hope we can do lunch again sometime."

"Yes," she said, and reconsidering, "Yes, absolutely. I'd like that."

***

Most of the business owners she helped were not as interesting as Martin and the Lorca women, but the occasional sparkler made her job interesting. There was Jay Endicott, owner of Blue Jay's Cakes, who also operated a small soap bar business with his wife, Wendy, from their home. At his invitation, the couple spent an hour showing her the process, and telling her about natural fragrances, the way they were gathered and processed.

"How many bars can you produce per week?"

"Oh, heck," Jay said, "it's a small operation. We just enjoy creating them. Each batch is unique."

Wendy chuckled, "At the end of the month, we probably average a dollar or two an hour. But they're pretty, and other people also find pleasure in them."

Over coffee, Wendy enthused about raising tulips in her spare time. As Cecilia was leaving, they gave her a couple of multi-colored bars.

Another businessman, Bill Sutherland, recounted his year spent in a Japanese home. He leaned forward, enthusiastically describing the arrangement of rooms, the details of the furnishings, modern versus traditional – particulars that her vacations in Japan, with their hotel accommodations, had missed.

The next time she attended a play with Renee and Lois, they took her backstage after the performance.

"It's okay. They know us. Craig, the guy who plays professor Wobbly? He's a friend."

Cecilia watched with delight as the crew scurried about, removing makeup, putting away costumes, combing out their hair, chattering like a windstorm, helping stagehands put away props. It was chaos. And in a flash, she realized that was the context that made it so wonderful. Suddenly, she felt what the troupe felt – the play's joy included all this hidden turbulence whose flower was the semblance of life displayed onstage. It had nothing to do with status, certainly not money. It was like Jay and Wendy transforming colors and scents into something intrinsically beautiful. And for Martin, a building was more than a building; its design held mysterious, essential meanings. And without warning, inexplicably, she felt like a child again, and though she could not help maintaining her smile, tears began running down her cheeks. She was happy. Actually happy, not just appearing so.

Renee spotted her first. "Cecilia! What's wrong?"

Cecilia opened her mouth, but had trouble speaking. "I...I'm not sure...but...I think I feel happy."

Renee wrinkled her brow. "What? Then why...?"

Lois ran up. "What's the matter?"

"I don't know," Renee said.

"Talk to us," Lois said.

"I...don't know either. I'm not sure I understand, but all these people, they work so hard, and...for little or no pay, and they're so...connected and alive."

Lois looked at Renee, who looked back, equally puzzled.

Craig arrived with a box of tissues. "What's going on?"

"We're not sure," Lois said as she grabbed a tissue and began dabbing Cecilia's cheeks.

They led her to a chair. After several seconds, Cecilia said, "My whole life hasn't been mine. I've married well and I have all these luxuries and a rich husband – a rich boring husband with all his boring friends who aren't friends, and all their insufferable chatter and their rich zombie wives." As she spoke, her tone had become increasingly emphatic. She collected herself. "Please don't take it wrong. It's not a 'poor little rich girl' thing. But ever since I started working in Nancy's office..." her voice began to squeak, "...I've met a few people, people like you, and I've caught a glimpse of what it's like to be a real person."

Lois grabbed her hand. "Oh Cecilia, we love you too."

Craig grabbed her other hand. "And I do too...and I'm gay."

Cecilia laughed, leading the other two women to crack up.

Renee slapped his shoulder. "It was your bad acting that upset her."

"No," Cecilia said, "not at all. Your character was wonderful. I'd love to do this again."

It took her a second to realize how risible was her statement. Everyone roared with laughter.

When they had settled down, Craig said, "Would you like one of us to take you home?"

Cecilia inhaled deeply. "No, but thanks. That's most kind of you. I'll be fine tomorrow."

"What's tomorrow?" Lois asked.

"Tomorrow I will tell my husband I'm divorcing him."

The other three came to a full, brick-wall stop. After a long pause, Renee said, "Really? You want a divorce?"

With an intensity Renee had not witnessed in her before, Cecilia said, "No. Not want. Tell."

Lois' gaze lost its focus. "Wow." She looked at the other two, then back at Cecilia. "How do you think he'll react?"

"I don't have to think. I know. He'll work a sales pitch. Then he'll remind me of the prenup, that I'll only get to keep the money I had when we married, while he gets everything else."

"Nothing about love?" Renee said.

"Maybe the usual cliché dribbled in there somewhere, like a second-rate script."

"He sound's callous," Craig said.

"Don't pity me." She looked at each of them. "I'm alive. I'm alive."

What the Shadows Say

The Soul of an Artist

Arthur Lancer finished the routine of turning off lights, setting the alarm, and locking the door of Lancer's Gallery. As he walked toward the public parking lot, he glanced across the street at Demain Today, the avant-garde gallery owned by Franklin Garrison – he hated people calling him 'Frank'. It specialized in experimental work. In the past, their less quirky paintings overlapped with Lancer's more modernist pieces. However, over time, Demain's offerings drifted from novel, to eccentric, and finally, to grotesque. Yet, it had brought them success. Arthur had witnessed their gradual increase in prices. It seemed the "whales" – customers well lacquered in several layers of money – saw in the bizarre the hope for the 'next big thing'; of getting in on the ground floor of some unknown artist who'd be discovered by some excessively well-known curator. And even if the artist ended a couple of brushstrokes short of fame, the whales could still display to their social clique evidence of their proper avant-garde tastes.

A hundred yards farther, Arthur passed in front of the Assemblage Gallery. As usual, a pair of "featured" paintings were prominently displayed near the window. The Louis Quinze frame made the hackneyed kids-at-the-seashore painting look even more ridiculous than the other – two cats with oversized eyes staring at him. *'Still, better than that velvet painting of the truck – the old Ford in the old overgrown grass outside the old homestead.'* He smiled, remembering how Mrs. Wilson had proudly pointed to it. "And watch the taillights. They turn on every now and then." He stopped smiling when he remembered that their gallery was fairly successful. *'Not as much as Demain's, but still.... Hell, the whole country's going the way of Assemblage and Demain.'*

As usual for the last few weeks, Lorraine gave him a cheery "Hi!" from the kitchen, then peered at him. "How you doing?"

"It's like having a tooth pulled – I'm glad it's almost over. One more week, and the doors close for good."

She shook her head. "Makes you wonder if there is a god."

"Oh, I believe in God. Unfortunately, He doesn't believe in art."

She smiled. "Didn't you once say that art was an expression of the spiritual?"

"Yeah – the reason I believe in art for art's sake. Unfortunately, the landlord believes in getting his rent each month – not to mention the utilities, property taxes, plus all the yada yadas." He paused to consider. "Besides, I should have said, '*can* be an expression of the spiritual'. Somewhere in the past, our country came to a fork in the road. One fork sauntered into the triteness of *Assemblage*; the other detoured into a swamp as we chased novelty all the way to Bizarre City, USA. And now we have *Demain*."

"I was browsing the Kandinsky book the other day. I like a lot of his work."

"Yeah. And Clyfford Still's another. But they weren't just trying to be different. Like Chagall, they had an inner vision they wanted to externalize."

"Do you wish now that you hadn't followed art as a career?"

"I've thought a lot about that these last couple of months, but like I've said, I've always loved art, even as a child. It's who I am. You might as well ask me if I ever considered not eating."

"That's not really my question. Of course you're an artist. I knew that on our second date. But you could have painted and sculpted as a hobby." She realized her mistake before the word had traveled an inch from her mouth.

He eye-darted her. "Hobby? Are you kidding?"

She dipped her head and spoke slowly. "No, not *hobby*. I should have said, *avocation*. You know, then have a day job in something else – one to feed the body, the other, the soul."

He paused to settle himself. "It looks like that's what's in the cards, Lorraine. But then again, I'm not really sorry for opening the gallery. If I hadn't, I'd always wonder, 'What if?'"

She nodded. "Yeah, that's true." She was quiet for a few seconds. "What do you plan to do after the it closes?"

"Rest up, put myself back together, then figure out my next act. Forty is not too old for a new career. Hopefully, it will be something as interesting and useful as your work."

She shook her head. "Not always interesting. And I've told you about my sporadic issues with clients; and sometimes with our lawyers."

"Sure. That's just part of life, but your architectural work involves art. And it fills a need. It produces tangible results."

"Architectural work?" She chuckled. "I don't design anything. I'm just a compliance manager, making sure projects adhere to regulations and safety standards. Heavens! Some of the structures look as ludicrous as the sculptures at *Demain*, except our ugly costs millions instead of thousands."

"Agreed. But at least *some* of the buildings are nicely designed."

She turned and tilted her head toward him. "Arthur, I'm just a lawyer."

A week later, Arthur was wandering the internet, seeking inspiration for his future direction. He didn't pay much attention to the ads along the sides of the screen. However, two mornings later, he woke with a surprising thought. He hadn't been dreaming about it, and certainly hadn't considered the idea over the past two days, but there it was – a fully formed plan. He remembered some ad about renting pets. Later that morning, he began an internet search. He recalled part of the name, and soon had located *Murphy's Rent-A-Pet*'s online page.

"Hi. I saw your ad for renting pets. By chance, do you rent monkeys? Uh, yes. it's for my nephew's birthday party...a small one, like the old organ grinders' monkeys...capuchin? Is that what they're called? And how much do you charge?...by the day, yes...I see, and does that include an outfit? Yes...clothing...the name is Lancer. I'll have to get back to you about the date. Thanks."

Next, he called his sister. "Sally, I need a favor from you. I'll need you to do some sewing for me."

"Sure. What, a shirt?"

"No. A suit, but a very unusual one." Sally ran a business out of a small off-the-boulevard store, designing and making custom clothing for slightly upscale women. Her business, moderately lucrative, allowed her and her husband to live their own slightly upscale life. Arthur often remarked how they shared the same art gene. He explained his plan.

The following Saturday, Sally arrived with a couple of yards of cloth and some sheets of oversize tracing paper. When she saw the monkey, she broke into a smile. "Oh my gosh! He's so cute."

"I've decided to call him Stanley."

After she had cooed over the animal for a few minutes, Arthur handed her Stanley's outfit. "It doesn't have to fit perfect. It's just a protective cover."

"This shouldn't take long. I'll have a pattern drawn up in less than an hour. Then I can do the sewing at home. Is this cloth okay?"

"Yep. That should be perfect."

"At first, I thought you were kidding. You really want to do this?"

"Yes." His terse answer evinced a determination that echoed their phone discussion. "I know you think it's childish, and Lorraine wants me to let it go, but…"

"You should. Just put it behind you."

"That's what I intend to do; and this is how I'm going to do it. I wish I could just walk away from it, but I need to do this."

The next weekend, he rented Stanley again, took him into his art room, and changed him into Sally's outfit. Then he knelt down beside one of the two pieces of bare Masonite on the floor. He grabbed a brush, dipped it in some paint and brushed on a few colors as the monkey watched. Then he grabbed a brush lying beside the second board and handed it to Stanley. The monkey just looked at it. Arthur prompted him by manipulating Stanley's arm to dip the brush in one of the paint pots. The monkey just looked at it. Arthur moved Stanley's hand with the loaded brush and stroked it across the board.

That was all it took. Stanley began making his own strokes. He changed colors spontaneously, squealing with delight as the board filled with different hues. Arthur began making broad strokes – lines, circles, dots – on his board, demonstrating possibilities to his pupil. Stanley did not merely learn fast. He improvised. Arthur's smile stretched wide. He switched Stanley's board for one that had been primed. Within 15 minutes, Arthur had his first piece of simian art. Three more followed, while Arthur made a video of the activity. When Arthur tried to separate monkey from brush, he encountered feral resistance. Two more pieces followed before Stanley could be coaxed away with a treat.

Arthur removed Sally's creation, sponged off Stanley's hands and a few spots on the fur, and dressed him in his original outfit.

On the following Tuesday, Arthur entered Demain Today with a portfolio case.

"Arthur. So good to see you." Renee Lantier's frozen smile annoyed Arthur, but he had to admit it added to the dignity of her age and bearing. And her tall frame and perfect apparel conveyed elegance. She was Demain's full-time docent, and had become as integral a part of the gallery as its owner.

"Is Franklin in?"

"Yes. I'll tell him you're here. By the way, we were both sorry to see you close. You had some truly talented artists." Her condolence possessed all the comfort of a stone pillow.

A few minutes later, Franklin entered through the curtained opening. "Arthur, Glad to see you." His smile was more genuine than Renee's, though his words weren't. "We miss having your gallery on the street. So, what are you doing these days?"

"Actually, I've gotten back to painting. I thought you might be interested in taking a look."

"Sure. Absolutely."

Arthur opened the portfolio case and extracted the first board.

Franklin stopped smiling. "Interesting. No – more than interesting. This is quite good." He turned to Arthur, "I didn't know you did abstract. Everything of yours I've seen was realist with a touch of impressionism."

"Yes. Of course, this was not the kind of thing I'd show at my gallery, but abstract has always fascinated me."

"Let's see what else you have."

That afternoon, Lorraine arrived home in a cheerful mood. "So how did it go at Demain?"

"Franklin liked them. He's going to display them all."

"Really? Well, that *is* funny. But if he sells some of them, what exactly are you going to do? Go to the press? Talk to a TV reporter?"

"That's the plan."

"You do realize you'll destroy your friendship with him." It was as much a question as a statement.

"We've talked about this last week. I'm not after Franklin personally. It's the state of art – of esthetics – in this country. I just want people to wake up."

"But it will embarrass him," she persisted.

"If it breaks us apart, then so be it. It's a price I'm willing to pay." He paused, then looked at her directly. "I'm sorry, Lorraine, but esthetics is my life. It's my soul. It's the ability to distinguish between quality and crap. And it's a barometer of society's values."

She thought, '*Here comes the speech.*'

"Our whole country has been going downhill for decades because it lost the ability to tell the difference between good ideas and bad."

"And you blame it all on art." She spoke with the tolerance of an unbeliever.

"No, art isn't the cause, but it is an indicator. Our country has been deteriorating since the 50s – think of the god-awful architecture, the monstrosities at MOMA and other museums, and the unwalkable cities with their sterile glass and steel flatness. And the suburbs too – their ugly hodgepodge of shapes and billboards and patchwork shops. They're signs of something gone terribly wrong in our culture. It's a kind of Day-Glo rot, and I'm trying to wake people to recognize it."

Early in her life, Lorraine had come to understand the futility of arguing with true believers. "Promise me one thing, Arthur."

"What's that?"

"That after a few of your pieces sell, you'll discuss with me and Sally exactly what steps you're going to take."

He knew they were not going to change his mind –
he had thought too long and hard about it. But she was
talking about the future, and at the moment, he had
almost finished preparing dinner. "Sure. I can do that."

***

Three weeks later, Franklin called. "I need to see
you."

When he entered Demain's, Renee's smile was wide.
It actually looked genuine. "I'll get Franklin."

Franklin smiled and hesitated. "Well..." He
coughed. "Actually, we had our annual auction last
weekend, and uh, well, I decided to include your new
pieces. So...*ahem*...we took off the price tags. You know,
the ones we had decided on...uh..."

"You mean the one's *you* wanted. Higher than the
ones I wanted, as I recall. A thousand dollars, weren't
they?"

"Yes, well, with the auctions, we always remove the
tags temporarily. We replace them on the ones that
don't sell at auction...uh...or don't bring high enough
bids."

Arthur waited impatiently for the bad news. It
wouldn't wound too deeply. After all, they were
Stanley's paintings.

"Uh...well, we sold three of your paintings."

Arthur smiled, but not for the reasons Franklin
would suppose. His plan was working surprisingly well.
"Really? Not just lowball offers?"

"Uh...no."

"Okay. So how much?"

Franklin looked at his list. "*Genome* sold for $8,000, *Pratfall* sold for $6,000, and *God Eats A Sandwich* sold for $18,000." Franklin looked up. His brow was wrinkled, waiting for Arthur's reaction.

Arthur mouth was open, but he couldn't find his thoughts, much less any words.

Franklin broke the silence. "Thirty-two thousand in total."

Arthur's mouth had closed, but his mind was still spinning.

"Of course, we take a third, but that still leaves a little more than 21,000."

"Wow. I never thought, I mean…"

"And I never realized you had so much talent. I want to propose something to you. Show me some more of your abstracts, and next month we will put on a show exclusively of your work. During single-artist exhibits, we take offers. Of course, you can accept or reject any offer, but I suspect you'll have quite a few acceptable ones." He paused to gauge Arthur's reaction. "And it will help spread your name." He waited, then into the silence, explained, "Getting press and TV coverage shouldn't be a problem."

"How many more do you need?"

That night, Lorraine laughed at the news. "I guess God does believe in art."

He raised his eyebrows. "Maybe, or maybe he just believes in monkeys."

Her lawyer mind began turning. "You can't go forward with your plan now. If you go to the press and reveal the truth, it will cost us a lot of money. Obviously, all future sales will evaporate. More important, the three people who bought your monkey art could sue you for fraud."

"I feel like a traitor, but you're right."

She shook her head. "You're not a traitor. You're like the Ferrari salesman. If people have more money than sense, he's not going to tell them they're fools. And if the people can't tell monkey art from people art, let them turn it into money art. Arthur, the stars have aligned in our favor."

As they lay in bed that night, she was bothered at how easily she had convinced him. Was he really willing to choose money over his esthetic values? Perhaps the business failure bruised him more than she had realized. *'Or was it me serving as breadwinner these last five years?'*

And so began a three-year run of their simian art caper. Arthur's work and fame went international. To own a genuine Lancer was a badge of status and wealth. The money gushed into the Lancer household. Even print reproductions generated high profits. Lorraine quit her job to become his manager – scheduling exhibitions, filling orders, managing sales and promotions. Both of them were kept furiously busy. He even considered buying a Ferrari – but after Lorraine's fit, he settled for a Mercedes.

However, one day, the stars began to drift.

He walked distractedly into Lorraine's work room. "I just got a call from Roger."

She saw the worried look on his face. "Roger from *Rent-A-Pet?*"

He nodded. "Stanley died."

"Died? What happened?"

He said it was pneumonia. And age."

"Wow. I mean, wow." She paused before asking, "What are we going to do?"

"He says he'll have a replacement in about two weeks."

"But how do you know the new monkey will be able to learn to paint? I mean, Stanley was exceptionally smart. What if the replacement is…well, you know, slow?"

He felt like laughing at her PC. Her legalistic mind couldn't bring herself to apply the word *stupid*, even to a monkey. "I don't know. Capuchins are supposed to be smart, but like people – some are probably smarter, some dumber."

"If the new monkey can't paint, what are we going to do?"

"Retire, I guess. We've got money, and the reprints bring in a lot."

"If all we have left are the reprints – no exhibits, no museum events – I'm not going to have much of a work load."

However, a few weeks later, when Arthur rented the new monkey, he found him trainable. While much slower to learn than Stanley, once he picked up the gist of the task, he proved capable. Livingstone, as Arthur decided to call him, was soon producing artwork, though at a slower pace than his predecessor.

Lorraine was relieved. "How do they look?"

"Just as good. Can't tell much difference in style."

He delivered a half-dozen of the new paintings to Demain. Franklin and Renee immediately looked at them. "We should have these framed and hung within a week," Franklin said. "Just in time for our spring event."

When he arrived home following his next Demain show, Lorraine asked, "How did it go?" She was smiling until she took a good look at him. "What's wrong?"

"Didn't sell a single one."

"None?" Into the silence, she finally said, "How high was the starting price?"

"Not high. In fact, I was miffed that they were a bit lower than the last batch. After all, they're the same quality as Stanley's."

"Are you saying you didn't get *any* bids?"

"Not a single one. It was embarrassing."

The next morning's paper was more than embarrassing. "*Is Arthur Lancer losing his touch?*" It went on to tell of the sudden deterioration of his style. "*The spontaneity we have come to expect from a Lancer painting was entirely missing. When asked about it, art critic Brian Rhesus said, 'Perhaps he's merely entering a new phase – like Picasso moving from his blue to his rose period. Hopefully he'll either improve his new style, or advance to a more artistic one in the near future.'*"

Arthur and Lorraine both slowly shook their heads. "Can you believe this?" he said.

"Arthur, I'm no artist, but I can't see any difference between Stanley's and Livingstone's artistry."

"That's because there isn't any. They're the same style – monkey style. The same quality, too. Livingstone's strokes are slightly different, but not enough to spit at."

She shook her head. "As far as 'spontaneity' goes? Good God! It's a monkey. What do they think — his painting is preplanned? Or maybe he's copying human art? It's laughable."

"I'm not laughing," he said.

"Let's check online."

The web reviews were worse. Besides the professional critics, the public comments were entirely negative.

> *"It was bound to happen. He's been producing too many paintings. He probably wore out his art neurons."*

> *"The new work is so different. It's like another artist painted it. Maybe he has multiple personality disorder."*

> *"Lancer's probably getting on in years. How old is he, anyway?"*

> *"I'll bet he started using someone else to do his art. Kind of like a ghost-writer."*

> *"We want the old Lancer back."*

The reactions were the same at his next two shows. After that, the invitations from galleries and museums evaporated.

After his final show, Lorraine asked, "What are we going to do, Arthur?"

"Well, it's obvious our art stardom is in the rearview mirror."

"Yeah." She nodded slowly. "But we've had a pretty good run. I can always go back to work, but what are you going to do?"

"We have plenty of money. You don't need to work."

"Yes, I do. Remember how you once said everyone needed to feel useful? Pardon the ditto marks."

He smiled. "Touché." He was silent for a while, then said, "You know, it seems like the need to be useful is a lot like art. Even when it seems unnecessary, it actually isn't."

"Have you got anything in mind?"

"Yeah. I'm thinking of entering the world of fashion design – for women. Max Gillian, one of my old gallery exhibitors, is also a part-time designer of women's fashions for small clothing manufacturers. Like what Sally does, but at the wholesale level. He's long wanted me to work with him to build an online store. Basically, we would do the designs, then outsource production for online sales."

"Good. We can leave the world of galleries behind."

Except they couldn't. A couple of Saturday's later, the doorbell rang.

"Arthur Lancer?"

"Yes." He took the manila envelope the stranger handed him.

"Consider yourself served, sir."

After reading the contents, Arthur went out to the backyard. "You won't believe this."

Lorraine looked up from her gardening. "Believe what?"

"I'm being sued."

"Sued? What for?"

"Supposedly for copyright infringement. It says I copied Kirkland Horship's paintings."

"Who?"

"Kirkland Horship. He's a well-known modern artist. His work is hanging in museums all over the world."

"Is that really his name?"

"It is. And if you saw his work, you'd be less surprised at his name than the hundred thousand dollars it fetches at auction."

"Which paintings?"

"I'm going to look online. This is ridiculous."

She followed him inside.

He looked at the list and typed in *Licked Cone*. "Hmm. You know, Livingstone's *Broken* does look a lot like it."

"Uh…yeah. Almost an exact copy."

The next image search showed that Horship's *Esther's Pickle* did indeed resemble Livingstone's *Nosey Moss*. And two more of Livingstone's creations were near-exact copies of Horship's work.

"How is this possible?" Lorraine asked.

Arthur was silent for a half-minute before quickly raising his head. "Take a drive with me." After he had printed the four images, they drove to Murphy's Rent-A-Pet.

Lorraine had never been inside the store. "Wow. It's like a mini zoo."

But Arthur wasn't listening. He took each image and compared it to the various prints hanging in the random open spaces along the walls. By the time he had traversed the entire store, they turned toward each other.

"How do you explain it?" she asked.

"Only one thing I can think of. Livingstone spent day after day in this store. He must have seen all these prints a hundred times. I'd guess he copied them from memory."

"That makes sense. Unlike Stanley, he was a copycat." She paused, then smiled. "A copy-monkey, actually."

"It's not funny. Horship's got us dead to rights."

Her smile widened. "Not really. There's a way out of this."

"What way?"

"We'll need to set up a meeting with Horship's attorney. I'll explain on the way home."

A week later, the four of them sat around a table in the conference room of Listy, Worte and Golem Law Group.

"Ms. Lancer, are you certain you want to be attorney in this matter?" Worte asked. "You do understand you could be called as a witness at trial."

"Of course, Mr. Worte. However, I doubt this will ever get to trial."

"And why is that?"

"May I address your client directly?"

Worte paused. "Alright, but only until I decide to call a halt."

"Fair enough." She placed some papers on the table. "Mr. Horship, these are images of the four paintings in question. Is that correct?"

Horship remained in the lean-back position with arms crossed, a display of nonchalance polished into habit by eight years of public infatuation. "Those are the ones."

"Actually, it may interest you to know that my husband did not paint them."

Worte spoke up. "Then who did?"

"A monkey."

Horship smirked. Worte half-smirked.

"Lorraine continued. I have a video you might find interesting." She turned her laptop toward them and played some of the footage of Stanley's first painting session.

The smirks faded. Finally, Worte spoke. "That certainly is amazing, but I don't see how this forms much of a defense. Your client still exhibited copies of my client's original work. That's copyright infringement. You're only adding misrepresentation to his list of misdeeds. It seems to me that this would impugn his character even more."

"It would," Lorraine granted, "provided Mr. Horship was foolish enough to bring this suit to trial."

Worte paused as he considered the situation. "Okay, what is it I'm not seeing here?"

"If the public learned that even a monkey can copy his art, how would that impact his career?" She let the question hang in the air for a few seconds. "And how would it look that even professional art critics panned the works as…" She read from a document, "*totally lacking in spontaneity...devoid of energy...lost the artistic touch...*' Here. You can read the rest of the comments from Arthur's last show." She handed the document to Worte.

After a half-minute, Worte said, "We'll need some time to study these comments and research your hus...client's last show."

"Of course. And while you're deciding, I suggest you and Mr. Horship consider how his future shows – and sales – will be affected by whatever changes in public perceptions might occur from a very public trial."

Two weeks later, the plaintiffs agreed to drop the suit. It required a non-disclosure agreement by both parties, but it left the Lancers free to follow their new pursuits. It also allowed Kirkland Horship's fame to continue rising, along with the prices people were willing to pay to own a genuine Horship painting.

50

Waiting Room

As he sat in her living room, Mark was on the verge of tears. "I don't know what I'm going to do."

Rachel took his hand. "Mark, we'll figure it out. Together. We'll solve this.

"It's just so difficult. Mom and dad won't understand. Dad already thinks I'm a bum, and Mom doesn't know what to think. How am I going to tell them the real reason Caruso's Pizza fired me?"

"Yeah. That was pretty extreme. Deliver a stack of pizzas to a business party in Santa Monica, and wake up in Chula Vista."

"I'd have been fine if they hadn't made me wait while they looked for the key to the petty cash drawer." He shook his head. "If I tell them the truth, Mom and Dad won't believe me. Nobody would."

"I believe you." She gently squeezed his hand.

"That's only because you witnessed it in Dr. Lancer's waiting room. Look, we love each other, but admit it – you didn't believe me before..."

"Okay, okay. But you have to agree – if the situation were reversed, would you believe me?"

He shrugged, then nodded. "Probably not. I'd figure you were having some kind of breakdown."

"Exactly. And I'm glad I was there." She shook her head. "I'm sorry I doubted you."

"Can't blame you, Rachel. I must have sounded like some whacko. I'm also glad it happened with you there. I need someone to believe me."

She shook her head and chuckled. "Yeah, that was something, you calling me to pick you up 40 miles away. After I'd been only a few minutes in the restroom."

"The thing is, my parents wouldn't believe me. They'd want to send me to a shrink – not that they could afford one. They really needed my paycheck to keep Pete in college. Now that's gone. And I can't just sit around at home."

"I could help out a little."

"No, no. Thanks, but I just can't let you do that."

"How's he doing, anyway?" she asked.

"Okay. He says he's acing some courses. We're just worried we're going to run out of money before he graduates."

"That would be terrible."

"Yeah. He's the one hope for the family. The smart one; the one who will be successful."

"Mark, I love you and it hurts me to see you put yourself down like this." She rubbed his hair. She loved running her hands through the light brown waves. "You're very bright. You just have this little problem."

"Thanks for believing in me. It means a lot."

"No problem. Hey – here's an idea. My sister started a dream journal. Maybe you could do something similar."

"A dream journal?"

"Yeah. She never could remember her dreams. Now, when she wakes up, she immediately jots down what she's just dreamt. After a couple of weeks, she began to see patterns – repeating themes. Also, some connections between her days and the night's dreams. Even better, she had a few dreams that foretold things later in the week."

"A journal...hmm. Not a bad idea. If there's a pattern, I'd like to know what it is. Yeah...good idea."

She smiled. "We'll get to the bottom of this. Anyway, I've got some leftovers for lunch."

He genuinely loved her. Not for her concern, not for her efforts to help him. He loved the way she moved – direct, efficient, a contrast to his easygoing manner. Some might not find her beautiful, but he did. She had broad shoulders, not the petite figure some men found attractive. *'Broad shoulders and a big heart.'* He loved both. But he wished he wasn't a burden. She might accept it for their future – assuming it would be *their* future – but he would hate to be her albatross.

Mark had learned to carry a backpack wherever he went. It was like a bug-out bag, except packed for the purpose of returning home instead of leaving in emergency evacuations. He had come upon the idea after he had been waiting to fly out of LAX to Oregon, but suddenly woke up in a train station in Kingman, Arizona. And there was that MRI appointment in Pacoima, when he awoke in a Tulare bus station. *'A bus station?'* he had thought. *'Who the hell takes a bus for a long trip?'* Actually, that turned out to be him, all the way back to Los Angeles. His real worry was ending up in Mexico or Canada without his passport. So, he always kept it, along with other potential necessities, whenever he knew he'd be in a waiting room.

And now he added his thin notebook. The first use came a week after the encounter with Dr. Lancer. He was waiting for the service man to finish the oil change; the next thing he knew, he was being awakened by some woman. "Are you here to see Ms. Maher or Mr. Chase?"

"Huh? Where am I?"

"You're at Maher, Chase and Associates." As Mark looked around, she added, "We're a law firm. Do you have an appointment?"

"Uh, what city is this?" Her obvious discomfort prompted him to repeat the question.

"Santa Barbara," she replied, obviously doubting his sobriety.

"Thank God," he said, which added to the woman's confusion. "It's not that far to get home," he explained, rather unhelpfully.

As he left the office and considered how he'd get home, he remembered the journal, and quickly jotted down as much as he could remember about the auto repair place.

On a Sunday morning a few months later, he showered and sat down at the kitchen table.

"Bacon okay with you?" Rachel asked. "I'm out of sausage."

"Sure, bacon's fine."

As she poured the orange juice, she asked, "What about the journal? Learn anything useful?"

"I can't see any pattern to it. Maybe you can take a look after breakfast."

Later, Rachel buried her nose in the notebook. He looked at her face – the tall oval shape with a prominent jaw, and the intensity of her attention. After several minutes, she shook her head, sending her straight black hair dancing from side to side. "You're right. Not much here. Maybe it's incomplete."

"Incomplete?"

"You've got your transport events listed, but not your non-transport ones." She looked up and noted Mark's bafflement. "What about all the times you don't get transported?"

"Why would that matter? I mean, that would just be normal, wouldn't it?"

She handed the book back to Mark. "What we're trying to do here is find a cause – no, not a cause. A correlation – the conditions that are present just before you transport."

"Yeah, that's true." He appreciated her logical mind. He knew she'd be successful as a chemist.

"I just think it would help to list the conditions when you don't get transported from waiting rooms. Maybe we could find what was different."

"Yeah. It might also explain the other question – why waiting rooms?"

"Look, I hate to push you out, but I have a midterm on Wednesday. I've got to study."

"Okay. I'll call you Thursday, find out how you did."

As he drove home, he tried to imagine their future, but all he could see was a shadow in a fog bank. No, he couldn't marry her, not as long as he had this problem.

During the next two months, he was transported twice – once from an optometrist's waiting room to a DMV office 50 miles away; and once from his tax preparer's office to a gynecologist's. He didn't even attempt to fake an explanation to the receptionist.

During the following three months, he carefully entered every waiting room experience into the journal. Luckily, he had only a single incident of transport.

One morning, he told Rachel, "I even recorded the kinds of potted plants. I still can't see a pattern. Here. Maybe you'll spot something."

Rachel went through the journal in her usual meticulous way. Mark, in his usual way, became antsy. He slouched back and fiddled with his cell phone. After a while, she went to her desk and retrieved a package of colored tab markers. After reading each page, she attached a marker to the edge.

After another quarter hour, she finally spoke. "I've put a red tab on the pages when you were transported, and a yellow one when nothing happened. I think I found a pattern."

Mark sat straight as a flagpole. "You did? Fantastic." He put his phone in his pants pocket.

"On May 7, you say you were transported just after two women in the room were called in. Also, that there had been a man, but he had gone somewhere else — you're not sure where. On May 22, you were the last patient for the day, and the room was empty. And at the end of June, you were at the hospital to drive a friend home, and everyone in the waiting area had already left."

"You're saying it only happens when no one's around?"

"That's what didn't quite fit, at first. In the hospital, nurses and doctors are always walking up and down the corridors. Also, in Dr. Twig's waiting area, there had to be a receptionist not that far away. Can you recall her location relative to yours?"

"Yeah. She was, like, around a corner."

"Couldn't see you?"

Mark rocked forward slowly as the point was becoming clearer. "That's true."

Rachel nodded briskly. "And at the hospital, doctors and nurses would be focused on their destination – a room or a clinic. No one would be aware of you."

"You mean, no one was actually looking at me."

"Or probably even aware of you."

"Mark shook his head. "But…that's crazy."

Rachel raised her eyebrows.

Mark looked at the floor and nodded. "Okay, okay. You're right. Getting transported isn't exactly run-of-the-mill stuff either." After a few seconds, he looked at her. "Then, what you're saying is that somehow, if people see me, they hold me in the room?"

"I'm not even going to try explaining it, but from your notes, that's the pattern I see."

Driving home, Mark kept turning the conversation over in his mind. And then he remembered one small thing – the kind of trivial detail easily overlooked because it seems – no, *is* – so common, so much a part of everyday life. He turned the car around.

Rachel opened the door. "Mark? You forget something?"

"Definitely," he said as he entered. "You're going to want to sit down to hear this."

Once on the couch, he said, "You remember my visit to Dr. Lancer? When I was transported to Castaic Lake?"

"Sure." She smiled. "Not exactly an easy thing to forget."

"Driving home just now, I remembered that a couple of guys next to me had been talking about fishing. One of them mentioned Castaic Lake. Then they were called to the pharmacy."

"So…you're saying that's what determined where you went? The destination?"

"It's the only connection I can think of. It's got to be the key."

"Did that happen on your other transports?"

"Not that I remember, but maybe I overheard it. Unconsciously, I mean."

Rachel looked at the table for several seconds, then knitted her brow. "That doesn't make any sense. That time at the hospital. You said that everyone had left the waiting area."

He rubbed his chin. "There were people walking in the corridor, but…hmm. Maybe it's not the spoken word."

Rachel tilted her head.

"I'm saying that maybe somehow I'm …I know it sounds crazy, but maybe somehow I'm picking up their thoughts – thoughts about places they've been."

"Okay. Let's stop right there. This is becoming scary-movie stuff." She paused as she looked down. "Then again, maybe it already was." She looked at him with knitted brows. "You know, Mark, maybe that explains why you never transport from home."

"Meaning?"

"At home, the thoughts...no, the emotional attachments are too strong. Yours and your family's."

"Yeah. That makes sense. But even if people's thoughts explain the 'where', what about the 'how'?"

Rachel turned her palms upward. "We might never figure that out. The real question is, what do we do now?"

"I don't know."

They were silent for about a minute before Rachel spoke up. "There's something else. In a hospital, people come from a larger geographical area. Why don't you ever end up in New York or Dallas, or South America?"

He smiled. "Cheaper than coach, and more legroom." They both chuckled. "A good question. Actually, I did worry about ending up in some place like North Korea, but the farthest I've transported is about 300 miles.

"So maybe there's a range limit? Another part of the mystery."

He nodded. "And we're no closer to stopping it."

She grabbed his hand in both of hers. "I'm sorry, babe, but you just have to keep trying."

About a week later he was at the auto insurance office. A large man was sitting in the chair opposite him. An XX-Large man. He wasn't reading or watching anything in particular. Just staring straight ahead. He caught Mark looking at him. His, 'What the hell you lookin' at?' glare was miles beyond intimidating. Mark immediately looked elsewhere, then picked up a magazine. Its pages were even more uninteresting than the cover, but it helped avoid a staring duel with Mr.

XX-Large. Soon, an agent came to the waiting area, and Mr. XX-Large followed her to her office.

As he perused the ads, he wondered, '*Does anybody actually buy this crap? Why would anyone want soap bars in the shape of cars? The Model A one would be hard to handle, especially for a woman's small hands, and would she...*'

He abruptly woke in a much darker area. The chairs in this waiting room were old, and leather-covered. He couldn't tell which of the doors was the exit. He rose and opened the one on the left. He was looking at a small restaurant bar. Small and quiet, and not well-lit.

Two guys were playing cards at the table nearest him. One of them spotted him, and practically jumped from his seat. "What the hell are you doin' here?" He didn't say it loud, but the edge to his voice froze Mark's blood.

"I, uh, I got lost. Came in here by accident. Sorry."

"How'd you get in?"

"How?"

That was the wrong thing to say. Actually, anything would have been the wrong thing to say. Mark found himself swung around and pinned to a wall while the two of them searched him – first for weapons, then for identification. Then, without a word, the two of them – both only 'X-Large' – pushed him back through the door, and across the waiting room.

Mark tried to analyze his situation. '*Ah. Door number two. Somehow I don't think this one's any better.*'

One of the X-Larges knocked. A voice said, "Yeah?"

Inside the room, sitting behind a ridiculously over-sized desk was a man, who would have been imposing even without the scar on the side of his brown face. He was less muscular than the X-Large men, but his eyes were more intimidating. They were simultaneously passionate and cold. Mark's fear level reached two thumbs up.

"Who's this, Nando?"

"Some guy named Mark Slider. You know him boss?"

"No. Where'd you find him?"

"In the waitin' room."

"How'd he get there without you stoppin' him?"

"Don't know, boss. That's why we thought we'd check with you." The boss stared at Nando. "No guns or knives on him, boss."

At five-eleven and 150 pounds, Mark didn't look dangerous. But to them, he was an unknown factor. The boss didn't like unknown factors. He pointed to a chair in front of the desk. Mark found himself lifted up and set in the chair.

"What's your story? Whaddya you want here?"

"I don't want anything. I got here...accidentally."

"How'd you get in without Pedro or Nando seein' you?"

"It's complicated, Mr. Boss."

"You tryin' to be funny? Huh? Some kind of comedian?"

"No...no, not at all."

The boss stared at him long enough and steady enough for Mark's arms to begin shaking.

"The name is Mr. Piña. Raul Piña. You mighta heard of me."

"Uh, no sir, I can't say I have."

Piña paused for about a quarter-minute, never taking his eyes off Mark. "Okay, Mr. Slider. Tell ya what. I'll give ya two minutes to explain how ya got here and what's your business with me. If I am not satisfied with your answer..." At this point he leaned forward with his elbows on the desk, "some very bad things are gonna happen. You understand?"

"Absolutely...but, you're not going to believe it."

Piña leaned back. "That'd be very unfortunate."

"I have these strange experiences..." He went on to describe his problem.

After a while, Piña stopped him. "I've heard enough. Break him," he said to Pedro.

"Boss, something's wrong here. We wasn't sleepin'. I swear. He never walked past us."

Piña stared Pedro down. Nobody refused his orders.

"I'm just thinkin', boss, maybe it wouldn't hurt to look at the video."

"Wouldn't do no harm, boss," Nando said.

Piña's eyes punched from one to the other. "Okay. Let's look at the video. But it damned well better not show him sneakin' past you." He tapped on the keyboard in front of him. Nando went around the desk and they both watched the video recording from the outside camera. They fast forwarded an hour's feed.

Then Piña looked at Mark. "What happened today that got you into my waitin' room? Specifically."

Mark described his morning at the insurance office.

"What'd the guy look like?"

Mark described Mr. XX-Large as thoroughly as he could.

"Cesar. And where was this office?"

"Lekron Insurance, on Sepulveda."

Piña picked up his phone. "Cesar...Raul...Were you at Lekron Insurance today?...What time?...Did you notice anyone else in the waiting room?...Describe him...Uh huh...What time was that?...I'll explain later."

He set down the phone and looked at Mark. "He confirms what you say. Even the time. And the outside video seems to confirm it. So, Mark, how do you explain it?"

Mark told Piña everything he had discovered about the phenomenon.

"What kind of work do you do, Mark?"

"Actually, I'm between jobs."

Piña chuckled. "Between jobs. Heh, you like that Pedro?" Pedro and Nando laughed. Piña stopped laughing. Pedro and Nando stopped laughing. "That's funny," Piña said. "What you mean is you're unemployed."

"Yeah. It's kind of hard to hold a job when you might suddenly find yourself a hundred miles away."

Piña nodded. "A definite liability. I can see that." He paused for a while before continuing. "Then again, it could also be an asset." While Mark tried to comprehend his meaning, Piña turned to Pedro. "Give him back his backpack and ID." Then turning to Mark, he leaned back and said, "How would you like a job?"

Mark's first impulse was to jump at the opportunity. His second reaction was more cautious. "Doing what?"

Piña opened a humidor well-proportioned for the giant desk. He turned it toward Mark, who raised a palm to decline the offer. Piña picked up a very large cigar, clipped the end and carefully lit it. He took a few puffs. "You would be doin' exactly what you're already doin', except gettin' well paid."

As Piña waited for his words to create interest, Mark was deciphering their meaning. Finally, he said, "You want me to transport money or drugs."

Piña raised his eyebrows and nodded. "You're a smart kid. But you think too small. It's money *and* drugs."

"You know, I really appreciate the offer, but I don't feel comfortable with that."

He had hardly finished speaking when the other three broke out in laughter.

"Don't feel comfortable?" Piña continued to chuckle. "Well I don't feel comfortable having an outsider trespass on my inner sanctum. Especially someone who might be called as a witness in some future trial. Comprende?"

"I see." What Mark saw was that he would be forever married to the mob...or cartel...or whatever this was.

"Look, all I need is for you to have skin in the game. That way, you don't rat us out, because you'll be part of us." He leaned back and took another draw from his giant phallic symbol. "Besides, you'll be earnin' big time. How about...three percent of the value of each run?"

"Uh, how much is a run worth?

"The drugs from Mexico are uncut, worth about a hundred grand per trip. You'll carry the cash to them, they'll send you back with the merchandise. So, how does six grand per round trip sound to you? Around 12 grand a month."

It was like looking at an optical illusion. One moment it's a rocky outcropping; then your vision shifts, and it's some kind of bird. Mark's enthusiasm was aroused. "I see only one problem. I always wear a backpack so that I have whatever I need, wherever I might land. The thing is...that is, what I've heard, is the cops use sniffer dogs. And drugs leave a trace."

Piña stopped moving. "Huh. Good point." He turned to Nando. "The kid's smart." He turned back to Mark. "We will buy you our own backpacks. Yours will stay here. The Mexicans will have their own backpacks with the drugs when they send you back here."

"Yeah. That sounds like it should work."

Piña nodded. "It's a *great* idea. It bypasses checkpoints, border patrols, border walls, and also the gentlemen in the black van across the street."

"The FBI is outside?"

"FBI or DEA. They got eyes on all our locations, and most of our people. Makes conductin' business difficult. You'll bypass those as well. They'll never even see you."

"We'll need a place to transport me from – one the DEA isn't watching."

Piña paused, then nodded. "Good point. Yeah, we have a Dr. Stone we use – just in case one of us needs emergency medical care..." He eyed Mark. "...with no questions asked and no one informed. His office will be your point of...what do you call it...?"

"Transport."

"Yeah. Transport. Your backpack and car will stay at his office." Piña paused as he tapped the ash from his cigar. "Like I said, Mark, you're smart. Probably smart enough to know what will happen if you choose to run off on your own with our goods or our money."

"Yes, Mr. Piña. Understood."

"Your phone number." He handed mark a pad of paper.

Mark handed it back, then said, "You know, phones can be tracked, and their owners ID'd."

"Yeah, we know. We'll make sure you get a few burner phones with fake account names. You'll carry one of them to and from here. And also to our supplier across the border. I guess that covers everything."

"Yeah, except the money."

Piña eyed him. "Don't tell me you're gettin' greedy."

"No, it's just that I can't put it in the bank."

"Good point. Here's a card."

Mark read the logo. *Fane Photography.*

"Joe Fane's a buddy of mine. I'll call him and let him know you'll be there tomorrow. He's goin' to take pretty pictures of you, and issue you a half-dozen fake IDs. You open up a new account – a small one, mind you – under one of the fake names and in a new bank. Rent a safety deposit box, and transfer all your extra cash there."

"Yeah, that should work."

"Come to think of it, to make your cover complete, you're goin' to have to show a source of income. Dr. Stone is goin' to hire you as...as whatever employment position he can think of. On the record, he will pay you $500 a week. Of course, the money will come outta your cut, but it'll be a good cover in case anyone asks. Let's see...what else...I guess that covers everything."

"When do I start?"

"Weekend. The best time to get lost in a herd of tourists. Nando will call you on one of his phones. You'll meet him in Dr. Stone's waitin' room, and he'll make sure you transport here. Right now, go into our waitin' room."

Mark rose and left the office.

"Pedro, get him a boring magazine and start thinking about the Lekron Insurance office."

"Boss, I never been there."

"No? Okay, then one of your favorite places. After 10 minutes, leave him alone in there."

When Mark awoke, he was confused, then surprised to find himself in a topless bar.

***

Mark arrived 15 minutes ahead of time. He didn't want to mess this up. Dr. Stone introduced him to Hector.

Hector had a limp handshake. Limp and cold, like his eyes. "Piña explained this...thing of yours. Yeah. I been to where you goin'. Uh, huh. This better work. Yeah."

Dr. Stone led them to an empty room. After 10 minutes of thinking about the drug-maker building in Mexico, Hector left the room. A few minutes later, Mark woke to a dead-eyed man in a paint-peeling room. The man never spoke.

'Perhaps no habla ingles?' thought Mark. *'Maybe only speakee Bang-Bang?'* he wondered. It was more his good sense than his nervousness at this, his first run, that kept him as silent as the stranger.

The stranger traded backpacks with Mark, and repeated the process Hector had performed. Mark completed the run. He drove home with his stomach still churning. His subsequent runs became less nerve-racking, until they had transitioned into a routine – a green routine. After six months, he had managed to accumulate a large nest egg for himself. That was in addition to giving his parents half his 'official' weekly earnings, which covered the deficit for Pete's tuition. Feeling on top of the world, he called Rachel and invited her to dinner.

As he parked the car, she asked, "Are you sure you don't want to go Dutch on this?"

"No, no. I've got a job. I'll tell you about it inside."

After they had ordered, she said, "So what's the job? Don't keep me in excitement."

"I work for a doctor."

"Doing what?"

"First, promise me you won't breathe a word of this to anybody."

"What? Why? Is it something illegal?" Mark looked her in the eye, and said nothing. Her smile disappeared. Finally, she said, "Okay, I promise. But if I say, 'stop,' don't say another word."

"I help a guy who, let's say...crosses the line now and then."

"What line."

"The legality line."

Rachel took several seconds to digest his meaning. "Jesus, Mark. Please tell me you're not making drugs."

"Not making..."

Her eyebrows shot upward. "Selling?"

He was about to answer when the chirpy waitress arrived with their order. Once she had sped off, each of them forked up a taste.

"Mmm. This is good. We're going to have to come back here again."

"You still haven't answered my question," she pointed out.

"Not selling either. I just help him move them."

"You run drugs for a living?" It was a whisper, but a harsh one.

"It sounds worse than it is. I don't actually distribute. My boss orders, and I just fetch them. What he does afterward is his business."

"Besides the danger if you get caught, have you considered what happens to the drugs?" He started to answer, but she cut him off. "They end up in someone's veins, Mark. People die from this."

"People die from reckless driving. No one blames the car salesman."

The 'discussion' did not last until the end of the meal. They drove to her place in silence.

"Shall I come in?" Mark asked.

"No. I think not."

"Don't be angry, Rachel."

"Mark, I'm not angry. Just disappointed."

"What else can I do? With my condition, how many opportunities do I have? Even if I could depend on my parents, what happens when they pass on? What kind of life could I expect? This is all I have, my one chance to make something useful of my life. I love you, Rachel. Please don't judge me."

She nodded. "I love you too. And I'm not judging you. It's just that...I don't know."

As he drove home, everything felt inverted. Now the world was on top of him. However, he had his job, his lifeline to a life. He got back 'on the road' the following week.

But, like all roads, his eventually turned. He had just returned from another run, when the DEA raided Piña's place. Mark was caught in the net, this time carrying the ID of one Micky Jerome. They threw him into a cell awaiting formal charges. However, that night, just as the last of his cell mates fell asleep, he was awakened by a cold wind. He found himself on a hammock in someone's yard. It took him a few minutes to realize he had transported again.

He eventually made it home, and got some shuteye before calling a cab and reaching Dr. Stone's. He was about to enter, when he paused for a half-minute with an idea. He entered the clinic.

Before he could ask, the receptionist said, "I'll let the doctor know you're here."

Stone rushed out and ushered him into his private office. "I heard you guys got picked up."

"Yeah. I managed to get away. Hey, what's going to happen to the operation?"

"The Zinke organization has already moved in. But you're safe. I don't think they know about you."

Mark nodded for several seconds. "Maybe you could do me and them a favor. Let them know about me. Maybe introduce me afterwards. And a favor to yourself too – you know, get Zinke to use your services."

Dr. Stone sat back in his chair. "Not a bad idea. Piña was a good chunk of extra cash." Stone nodded to himself. "Yeah, I'll let you know."

Zinke liked the idea, though it took some verification from Dr. Stone and the cartel down south before he accepted. Mark now had a clear vision of his life – an unexpectedly successful one. No matter how many times he got arrested, he'd be out before the next morning with an alternate ID. And if his ID forger was arrested, his contacts could find him another. His curse had become his godsend.

There was only one gap in his life. He tried to reconnect with Rachel, but she didn't answer her phone. One day, he visited her home. Her mother answered the door. "Hi, Mark. Haven't seen you in a long time."

"Hi Mrs. Landers. Is Rachel in?"

"Oh. I guess you haven't heard. She graduated and moved to Philadelphia with Tom."

"Tom?"

"Her husband. They got married right after graduation. She started a new job there."

"I see. Well, when you talk to her, tell her congrats for me."

"I'll do that. Would you like to come in and talk? I'd love to hear what you're up to these days."

"Maybe some other time. Thanks."

The rest of the day was overcast, despite the sun. He waited anxiously for his next trip down south.

The arrangement with Zinke worked as smoothly as it had with Piña. The money continued to roll in. The system Mark had plugged himself into worked like the finely-tuned engine on his BMW. Of course, he could have paid cash, but that would have attracted attention. So, he put it on a five-year loan, keeping payments low enough to provide an explanation, in case the IRS should get curious.

One day he got a toothache. He had a 2:00 appointment at Garth Dental Clinic. He had chosen Garth because they had three dentists and a half-dozen hygienists. Several people were always waiting for their appointments. He would never be alone.

"Bad news, Mark," Dr. Tolson said. "It's a cracked tooth. Starting to get infected. You'll need an endodontist."

"Uh, maybe you could just pull it?"

"I'd be afraid to. Liable to come apart on me. No, it will need a root canal and crown." He handed Mark a card. "You'll want to call Dr. Lasky ASAP, before the infection reaches the jawbone."

Two days later, Mark sat nervously in the waiting room. He arrived on time, but Dr. Lasky was delayed. Worse, Dr. Stone's friend hadn't yet arrived to keep him company. And his tooth had begun to pound on his jaw.

A couple of women were looking at pictures.

"Oh, the seals are so cute," the too-redheaded woman said.

"Actually, those are sea lions," the more honest gray-haired lady said. "They look small because they don't let the cruise ship get too close to their beach. Roger used a telephoto lens."

Mark's throbbing jaw found the conversation annoying. *'What is it with old people and cruises? Boring.'* He inserted his earbuds and turned up the music.

"Where were these taken?" Too Red asked.

"This is San Simeon, and the other one, the one with the seals, is Cambria."

"Seems like a lovely cruise," Too Red remarked.

"And here's one of my favorites." Lady Gray held the photo up for both of them see. "This is the sunset Roger shot on our way back, just off the Channel Islands. Isn't it lovely?"

"My Gosh. Spectacular."

"My favorite," Lady Gray said. "In fact, as far as I'm concerned, this was the only photo that truly captured the way things looked. Not that I would tell Roger."

On his phone, Mark was fingering through the list of replacement rims for his car. *'Dang! That much? Good thing I'm raking it in.'*

The door to the treatment room opened. The young gal smiled. "Sorry for the wait, Mrs. Jackson. One of Dr. Lasky's patients had a complication."

Lady Gray walked into the treatment room, while Too Red continued to shuffle the photos. Mark couldn't decide between rims. '*The low-profile are trendy; but then, the cast-and-anodized actually look better. Sharper lines.*' Both had an avant-garde price. As he was pulled into the website's black hole of wants – actually, a green hole – he didn't notice when Too Red left for the restroom. After a few minutes, he dozed off.

He felt himself falling. Before he could open his eyes, the cold water slammed his senses. His body instinctively jerked inward.

"What the hell?!"

He looked around. Beyond the watery expanse, he could barely see the tops of the Channel Islands. To his right were the mountains behind the coast. It took less than a half-minute to understand...Lady Gray on the deck of her cruise ship. Except the ship wasn't there.

Somehow, he had to reach land. He began to stroke toward the island. He was a decent swimmer, but the currents...

Complications

"Diabetes? I've heard it's a terrible disease. A lot of complications."

"Not likely in your case, if you're disciplined in dealing with it." Dr. Parmunti handed her a large envelope. "Inside you'll find a list of instructions for tracking your glucose level. And Mrs. Dion, I can't emphasize enough the importance of tracking your glucose on a permanent basis."

Gail Dion felt the thickness of the envelope. "I guess you get a lot of diabetics."

"We do. Yours is at a low level, what we call pre-diabetes. If you're attentive and consistent at tracking your numbers, we'll be able to control it. The instructions are in the packet. At this point, it's not necessary to start you on drugs, but I'm going to write you a prescription for a testing meter. Your insurance should cover it."

When Gail reached home, she immediately opened the packet. The record keeping form had fill-in boxes for the time of each meal, the foods consumed, and the test results an hour-and–a-half after. '*Heck, I could do this easier on a spreadsheet,*' she thought. She took pride in her computer skills, which she had used extensively in her career as a logistics manager. Though retired for a few years, she had lost none of her ability. Within a half-hour, she had a spreadsheet set up to track all the required data and more.

Seven months later, she was having lunch with Rhonda Foster, a longtime friend and co-worker from their days at Hulcap Industries. "And no bread for me," she told the waiter.

"How's the diabetes? Got it under control?" Rhonda asked.

"Mostly, though the glucose level occasionally spikes. I've kept a record of the readings for each meal, along with the foods I ate."

"Sounds like the old Gail. You always liked data."

"I do, but there's something else – and this is going to sound weird, but just bear with me. As I said, I keep getting these occasional spikes – always after both lunch and dinner on the same day. Then the readings return to normal. I tried cross-referencing the spikes to what I ate, how much I ate, the meal times, even the day's exercise. But there wasn't any pattern."

"Have you talked to the doctor?"

"I see him in a couple of months for my quarterly. But here's the thing. Ralph and I were watching the news about them blowing up the London stock exchange the other night..."

"Just terrible." Rhonda said.

"...and then I remembered my numbers had spiked three days earlier. Later in the conversation he mentioned hurricane Chloe, and I remembered it too occurred three days after one of my glucose spikes."

"Interesting," lied Rhonda.

"Then I checked every spike I've had since keeping track, and compared the dates against the news events around those days. There was a disaster three days after every one. Weird, huh?"

Rhonda stopped eating. Now she *was* genuinely interested. "Are you saying your glucose spikes are somehow causing disasters, or..."

"Oh heavens, no. I just think it's an extraordinary set of coincidences. Once or twice I could ignore, but six times in a row? And no disasters when I don't have spikes? What are the odds?"

"What were the dates?"

"Actually, I have a printout." Gail reached into her purse, and began reciting the list.

Rhonda interrupted. "March 17? I don't remember anything happening then."

"Sure. The Texas gas refinery explosion was on the 20th."

"Can I see the list?"

"Sure. Keep it, if you want." Gail said. "I can always print out another one."

"You know, Gail, Keith told me last month…or was it the month before…anyway, he mentioned some experiments by a couple of cognitive scientists. He still reads the psych magazines, even though he's retired. What was it? Something about how they found most people sense the future without realizing it. I forget the details. I learned years ago to tune out when he starts talking shop.

"Actually, it sounds fascinating. I'd like to know more, even if it doesn't relate to my disaster list."

"I'll ask him about it tonight."

The next day, Gail's phone buzzed. "Hi Rhonda. What's up?"

"Listen, I asked Keith about that article – the one about people knowing the future? It's called 'unconscious precognition', and there were two experiments that confirmed it. The thing is, Keith said it's only a matter of minutes. No one has shown it to occur with a three-day lead."

"So, does he think I'm a quack?"

"It's hard to tell. You know how shrinks are: You ask them a question and they never give a straight answer. 'Doc, am I over-reacting?' 'Do you think you're over-reacting?' Anyway, after 30 years, I can read him pretty well. So yes, I could see he was skeptical. But just so you know, I changed his mind."

"Really? How did you do that?"

"By figuring out how the 'precoging' thing could connect with the glucose spikes. You know how Keith is – the scientific mind and all that. I came up with a mechanism that could explain it."

"So? Don't keep me in suspense. How? I've practically pasteurized my brain searching for a connection, but haven't been able to think of one. How does a plane crash affect my blood three days before it happens?"

"My aunt is diabetic. I remember her saying that whenever she had an anxiety attack, her numbers would rise – something involving stress hormones. So, I told Keith that maybe if you're unconsciously aware of the coming disasters, your body might be releasing stress hormones. Then Keith starts pacing the room, and says, 'That makes sense. The precognition is subconscious, and so is the release of hormones. She wouldn't be aware of either one.' Then he looks at me and says, 'Honey, that's brilliant! And the three-day precognition...why, that's incredible! Absolutely record setting.'"

Gail was bewildered. "Good heavens! You think that's what's causing it?"

"I do. And Keith does too. Do you know, that was the first time in 30 years that he ever complimented me on any remark I made involving psychology? It was always like he built a fence around the subject. He was very possessive about his field of expertise. Over the years, I learned to avoid the topic as much as possible."

"So, what do I do now? I worry about the spikes. Diabetes can damage the body's nerve cells."

"You can ask your doctor, but from what I've heard, occasional high readings won't cause damage. Otherwise, nobody would dare eat a donut or ice cream. But Keith says you should start posting your numbers on your Me&Mine page."

"Why?"

"He thinks there's something of a medical miracle here. It's like posting a doctor or clinic you recommend or a new herbal supplement that helped you. I think he's right. Maybe other people will begin tracking their readings and find similar precognition. Who knows how far this might go?"

"Post my glucose numbers along with my travel and family photos and friends' postings? Tacky."

"Just start a second page," Rhonda said. "Lots of people do it. That way, all the diabetes stuff could be on one page. Not just your readings, but diabetic recipes too. A lot of people have the disease. It could help them."

"Hmm. I'll have to think about it."

The next day, Gail decided Rhonda was right. Who could predict how far it might go? She created a *Diabetic's Discovery* page and listed her purpose, as well as information about her glucose reading's connections to future events. After several days, she still had only 28 followers – all of them her regular friends. Nevertheless, each day she dutifully listed her readings for all her meals.

Two weeks later, a plane crash in the Alps took 280 lives. From her glucose numbers three days earlier, she had known something was going to happen. She realized her discovery of her "Diabetes ESP", as she now called it, was more of a curse than a gift. Knowing three days ahead that some terrible tragedy would occur bestowed only a feeling of dread. She wished she'd never noticed the link. She even considered ceasing to track her numbers, but the doctor insisted it was necessary. After all, she did have an actual medical condition, one that could cause serious complications.

The next day, her phone buzzed. "Hi, Morgan."

"Hi, Mom. Have you looked at your Me&Mine page today?"

"Not yet. I usually record the numbers in the evening."

"You've got 500 followers."

"What?" She quickly opened her laptop. "You're right. How did this happen?"

"Word of mouth, I guess. Your followers linked your page to their family and friends, and they all did the same. It's gone viral."

"Oh, for heavens' sake. I've got 117 people who want to friend me. I don't even know these people. What do you think I should do?"

"Go ahead and friend them. It doesn't mean anything, anyway."

"You know, Morgan, this is getting to be more trouble than it's worth. Come to think of it, it doesn't pay anything, so it's worth nothing."

The air disaster was the first story on the news that night. Near the end of the segment, the news anchor said, "And for an unusual addendum to this story, we go to Ronnie Twift."

The face of a preppy 20-something woman appeared. "Yes, John. It seems someone out there can actually foresee disasters before they happen. Her name is Gail Dion, and she…"

"What the shit?!" Ralph said. Gail remained silent, unable to speak.

"…records her diabetes glucose readings on her Me&Mine *Diabetic's Discovery* page. More important, her readings seem to foretell disastrous events. Her readings go high for lunch and dinner three days before a major tragedy occurs somewhere in the world."

"Ronnie, is this Ms. Dion some kind of astrologer or fortune teller?" the news anchor asked.

"Apparently not, John. From what we've been able to discover about this mystery woman, she is an ordinary suburbanite living in retirement in Cincinnati. We plan to follow up on this story, and bring it to all our KWAK news viewers."

"Thanks, Ronnie. We'll be anxiously awaiting your report in the near future. And when we return from the break, we'll tell you about a dog who has adopted some orphan ducks."

Gail was incensed. "Let's switch channels. I'm never going to watch KWAK news again." However, other versions of the same story were on the other news channels.

The next day, the doorbell rang.

"Hi Mrs. Dion. I'm Ronnie Twift from…"

"I know who you are. I saw your dreadful broadcast last night."

"Dreadful? Why would you say that?"

"I'm not an astrologer or a fortune teller."

"I never said you were. John Stimmers was speculating, and I'm really sorry he did that. But I'll tell you what. You tell me in your own words, and we can stop all the speculations, rumors, and lies. This is your chance to tell your own story accurately. Will you help me get the truth out there?"

If Twift had been a guy, Gail probably would have closed the door in his face. But this was a chance to talk woman-to-woman. "Oh, okay, but he'll have to wait outside," she said, pointing to the guy with the video camera.

Gail made a pot of tea, laid out the tableware on the dining room table and filled the cups. As she was about to sit down, the doorbell rang again.

"Mrs. Dion, I'm Sam Peterson from the Cincinnati Howler. Would you mind me asking a few questions about your magnificent gift of seeing the future?"

She was about to refuse, but realized she was going to be telling the story to Twift anyway. *'Might as well kill two vultures with one stone,'* she thought. However, a few moments later, a woman walked up just as Peterson entered. "Hi. Mrs. Dion? I'm Ginny Moore from…"

About 10 minutes later, after she had taped a sign that read "Back At 5:00" to the front door, the six of them sat down at the table.

Twift kicked off the interview. "I'm curious. How long have you had this link between your glucose readings and the world's disasters?"

Gail described the train of events, ending with, "I have no more idea about the how or why of this link than you do. And before any of you ask, I've never been a fortune teller, a card reader, or an astrologer. And let me add, I have no psychic ability whatsoever."

The interview continued for another half-hour, with the questions becoming decreasingly germane and increasingly insipid. The next day saw a repeat performance with other media actors, and the third day would have as well if Ralph hadn't responded to her complaints by posting a "No Trespassing" sign in the front yard. Even then, he had to assume the duty of answering the door and driving off several media people with a few slightly abridged cusswords. Gail and Ralph were glad the media were gone. They naively imagined they could get back to their sedate retired lives.

A few days later, a scientist from Ultra Rose Labs called, and she agreed to let them test the magnetic fields around her brain. Though they found nothing notable, Gail didn't mind. The tests were short, painless, and even a bit of fun. And the scientists were very polite, unlike FBI agents Jim Goth and Rick Hun, who rang her doorbell the next day and announced their need to investigate her.

"Investigate? For what?"

"We think it's possible that "foreign powers" might be data-mining your readings."

"Are you serious? This is what we citizens pay you for?"

"We checked your purchase records. Your glucose monitor was made in China," Goth said.

"So are my shoes. So what?"

"We have a detection device with us. We'd like to have you take a test while we check around the monitor for transmissions. It will take only a few minutes."

"That's ridiculous. Get out of my house."

"If we leave, we'll be back with a warrant to seize your device for testing purposes," Hun said.

"We'd rather not have to deprive you of your continued glucose tracking," Goth added.

Gail brought the test kit to the dining room table and performed a blood test while the two agents moved a sensor around the monitor. She felt like telling them it reminded her of a séance, but she thought it best not to provoke them.

"Okay. We're clear here," Hun announced.

"Are you sure you don't want to check my shoes?"

The agents did not smile. Ever.

Later that day, she heard her name mentioned in a radio announcement. For his TV show that day, Wally Bunch was going to be doing an investigative story about her. She went out to the garage. "Ralph, you ever hear of Wally Bunch?"

"Wally who?"

"Bunch. He's doing some TV program on me. Did he interview you?"

"No. Never heard of him."

They went to her computer and did a search. "A UFO specialist?" Ralph said with the same expression as when he opened the garbage bin lid the day before pickup. "What's he got to do with your diabetes?"

They found the TV listing, and that afternoon watched his introduction. His coverage of the Diabetes ESP (by this time, the term had become part of the common American lingo) was sandwiched between stories of a haunted swamp and a child who played ball with ghosts.

"Jesus!" said Ralph. "Look at the company you keep." His humor took the edge off Gail's concern about her public embarrassment.

Wally Bunch had dramatized her story, and ended the segment with the most likely explanation of her "psychic phenomenon": "We have investigated, and we know for a fact that Gail Dion has had extensive dental work done through the years. It's clear to us that this resembles other cases we've investigated. Clearly, at least one of Gail Dion's modified teeth is picking up transmissions from the other side. The only questions are whether the spirit world is deliberately sending her these transmissions, and if so, why."

"Gail, this is getting ridiculous." Ralph said.

"No kidding. It's embarrassing. I never wanted this kind of attention. When does it end?"

She asked the same question the next day, after the Church of Our Lady of Lichtenstein declared her to be "a false prophet, a tool of the Antichrist".

"Who the hell are they?" asked Ralph.

"Oh, you know. That church out on the Westside district with an effigy of a roadrunner nailed to an orange cross?"

"That place? I thought that was just a joke – a mock church of atheists."

"No. It's a real church, but with some weird beliefs. They think this is the afterlife. They don't believe Hell is a pit of fire but an insane asylum, and that we're already there."

"That's not just weird. That's...well, insane."

The next day, Rashid Berry of GasFlix Pictures contacted her, wanting to do a movie on her life.

"What do you think, Ralph?"

"We'd probably make some significant money, but once you sign, you'll lose control of the story."

"I already have. And frankly, I'm tired of being in the public crosshairs."

He grinned. "Maybe they'd have Wally Bunch write the screenplay."

She was again grateful for his humor. It helped relieve the stress. She turned down the movie proposal, as well as a stock broker's offer to pay for her daily revelations, provided she keep them private. She talked about these events with Morgan.

"Mom, I'm going to make a suggestion."

"What's that?"

"Lie."

"What?"

"Keep the real readings for your doctor, but put fake ones on your Me&Mine page. You know, like keeping two sets of books when a business wants to hide income from the IRS."

"Actually," Gail said, "the IRS is starting to look pretty good compared to the media and some of the nutcases out there."

"List all the online readings as high, even when they aren't."

"What would be the point of that?"

"When everyone sees the high readings, and no disaster follows in three days, they'll figure out you're not a soothsayer after all."

"But how do I explain it?" Gail asked.

"That's the beauty of it. You don't have to. If anyone asks, you've merely lost the power. It just went away."

Gail discussed Morgan's idea with Ralph, and they both liked it. People would finally leave them alone. Over the next week, she entered numbers on her website 50 points higher than the actual readings. She was confident her actions could break the public's interest in her glucose numbers, and that she and Ralph could get back to their sedate life of retirement.

However, her quarter-million followers immediately panicked. The next day, security agencies in several nations went on alert. By the second day, brokerages around the world began a sell off that accelerated for two weeks, shaving 43 percent from the Dow Jones index. By the third day, churches began filling up in the evenings. By the fourth day, people on the coasts were selling their houses and moving to avoid the coming earthquakes and their attendant tidal waves. Housing prices plummeted. They streamed into rural areas to have access to food when civilization collapsed. The price of rural houses skyrocketed, as did the price of food. Devout people rejoiced that the End Times were near and that non-Christians would be cleansed from

the Earth; or that non-Moslems would be cleansed from
the Earth. Christians awaited the Messiah's Second
Coming; Jews awaited the Messiah's first coming;
Hindus awaited the end of the fourth cycle; Buddhists
complained that the end of the world was arriving
ahead of schedule.

While martial law was being declared in increasing
numbers of the world's cities, Gail and Ralph made a
decision. The next day, they went for a drive. They
parked their car at the curb, and walked a few yards
along the sidewalk before turning onto the walkway
toward the entrance.

"I've always wondered what it looked like on the
inside," she said.

"I hope they accept new members," he said.

Just before reaching the green- and purple-striped
doors, they bent their heads back for a closer look at the
roadrunner statue nailed to the cross.

Frailty

After tea was poured, Imam Hamid Bakhtiar said, "How may I be of service to you?"

Robert Stark had his presentation well-memorized. "I'm considering writing a book about the revolution in Kopanzia. Kopanzia is a majority Moslem country, and, of course, President Kikuru Holombe was Christian. I'm having trouble reconciling this act of prejudice with your religion's tradition of tolerance. I hoped you might shed some light on this for me."

Bakhtiar nodded for several seconds before replying. "You have made an incorrect assumption, Mr. Stark. President Holombe was not overthrown because of his religion."

The foundation of Robert's presentation had just crumbled. "My apologies, but all the news reports indicated..."

"Forgive the interruption, Mr. Stark, but correct me if I'm wrong. Haven't all your books been exposés?"

"Not all. Two were contemporary histories."

"Ah. Then almost all. Nevertheless, isn't the essential nature of an exposé to reveal information hidden from the public?"

"You're saying the reports were inaccurate?"

"Or more accurately, deliberate lies."

"The government's or the media's?"

Bakhtiar smiled. "You seem to believe those are two separate things." He waited as his words took effect. "I agreed to meet with you because you have a reputation. You are one of the few who write and speak publicly in a quest for truth, not just fame or money."

"I believe the two are not mutually exclusive. I've always thought that most people want to know the truth and are willing to pay for it."

Bakhtiar looked down, then raised his head, which held a wry smile. "Mr. Stark, I have a great deal of respect for you, as well as for your work. Your exposés have been a service to the world. However, I think your view of humanity is a bit too...charitable. Perhaps that is because of the difference in our ages – you in your early 40s I would guess, and I in my 60s. However, if you are truly interested in getting beneath the lies, I am willing to assist you."

Robert saw a new image of his next book begin to form, like shadows in a fog slowly assembling into something recognizable. "I would very much appreciate your help."

"I'm going to give you the name and address of a contact in that country. If you want to know the truth, you will need to meet him." He paused as he looked directly into Robert's eyes. "That is, if you actually want to know."

"I very much want to know."

"You must promise not to reveal my name. It could make my life difficult, but more important, it would be dangerous for him, and ultimately for you as well. And if he asks you how you got his name, tell him Mosaddegh gave it to you. He will understand."

Robert promised and Bakhtiar wrote a name and address on a piece of note paper. He reached into a drawer and pulled out a small object, and handed it across the desk.

It was an ordinary St. Christopher medal. Ordinary, until Robert noticed the saint was rowing a boat. Robert furrowed his brow. St. Christopher was never depicted in a boat.

"It is a safe-passage icon," Bakhtiar said. "Don't lose it. You will present it to this man." He handed the paper to Robert.

With this one action, Robert's interview was transformed into an odyssey.

***

The heat outside the terminal of Pchongo Airport wasn't as bad as Robert had expected. He went directly to the Joshuma Hotel, recently renamed to honor the new president-for-life. Robert wondered if the owner was ordered to rename it, or if it was just his way of kissing ass. Whichever the case, the accommodations were comfortable, and the décor interesting with its combination of Western flatness and reiterated African patterns. He had brought his laptop with some fake notes for an outline of a supposed book project titled *Kopanzia After the Revolution*. He'd been a muckrake writer for decades. He knew that to deceive, a cover story had to be clothed in the trappings of substance.

The next morning, he took a taxi to the address Bakhtiar had given him. "Hi. I'm here to see Moses Ungande."

The woman eyed him suspiciously, then said, "Wait." She closed the door.

About a half-minute later, a man opened the door. "Yes?"

"Mosaddegh sent me." He showed the man his St. Christopher medal.

Moses raised his head in recognition, then said, "Your phone."

Robert understood. Phones could be tracked. He handed it over.

Moses instantly shone a wide smile, as if they were old friends. He turned back into the house, mumbled something and handed the phone to the woman. He stepped outside and closed the door. "Come with me." He was about 45, with thinning hair. At six-feet, he was the same height as Robert, but his lean body and relaxed stride made him seem taller. Robert made a mental note to exercise more after he returned home. He followed Moses to a car parked at the side of the house. It was a tan Mercedes taxi, a bit muddy along the bottom, but in good condition. Robert guessed it was about a decade old. He tossed his overnight bag on the back seat, got in and fastened his seat belt.

Moses said, "Fifty dollars." When Robert hesitated, Moses explained, "Ten dollars for gas, ten dollars for wear and tear, and thirty dollars for risking my life."

He handed Moses the money. "It's good to know that your life is worth more than a tankful of gas."

Moses chuckled. "Good humor. We will get along good, but I must ask you not to talk until we are out of the city. Since the revolution, driving requires my full concentration."

Moses was constantly checking the rearview mirror and both sides of the streets until the road meandered into a landscape of shrubs and trees. Moses relaxed. He was open to questions about the city, the revolution, problems with the plain-clothed police, even the political conditions, but ignored any questions regarding his personal life. Robert didn't even consider inquiring about his family.

The border crossing into Talstonia was easy.

"I expected more guards and more delays," Robert remarked.

"They have many trade ties. Talstonia's main source of money comes from the mines, but the ore is shipped through Kopanzia, who probably takes a hefty transit fee. So, they need to get along."

"I had heard ex-president Holombe took refuge here."

"Perhaps. But if it's true, I am sure his host extracted a promise in return. I am sure he is not allowed to stir up trouble."

"Is that who I'm going to meet?"

"Not sure. But here is your first contact." He steered the car sharply into a garage parking lot. "This is as far as I go. When you return, I'll be here, all smiles."

They shook hands. Robert exited the car, retrieved his bag and waved to Moses as the car drove off. A few seconds later, two rather large men came out of the garage. They were wearing work clothes. Mechanics, Robert figured, until he noticed the overalls were spotless.

"Come," one of them said. He immediately turned around and walked into the garage.

'Not very talkative,' Robert thought, though their lack of social manners went well with their surly expressions. He followed them inside – inside the garage, then inside the trunk of a car as he was directed by the wave of a hand.

Soon he was bouncing along on the way to meet…who? Holombe? Some terrorist? *'Only a crazy person would have agreed to this.'* He began to miss his comfortable apartment, the night life, the… He snapped himself out of the mood. He was an ex-marine and an investigative journalist. This was his life. This is what defined him.

After a duration stretched by discomfort into the impression of hours, the car stopped. The trunk was opened and Robert got out. *'Definitely getting too old for this.'* He was inside some kind of giant windowless warehouse.

One of the men retrieved his bag, and the two bodyguards, as he assumed them to be, led him into an office, which led to another. Behind a desk sat a man who appeared vaguely familiar. Robert sat down and the two bodyguards walked out.

"Mr. Stark, I am president Holombe."

"Ah. Yes, I remember your face from the newspapers."

"Just think, Mr. Stark, if I had not been overthrown, you would never have heard about me. Then too, if I had not refused to sell our bismuth mines to an American company, I would not have been overthrown. And if I had not given a damn about future generations of my countrymen, I would not have refused to sell." He paused, then chuckled. "So you see, the chain to fame is long."

"I am familiar with that chain, though my story has not been so..."

"Unpleasant?" Holombe suggested.

Robert nodded. Holombe did not appear bitter. He possessed an intrinsic dignity. This was no overweight self-indulgent dictator. Nor did his eyes resemble those of so many evil African leaders, the ones who spray words like mist to hide the viciousness lurking inside, waiting to be unleashed if their power is threatened.

Robert estimated his age at 50, his short, curly hair barely showing signs of gray. With an elongated face and a trim body, Holombe seemed sober, perhaps stern. But there was something else, something that Robert, a wordsmith, could not put into words.

"Now, tell me why you have come here."

Robert reached into his pocket and handed the St. Christopher medal to Holombe, who gave it a cursory examination before sliding it back. "We know who you are, and are familiar with your contact. But ask your questions."

"Well, originally I was investigating the apparent intolerance of Muslims. Then Mosaddegh informed me that your overthrow had nothing to do with bigotry. So, it appears I have another story to tell."

Holombe slowly nodded. "I understand why Mosaddegh sent you. I am familiar with your books. He assumes, as do I, that you are an honest man who seeks honest answers. Very well. When I prevented the JRZ Mining Corporation from stealing our ore for pennies on the dollar, they went to your government and got the CIA to promote a revolution led by the puppet Joshuma. His army, financed and armed by your government, shelled the palace. They did not know that at the time I was away, in secret talks with the Chinese to develop the mines on terms much fairer to Kopanzia. However, my family was in the palace. All were killed. I hope that shortened version of my story gives you enough material to begin another book."

Robert could not form a coherent sentence. This narrative was too unexpected, Holombe's loss too tragic, the Americans too cruel. The bits would not link into a single thread. Finally, he said, "I am sorry for your loss. Truly sorry. Yes, this is a story that needs to be told —

not the story I expected, but a more important one. I would like the chance to interview you about the details. The American people need to know about this."

Holombe chuckled. "Mr. Stark, for a very long time, your country has stolen and cheated many countries. Most of your people did not know, or more likely, did not want to know. They were unconcerned as long as they had their comforts, their wealth, their cheap coffee and other cheap products and materials that came from the poverty and pain of distant others."

"Mr. Holombe, some will listen. Some will care. Otherwise, the perpetrators of these deeds will never be held accountable."

"And you think that exposing their deeds to public eyes will accomplish that?" Holombe compressed his lips and shook his head. "Perhaps that would fulfill your need for justice. Do you think it would satisfy mine?"

Robert remained silent, curious about Holombe's game.

"The deaths of Kopanzians was never the objective of your government. They were just...how do you say...collateral damage. When your country invaded Iraq, the war cost the lives of over 150,000 Iraqis. That too was collateral damage. Your government and your businesses – and, I might add, too many of your ordinary people – are only interested in profits. Money is their fixation. No, Mr. Stark, my goal is to make war on your country, a war that will cost your country a great deal of money. I will punish America."

Robert began to wonder about Holombe. He seemed calm, very much in control of his emotions, but did he really think he could hurt the world's mightiest nation? Perhaps the loss of power, and especially, the loss of his family, had been too much for his mind. Had he lost that too?

Robert was unaware his mouth was hanging open, until Holombe remarked, "I see you are shocked. But you of all people should have anticipated something like this – if not from me, then from someone else."

"I don't know what to make of this, Mr. Holombe. *You* are going to make war on the United States?" His tone of incredulity evinced the abandonment of his role as interviewer.

"Yes, with the help of others. America has made a great number of enemies. Several have pledged to join with me in this crusade, including yesterday's pair of recruits from Yemen and a Syrian." He paused to reflect, then resumed in a slower, more deliberate pace. "What you are thinking now is that you are duty-bound to report this to your government. However, if you do, they will not reward you. They will imprison you and defame you."

Robert was unnerved. Holombe had read his mind. He waited, but realized Holombe was going to make him ask. "And why would they do that?"

"First, you have visited with someone who is on their terrorist list. Second, you now hold a secret they do not want exposed. Third, they would like to know the identity of my intermediate – Moses Ungande. If I have judged you correctly, you recognize he is a decent man, and have no wish to bring harm to him. And so, you would refuse to divulge that information. Fourth, they will imprison you until you reveal my location."

"But I don't know where we are."

"Of course. But do you think they will believe you?"

"Then, why have you agreed to this interview? If I can't write about it...?"

"I've read every one of your books, Mr. Stark. I feel I know you. They tell about corruption within your government and among the largest businesses. Perhaps you could investigate the JRZ Mining Corporation. You might find a lot of other misdeeds. More than enough for another book."

During the return trip the next morning, nestled a bit too snugly in the trunk of the car, Robert tried to conceptualize the next book. JRZ's sins around the world? Perhaps American mining companies in general? He briefly considered a story about a deranged leader, but Holombe was right – it would be dangerous, totally radioactive.

He was glad when the trunk opened and he could see Moses smiling beside his Mercedes. Perhaps Moses was surprised at seeing Robert still in one piece? When he got in, Moses's first words were, "Fifty dollars."

"Now I know why you were glad to see me alive," Robert remarked with a wry smile.

Moses grinned. "Naw. I knew you would be safe." He looked at his skeptical passenger. "You think you are the first passenger I take?"

Robert remembered Holombe mentioning the Yemeni and Syrian. *'Probably a few others,'* he thought. *'Perhaps many others?'* When they returned, Moses fetched Robert's phone and a list of names. "This for the cover story – a list of all the people you tried to talk to for your book." He chuckled, then brought his face close to Robert's. Eyeing him intently, Moses spoke quietly. "Too bad that every one of them refused to say anything."

***

His return to America was ordinary – certainly less remarkable than the one between Kopanzia and Talstonia. He was happy when he spotted Melissa in the baggage claim area. Her flowered blouse reminded him of the land he had recently departed. She liked colorful clothes, a distinct contrast to his own preference for solid, often muted colors.

"Tired?" she asked.

"A little. It was a long flight, especially with the stopover in Paris."

"Get any good material for your book?"

"Maybe for a different book."

She waited. "Want to talk about it?"

"After we get in your car. And thanks for picking me up."

"For some reason, I was actually starting to miss you." She smiled.

Melissa Newton was a writer and assistant editor for Techphilia Monthly. Her long, light brown pony tail accentuated her supple movements, belying her capacity for intense activity. They had been good friends for three years. She didn't like the term 'girlfriend' but had been unable to think of a better one to describe their relationship. Lady friend? In the 21st century? Woman friend? Sounds like a label on a zoo cage. A couple? A thing? The last offended both of their literary sensibilities. However, they were definitely friends and sometime lovers. And colleagues as well, who often helped each other with first edits of rough drafts.

A quarter-hour later the shuttle dropped them off, and they soon were on their way.

"Ready to tell me about it?"

"I suppose so, but you might not be ready to hear. I need you to promise not to repeat this to anyone."

"Okay."

"Even if you're asked in a trial, a deposition, an interrogation..."

She looked at him with a wrinkled brow. "Jesus! What's with you? Okay, okay, I promise."

As they rolled down the freeway, he gave her a summary of his conversation with Holombe.

"Jesus!" she said again. And after a pause, yet again. "What are you going to do?"

"I turned this over in my mind the whole 20-hour trip back. The thing is, I have no idea what Holombe's plans are. Without that, there's not much point in alerting the government and risking my neck. So, for now, I'm not going to bother."

"And if there's an attack?"

"I'll cross that bridge when I come to it."

She turned toward him with one of her smartass smiles. "Just hope the bridge isn't their target."

***

A week later, a 737 went down on takeoff from Detroit Metro Airport, killing all 260 passengers and crew. On the same day, the Los Angeles Dodgers completed their fifth win in a row. Dodger fans spilled out of the stadium and celebrated in the streets of the city. Cubs fans tried without success to cheer themselves in Chicago's many bars. The baseball fans of America speculated about the World Series matchup.

***

The next evening, Robert drove Melissa home. He finally broke the silence. "It was a good play. The stage designer did an exceptional job."

Melissa looked at him, then faced forward. "Yes. The entire production was very thoughtful."

"I'll bet it wins a couple of Tony's."

She decided to stop playing pretend. "I'm sorry, Robert, but your idea sounds paranoid. Someone assembled a hundred or so mini-drones and deliberately flew them into a jet engine?"

"And I'm sorry I brought it up over dinner. I didn't mean to spoil the evening."

"Look, your exposés have been incredibly popular. But I think you've let your muckrake fame run away with your common sense."

He shifted his right hand to the top of the wheel and his left arm onto the arm rest. "You won't even consider it a possibility?"

"One of my articles last year was on drones, so yes, I know it's technically possible. But *possible* does not equal *fact*. What's your evidence? A blurry cell phone video?"

"Just watch the video, then watch one of birds flying in flocks. The motions don't match."

"Maybe I'll discuss it with Joe. But he's a tough editor. Which is only half your problem."

"Okay, I'm listening."

"Do you think any FAA people will go on record for an interview? Or airline employees?"

Robert's silence answered for him.

"Your only proof is Holombe's words, with you as the only witness. And that's a fact you don't dare reveal. And if you present it in a new book as mere speculation, you'll morph into yesterday's author and today's crackpot. You'll lose all the credibility you've built up over the last 20 years."

He remained silent. She was right. He now realized he'd not been driven by good standards of reportage, but by his own frustration. He was unaccustomed to feeling powerless.

He turned toward her, and quietly said, "Thanks."

She looked at him, her brow furrowed. Then, seeing his sincerity, "You're welcome."

Three days later, flight 127, another 737, crashed on takeoff from Ontario Airport in California. Speculations about design flaws assailed Boeing. The company immediately went into defense mode, implicating the flight crew. President Murtaugh assured the public. Congress scheduled hearings. The FAA promised a thorough investigation. And the latest Star Wars movie opened on Friday.

***

But everything changed the next day. Another plane crashed on takeoff from the Atlanta International Airport. The media began using the "T" word. Murtaugh addressed the nation.

> "My fellow Americans, I come to you tonight with grave news. In the last ten days we have suffered three civilian airline crashes and the loss of 800 lives. After thorough investigations and inter-agency consultations, our intelligence services have concluded that

these were acts of terrorism. America is under siege. Ruthless, murderous terrorists have chosen to make war upon America. The CIA, the FBI and the NSA have identified the attackers. They are members of Iran's Revolutionary Guards. We have not determined how they sabotaged the planes, but I have directed the TSA to expand their inspections to include the planes themselves. Tomorrow, I will send a request to Congress to increase the number of TSA agents by 50 percent.

I do not want war. I am a man of peace, as are all Americans. But when attacked, we will strike back with the ferocity of our national symbol, the eagle. We will no longer be prey to dark forces that threaten America, and therefore the world. As I speak, cruise missiles are nearing their carefully selected targets in Iran. The day of reckoning has arrived. To all the men and women in uniform who protect America, I say, we salute you. It is on your shoulders that the safety of our country rests, as you carry out your missions of retribution upon the enemy."

Robert and Melissa sat speechless, slack-jawed. She grabbed the remote and shut off the television. She leaned toward him. "They think it's the Iranians. Robert, you've got to let them know."

He looked at her for several seconds before saying, "Melissa, don't you understand?"

"Of course I do. It's going to cause you trouble, but if you don't, innocent people are going to die. And it's going to drag us into another war and..."

"Melissa!" Then, more quietly, "Melissa, it's bullshit." She was silent. "You're looking too closely at the details. But the big picture? It's just bullshit. Murtaugh has been looking for an excuse to attack Iran. And the NSA determined it was Iranian agents? You and I know it wasn't."

She tilted her head onto the back of the couch, looking at the ceiling. "Jesus! You're right. I'm sorry."

"It's okay. You're used to writing about tech. You deal with details, with facts. I write exposés. I've learned to spot lies and cover ups through a mile of fog. It's become a habit with me. Besides, I remember what happened to Steven Hatfill."

"Hatfill...Hatfill..."

"The scientist accused in the anthrax powder attacks?"

"Oh, yes. Now I remember. The government dragged his name into the mud on the flimsiest evidence."

He nodded. "Yep. And after promising to keep his name from the media, they notified the press. Eventually, they discovered the actual culprit, but not before they had smeared his reputation."

"And then there was Wen Ho Lee," she said. "Shackled in solitary confinement and denied access to lawyers. God's sake! He was 60 years old."

"How many charges was he accused of?"

"Fifty-eight, if I remember correctly. No, it was fifty-nine. In the final plea deal, fifty-eight were dropped."

He turned his palm upward. "Well, there you have it. What do you think they'd do to me?"

"You know Robert, this opens up another question. Do they actually know it's Holombe?"

He tilted his head for several seconds. "Hmm. Maybe not. Even if they did, Murtaugh would still attack Iran – kind of a 'just because' opportunity. But it's a good question. Holombe is lying very low. Beneath the radar, I'm sure." He paused again. "Notice how nobody's claimed responsibility for any of the plane crashes?"

"And also, Murtaugh implied the planes were sabotaged. Earlier, they said it was birds, so now I'm thinking you were right – that they were taken down by drones."

"What does your editor think?"

"I haven't told Joe about your theory."

"Why not?"

She raised her eyebrows. "Oh, I don't know. Maybe because I like my reputation at the magazine – not to mention within the journalism community."

He shook his head. "You actually thought he'd consider you paranoid?"

"Well, gee, maybe that did cross my mind once or twice." She saw his irritation. "Robert, you don't go to your editor with every Outer Limits story that crosses your path. I needed some evidence before bothering him."

"Now you have it."

"No, now we have Murtaugh stating it was aircraft sabotage. Even after Murtaugh's nose grows an extra ten inches, do you think Joe is going to let me contradict the president? Without a coffee grain of proof? And I'm not talking about some blurry cell phone video someone posted on YouTube. Maybe if I worked for the National Juicer, where they run stories about White House aides from Mars. And I don't dare tell him about your prom date with Holombe."

Robert's face sagged. "Melissa, I've never felt so helpless. I mean, I know so much about this, plenty for another book. But I can't write a single paragraph of it." He shook his head.

She caressed his hair. "Remember my story predicting Arthur Lash would go broke? How this billionaire inventor, who everyone practically worshiped as a tech-savior, would be bankrupt before he accomplished his goals? You know how much flak I took from it? I know Joe was irritated at me for months."

"But he approved it, didn't he?"

"Well, maybe he was irritated at himself for letting me write it. Anyway, after Lash went belly up, with few promises fulfilled, do you think I got any congrats from Joe? Or the public?"

"Life is unfair," he agreed. "The life of a writer is more unfair."

She shrugged. "What's a writer to do?"

"I know what I want to do." He pulled her close and prolonged a kiss into a whirlpool, ending yet another discussion in the same unwriterly manner.

***

The next morning, he said, "I have an idea."

"Another position?"

"No, a book."

He enjoyed her raillery. She enjoyed his pretense of ignoring it. After three years, it had become an unspoken, yet defined routine.

"The one about JRZ?" she asked.

"No. That one's a dead horse. All I could find were industry journal articles and corporate puffery with the usual accolades. It looks like the government has classified most of the material on the company's dealings with foreign governments. National security, my ass."

"Your ass and my stomach. I'm starved. Let's get some breakfast."

Dino's Diner wasn't a diner. It was an upscale, trendy restaurant pretending to be a folksy cubbyhole. Robert and Melissa liked it for the small windows at each booth – big enough for a view of the outside world, small enough to avoid the ambience of a fishbowl. As he finished his eggs, he said, "You're a tech writer. Just for speculation, how would you stop the drone attacks?"

"Well...good question. The cell phone video indicates it wasn't one drone, but a flock of them. So, someone has to control it with radio...no, wait. There are probably some autonomous ones out there."

"Like self-driving cars?"

"Yeah. I saw a video of a radio-controlled plane that took off and landed itself after a five-minute flight. It even avoided trees and power poles on its own."

"Image recognition," he suggested.

"Sure. But then, I have no idea how I'd stop them. One operator could launch a flock of them with a single signal, and the drones would do the rest on their own. They could be programmed to aim for a specific shape."

"You mean, like a jet engine hanging below a wing."

"Exactly."

"How many would it take?" he asked.

"How many? Just one if it hits the right spot. I'd guess the chances would be one in five. And they wouldn't have to be that big."

"Wait. You're telling me a wide body jet weighing...however much they weigh, you're telling me a single tiny drone can..."

"Yes, exactly. Jet turbine blades are vulnerable. A couple of drones enter the intake and they can damage the blades. Worse, if the drones break apart, their pieces become shrapnel, jamming the blades behind them. They're more delicate. And that assumes they aren't carrying something even more damaging. They'd be even more dangerous than bird strikes."

"Can't they fly on one engine?"

"Sure, but if it's a flock of drones, they could aim at both engines."

"Quite a metaphor, don't you think? A bunch of small aircraft bringing down a giant?"

The waitress refilled their cups. Robert looked at her, then at the other patrons. He wondered if any of them felt a hint of the difficult future ahead. After the waitress left, he said, "I don't know for sure, but I strongly suspect it's all Holombe's work."

"Either that, or it's a hell of a coincidence," she said. "Though there are a lot of others out there who want to hurt us."

"Yeah. That too is something Holombe said."

"In any case, I think your suspicions were correct. He's probably gone off kilter. His anger, the loss of his family, his country. It could lead anybody into delusions of power."

He pursed his lips. "Maybe not."

She lowered her head and raised her eyebrows. "Oh?"

"I'm beginning to think Holombe isn't crazy. In thinking about his wild ideas, I keep remembering this image – his calm and deliberate manner. So, let's analyze it from his side of the table. A plane is less than a hundred million dollars. But shutting down an airport is tens of millions more. Not only is every flight from the airport canceled, but every one *to* the airport. And then there are the connecting flights."

"Okay. I can see that."

"But Melissa, what if people are afraid to fly? The airlines would lose billions, not millions."

"You think this is what Holombe has in mind?"

"I do. At the time, I thought he was just a mad dog."

"Maybe you were right, but a mad dog can be more dangerous than a sane one."

"I realize that now. I want to get my book out before the economy drops into a hole."

"Hope it won't mention where Holombe is hiding," she said. "Some nice men dressed in black might want to ask how you know. Oh, did I forget to mention their sunglasses?"

"Actually, I don't know his location."

She laid down her fork. "Did I miss something? I thought you said he was in Talstonia."

"I've thought about that too. Once I was in the trunk, I had no way of knowing where they went. They might have taken me back across the border, or driven into Borudo. I would guess we drove for about an hour. Holombe is a very clever man."

"So, what's your idea for a book?"

***

A year later, Robert sat under the glare of stage lights.

"Good evening. I am your host, Martin Urban, and I thank you all for joining us for this week's edition of *Art for More Than Art's Sake*. Tonight, we have a very interesting – and I must add, renowned – guest, writer Robert Stark." He held up a book. "He is the author of this recently published novel, *The Wrath of Juan Valdez*, which has become a best seller around the world, now translated into four languages. He is also the author of several exposés, most about government malfeasance." As the camera zoomed out, he turned toward Robert. "Good evening, Mr. Stark, and welcome."

"Thanks for the opportunity, and also for that warm introduction. However, my publisher called me this afternoon, and it is soon to be five languages."

"In that case, congratulations. I'll begin with the question on everyone's minds. Is the plot depicted in this book true, or is it mere speculation?"

"Actually, neither. It's just a novel – which, by definition, is a work of fiction – and it tells an exciting story."

"But you do recognize that the plot suggests the motivation behind the terror attacks in America."

"Not really. The news events of the day inspired the general plot idea, but authors do that all the time. Contrary to some popular notions, most fictional plots do not arise out of thin air. Like a pearl, they need some grain of reality to instigate the process."

"Then let me ask you straight out. Do you believe the terror attacks in America are the work of some deposed leader of a foreign nation?"

"I don't know, though perhaps you are right."

"I was not suggesting it, but your book does."

Robert could see that Martin was not going to be easily deflected. "This is not *Animal Farm*, which Orwell wrote to make a political point. The *Wrath of Juan Valdez* is a novel, not unlike, *The Day the Sun Died...*"

"By Yan Lianke, a Chinese writer."

"Correct. His book addresses the human condition. But do you think that Lianke is suggesting that people habitually dream walk?"

"But, of course, Lianke's plot does not reflect events in the real world, particularly in the news of current events."

Robert was perturbed by Martin's persistence; even more by his discernment. '*But then,*' he thought, '*that's why his interviews are so popular.*' He took a deep breath. "We don't know that. I have no idea of Lianke's inspiration, but I'm certain that in some villages of the world, the social order has actually fragmented. Perhaps he had read of such an event, one that inspired his novel."

"And you were inspired by the terror attacks in your own country?"

"Precisely. But, of course, the location of my story is in South America, not Iran. And also, the United States bombed Iran, rather than starting a revolution and overthrowing its president."

"Would it be fair to say that copying reality made your task easier."

"Perhaps it would have if I had waited six months longer to begin the writing. That would have given me a more thorough picture of how it would play out."

"Could you give our viewers an example?"

"Sure. Originally, I thought the attacks would damage the airline industry. I had not made the connection to the other business sectors that would be hurt – hotels, rental cars, even cruise ships. And, of course, there were the scattered attacks on the electrical grid. America was especially vulnerable to airline disruptions."

"More so than Europe might be?"

"I think so. We – meaning Europe – have a good rail transit sector."

"Mr. Stark, you depict Juan Valdez very sympathetically. Does that reflect your feelings about the terrorists operating in your country?"

Robert had hoped Martin would ask that question. It was a chance to counter some of the criticism he had endured both online and in print media. "Absolutely not. Murder is murder. How can one justify that? However, my novel is in the well-established genre of the best revenge stories – those that explore the psychology and character of both opponents."

"Another question that fascinates me is, why a novel? This is your first work of fiction, is it not?"

Robert was relieved by the question, one of the few he could answer without pretense. "It is. I always wanted to write a novel, but novels require background research – the details of locations, occupations, and such. My first attempt at a novel immersed me in those kinds of elements, and sidetracked me into non-fiction. And again, with the second, and so on. Finally, I decided I was not going to put it off any longer."

"Every successful novel is inspired by some idea. But other authors have described a linchpin, a specific concept or event or person that pulls the plot elements into a coherent narrative. What was your linchpin for this book?"

"A good question. I suppose I'd have to say it was the drones. When I talked with Melissa..."

"Your wife, we should mention, and writer for *Vores Teknologi*."

"Yes. At the time we were just friends, and she was a successful writer for an American technology journal. She explained to me how a drone could enter a jet engine and destroy the turbine. I was surprised at how a small object could bring down a giant aircraft, and that struck me as a metaphor, and the seed of a new book.

"Before we take the phone-in questions, I'd like to ask you about one issue that I know all our listeners have in mind. Why Denmark?"

"Actually, I had contemplated emigrating to Europe long before the terror attacks. However, once Melissa and I decided to marry, we had to plan the specifics for our future. We were impressed with the people of Denmark. Your citizens are so creative, and the quality of life is superb. And I should also add, Danes are very welcoming. You made Melissa and me feel at home, and we are grateful."

Martin recognized the cozy PR talk. It was, after all, part of his broadcast business. "Did the deteriorating American economy play a part in your decision?"

"Not at all." Robert had known the question would come, and as with Bakhtiar, he had a well-memorized presentation, except this one would work. He had even practiced it in front of a mirror to ensure the prevarication remained invisible. "Martin, my earnings arrive monthly, regardless of the state of the American economy, and regardless of my country of residence."

Martin nodded, but Robert knew he hadn't bought it.

On the other hand, Martin knew there couldn't be much of a payoff in pursuing the question. "We'll go now to the phones. We have Lars Nielsen from Niborg on the line. Good evening Mr. Nielsen. What would you like to ask Mr. Stark?"

***

On the drive home, Melissa said, "It was a good interview, but you shouldn't have let Martin get under your skin."

"You think he did?"

"You were frowning." After several seconds, she turned toward him, her brow knitted. "Actually, you seemed somber from the beginning." When he didn't respond, she changed the subject. "Do you think Holombe will ever see the show?"

"Unlikely. I doubt he watches interviews with artists, but I'm sure he'll end up with a copy of the book."

"How do you think he'll react?"

"He'll like it."

"You seem awfully certain."

"Melissa, think of his motivation. He agrees to see me, and discloses his intentions against America. Then he tells me why I'd better not reveal what he just told me."

"Yes. I've thought about that from time to time. It seemed odd. But you said he wanted you to write a book about the JRZ Mining Company."

"And I took him at his word, but I began doubting that last year, while writing the book. The deeper I got into the Valdez character, the clearer it became. Holombe played me." He hesitated, as if confessing a sin. "When you turn the chessboard around, the layout looks different."

She checked her impulse to respond, uncertain about the emotions he was feeling.

"If he wanted revenge against JRZ, why not just kill their executives? Or blow up some of their operations? His network certainly has the means. And then there were the remarks he made about the American people not actually caring. Then why have me tell them about JRZ? And he must have known that my research would lead to a lot of dead ends."

"Then why invite you for an interview?" she asked.

"Honestly? He knew I couldn't help myself – that I'd feel I'd have to write the story. And he also knew I'd figure out the only way I could tell it – a fictional narrative. His goal was to let the government know the reasons behind the attacks, without revealing his identity."

"Why would he care about that?"

He looked at her. "You're a forgiving person, Melissa. You don't understand revenge. It's satisfying only if the victim knows it's retaliation, that someone out there is paying them back." As he paused, he nodded his head. "He had it all figured out ahead of time. I thought he was using me for a knight, but I was just a pawn. And I've got to say, he played like a chess master.

She looked at him, her mouth open. "Robert! You seem to actually admire him."

"Admire? No. Just respect."

"Even respect!" Her voice rose. "Jesus! He's killed over two thousand people, not to mention the disruption of our way of life, the impoverishment of half the country. How can you..."

"For God's sake, Melissa! I don't excuse the killing. His actions are horrible, and he's caused wholesale death and suffering. But I do respect his ability to see clearly. He knew what I would do, he knew the economic effect of bringing down aircraft. Perhaps he even knew how America would react, getting mired in another war. He knew our vulnerabilities better than we did, certainly way better than I did. You have to respect that."

Her voice had become strained. "Robert, he's still a murderer."

He pulled over, turned off the engine and faced her. His words came out flat and slow. "Yes. He is. But he was right about one thing. He said the problem wasn't that the people didn't know about America's misdeeds, but that they don't want to know. Melissa, I've spent my whole life writing exposés, thinking I was Paul Revere waking the people to their country's sins. But Holombe spoke the truth. The people aren't interested as long as they have a full stomach and a warm bed, even if it's bought at the pain of others half a world away."

Her mouth hung open for several seconds, before she said, "The people do care. Why do you think they bought your books?"

"*Some* of the people cared, and some of them even changed their lives – joining demonstrations and organizations, or refusing to buy certain products – but the majority of them? No. Most bought my books because they wanted to believe they really gave a shit. Most of them never made a serious effort to change their country. I won't say I completely wasted my years tilting at windmills, but when I look back, all I can see is an inflated sense of self-importance."

He turned, again facing forward. The dark of the night seeped into the car. He had expended himself; and she had trouble digesting the revelation.

Finally, she said, "Robert, you can't think this way – this self-loathing."

He continued as if she hadn't spoken. "You know, Bakhtiar was right. The people don't want to know the truth. He called my view of humanity 'charitable'. That was just politeness. What he really meant was *naive*. He was right."

Silence filled the car once more. He started the engine and got back on the road.

She finally understood what he admired about Holombe – the clarity, the deep-rooted cynicism that shielded him against the disillusionment now pummeling Robert. After several minutes, she said, "You feel your work has been futile. Tell me something. If you could live your life over again, what else would you do?"

He looked at her, then back at the road. A mile or so later, he replied, "I don't know. I'm not sure."

"Most people's lives are less meaningful than yours. Less purposeful. Maybe you're right. Maybe you are naive, maybe your efforts were futile. But honey, you tried. At least you tried to do something good. You weren't one of those who live their lives for a full stomach and a warm bed, and that's something. It is what good people do."

He looked at her for several seconds, then realized the car was drifting. He drove on. His eyes moistened. He took a deep breath. "Thanks, but I don't think I have another exposé in me. There's no more motivation. It's gone." He looked at her, but she said nothing. "What's my future – living off old royalties for the rest of my life?"

"Or..." was all she said.

"Okay. I'll bite. Or what?"

She looked at him, eyebrows raised. "*The Wrath of Juan Valdez* got great reviews."

"True. Yes, that's true." He paused for several seconds, nodding. "And actually...actually, I enjoyed writing it." He was silent for a half-minute. "You know, an interviewer like Martin would make a good protagonist..."

The car continued through the dark, following the road lit only by its headlights.

Whatever Happened to Batman?

Stephen Cressy tried to calm himself. He almost wished he'd brought chewing gum, though that obviously would have looked unprofessional. He realized that, in reality, his new position required a certain comportment. Intellect and knowledge alone were insufficient. He had to look the part. And chewing gum would definitely belie that image. And so, Stephen Cressy hoped no one would notice him tapping his left heel.

Finally, it was Preston Drake's turn to speak. "Mr. Bigley…"

"You can call me Dick. No reason for formalities here, Preston. We've known each other for a few years."

"Uh, yes, of course Dick, if that's okay with you." Preston Drake continued: "For the first time anywhere, I'm announcing to you that TinkerGen Corporation has achieved the ability to recreate an entire genomic sequence – or, to use the common expression – to clone a human being."

Stephen could sense the electricity as everyone instantly stiffened. Dick Bigley finally broke the silence. "That is interesting news. It sounds like a tremendous scientific breakthrough. But why did this warrant a meeting with state government officials?"

Drake's corporate all-knowing smile didn't move a millimeter. "Because it is the state that bears the responsibility for incarcerating long-term prisoners; which also means the state bears the expense. Everyone here understands the strain it places on that annual melee known as 'passing a budget'. I'm certain all of you as well as the governor would appreciate making that process easier and quicker."

"You do know that cloning humans is illegal in this state, don't you?" Kylie Sanders asked.

"Of course, madam Attorney General."

"Then I have two obvious questions: First, how will cloning humans reduce our prison expenses; and second, are you intending to break the law? Because if you are, I'd expect our prison expenses would rise by one person."

"To answer your first question, we have in mind a limited but carefully chosen subject for cloning – one whose record of crime fighting is both effective and heroic."

The silence that followed was part of a well-understood negotiating tactic: Whoever breaks the silence, loses; which in this situation meant that if Bigley's team asked for the unknown clonee's identity, they would cede control of the conversation. After two minutes, everyone was growing uncomfortable. After four minutes, stubbornness had turned to stone. After six minutes, one of the state officials began playing Tetris on his phone. At the nine-minute mark Wayne Small's cell phone rang. The Commissioner of Corrections picked up his phone and left the room. After 12 minutes he returned. After 15 minutes, Dick Bigley rose and began to collect his things. The other state officials followed suit.

"Okay, okay," Drake chuckled, "you win. Do you want to know the identity of the person we intend to clone?"

Bigley and the others sat down. "Well, yes. Now that you mention it, that would be nice."

Drake swallowed his pride. '*You can't win them all,*' he thought. Besides, he was in it for the long game. "The person we intend to clone is the greatest crime fighter of all: Batman."

The silence that followed was of an entirely different kind – more like shock. Finally, Bigley spoke. "So, you intend to produce – grow or create or whatever – replicas of Batman?"

"Precisely," Drake replied with a terseness that returned control of the conversation to his side of the table.

"I have to admit," Bigley said thoughtfully, "the idea is intriguing. The real Batman is getting on in years, and lately he's lost a few fugitives…seems he can't run fast enough anymore. Our CCTV cameras have recorded his flights – well, actually glides – and frankly, his age is definitely showing."

Drake jumped at the opening. "Actually, we've already talked to him, and he agrees with our proposal, and is willing to give us some bio-samples to start the cloning process."

"But you still have the problem of state laws," Sanders interjected. "And frankly, it would take a referendum of the voters to overturn the relevant statutes. That could be problematic, and would take years."

Drake replied without hesitation, "And, it would also require us to reveal our intentions, allowing time for the criminal elements to find and kill the clones before they reach adulthood." By demonstrating his grasp of the subject and the thoroughness of his planning, Drake had definitely regained control of the conversation. "That's why we'll be performing the cloning in Japan."

"Then what do you need from us?" asked Bigley.

"We believe that reproducing Batman will require the clones to be raised in the same culture as the original. So, once the clones are born, they'll be transferred to this country, and adopted out. We also believe the adopting families should match Batman's as closely as possible. That should assure us the same results."

Bigley nodded. "Makes sense. You want to control both nature and nurture. But again, what do you need from us?"

"I'm sure you're aware that the adoption process is long and uncertain for prospective parents. We need the state to expedite the process for all 24 clones. This could be done through minor string-pulling – no necessity for new laws or regulations."

Sanders nodded. Bigley paused as his political mind raced ahead. "OK. I see a couple of hurdles – one small and one very large. The first is discussing this with the governor. I think he'll be as inclined toward the idea as am I. The second hurdle, however, is not flexible."

"I assume you mean the time factor," Drake said.

"Exactly. This whole process will take 20 years. None of us will be in office by then. Hell, some of us won't be alive. And that might include you, and even your corporation. How does this project survive that kind of time horizon?"

"That's exactly why I've brought Mr. Cressy to this meeting. He's in his 30s, so he's likely to outlive both us and the project. Stephen, why don't you explain how this project will work going forward?"

Stephen stood up, hoping his nervousness wouldn't show. He'd never done a presentation at anywhere close to this level of an audience. "Lieutenant Governor

Bigley, fellow officials, I am the designer of this project. I hope this presentation will answer your questions – most of your questions – perhaps all of your questions." He smiled nervously. *'Breathe,'* he told himself. *'In goes the good air, out goes the bad.'* There. He felt better. "Could we lower the lights? Thank you." He began the slide show, mechanically reciting the same points Drake had already introduced.

"Stephen," Drake prompted, "why don't we go directly to the project organization and timeline charts?"

"Yeah, sure." Stephen jumped ahead to the next section. "Basically, TinkerGen has created and funded a trust foundation, Junior Gen, with me as chairman."

At this, Dick Bigley looked at his fellow officials, all wondering at a 34-year-old apparently made into a corporate chairman by the stroke of a pen.

Stephen continued. "Junior Gen will have three employees whose sole job will be to collect data and track the progress of the clones. The purpose is to ensure the project will continue uninterrupted for the next 20 years."

At this, Drake interjected, "Actually, Stephen is being a bit modest here. He's the one who invented the main genomic method that became the final breakthrough. As the key innovator, and given his relative youth, he was a natural choice for chairman. Sorry for the interruption, Stephen."

Stephen continued right where he'd left off. "If something should happen to prevent my continuance with the project, the foundation has provisions for others to carry it forward. I've also constructed a schedule – item 'B' of your packets – for interceding in the clones' education at key points in their development. We believe this is required to ensure they accumulate the correct frame of reference by the time they reach adulthood.

Wayne Small, interrupted: "Correct frame of reference? What exactly does that mean?"

"Batman became Batman partly because of his inherent nature. He tends to divide the world bilaterally – his good guys/bad guys viewpoint is a manifestation of this. However, he was set on his anti-crime path by witnessing the death of his parents, and also by the possession of great wealth. Therefore, we're going to have to interdict the clones' normal upbringings at particular points and in particular ways. That will align their understanding of how the world works with that of Batman's."

"Surely you're not intending to kill the adopting parents!"

Stephen chuckled as he shook his head. "Oh, heavens no, Ms. Sanders. But we intend to make each clone believe their parents were killed in a criminal act. It should achieve the same effect. Each set of parents will agree ahead of time to this condition, along with a non-disclosure agreement that includes both a high payment versus a high penalty for reneging – in other words, a large carrot and an even larger stick. In addition, each clone will be told that a large trust set up for them was funded by the 'deceased' parents' life insurance policies."

Bigley was impressed. "Goodness. It seems you've thought of everything."

"Well, in fairness, credit belongs to our project coordinators. My specialty only lies in the biological area – the cloning process." Stephen realized his tone was sounding a bit wimpy. "The coordinators do the actual *grunt* work." '*Nice recovery*,' he said to himself.

After a short pause, Bigley asked, "Do you have any figures on how much this would save the state?"

Drake answered for Stephen: "Our comptroller has a list of figures. They're in your Packet C." Then turning to Stephen, "Thanks. Stephen." The latter sat directly down, feeling relieved about his performance. Drake continued, "On page 3, you'll notice the two lines with and without our program. Of course, assumptions had to be made about future conditions, including economic growth, technological advancements, and the future size of police forces, but I believe if your comptroller's office looks them over, they'll agree the assumptions are reasonable."

"Christ!" exclaimed Bigley, "Even if these are off a bit, the savings would be huge over a 20-year period. So, let me guess, you'll want funding."

Drake raised his eyebrows. "Well, TinkerGen is not a non-profit corporation."

"I think this is totally doable," Bigley said. "Only one thing: If we're going to keep the undertaking from the public, we'll have to rename the project and fund it through one of our many agencies. TinkerGen will be listed as a private contractor."

"And what will be the program's new name?"

"Oh heck, Preston, that's no problem. We've already got so many programs with specious names that I can't remember half of them. Remember: This is politics."

With that, the meeting wrapped up with smiles and handshakes all around.

***

Matthew Bodine kept the suspect in sight, but at sufficient distance to prevent being spotted. Sure enough, Randy Goody met a guy on the street, spoke to him and quickly moved on. The second guy looked like a gang enforcer. Which one should he follow now? Bodine decided on the enforcer. He already knew where Goody lived and could always find him again, but he didn't recognize this new guy. In 2042, the police and most private eyes depended on the internet and electronic surveillance, but even as a child, Matthew always seemed to have an instinct for tracking people on the street. Call him old fashioned, but he'd bet he was the best, even when not dressed up in his crime-fighting gear.

A week later, Ronald Johnson was checking images on the SSC (street surveillance camera) recordings when he noticed someone at the edge of the frame. He was stunned to see…himself! *'But I wasn't near there that day. No wonder the bomber has been so successful! He's pretending to be me! If he makes me look like a criminal, he neutralizes me. He'd be able to run rampant. Clever…but not clever enough!'* Using the SSC recordings from several cameras, Johnson traced the guy back to his car, searched the records for the license plate, and found where he lived. *'A mansion! The guy's rich, huh? Well, let's see how much his bodyguards can protect him.'*

The next day, as Matthew Bodine exited his driveway, a single bullet through the windshield killed him instantly. The following day, Joseph Sumpter read of the killing, including the suspected location of the shooter – a church bell tower across the street. *'Using a church to commit murder? What a monster!'* Checking images on the SSC, he saw an individual entering the church two hours earlier carrying a large satchel. Searching through other images, he was able to find one showing the perp exiting his car. License records provided his address.

Two days later, the news reported a small explosion had destroyed a car belonging to one Ronald Johnson. The occupant of the car could not be identified, pending-DNA testing of the scraps of tissue that could still be recovered.

Bruce Carruthers was outraged at this act of terrorism, but was able to trace information back to the perp, one Joseph Sumpter. And so it went on for a month, with each Batman clone killing off one another until only Paul Hallet remained. He still found it rather surprising that Mitchell Rangel, the guy he had pushed off the parking structure, looked so much like him. He was reflecting on this fact as the gates to his driveway opened and he pulled into his 10-car garage. As usual, it was after midnight. Hallet was used to working late. *'After all, that's when the bad guys come out from under their rocks,'* he thought as he entered his house. He ascended the circular stairway to the bedroom. When he opened the door, he found his wife holding a gun.

"You bastard! Out late again? Don't bother with an excuse! This is the last time you cheat on me!"

Even in the large bedroom with the many tapestries covering the walls, the sound of the gunshot was deafening.

What the Shadows Say

The God Syndrome

"What? What do you mean cancer? What in the hell are you talking about?"

"I'm...I'm sorry, Rita. It just came out. I'm not sure why I said it. I just got a picture of it...or a feeling..."

"Jesus, Leonard, you're turning weird. You're a personnel manager, not a doctor. Would you just sign off on the vacation?"

"Sure, sure. April 6 through the 18th. You got it. Mind if I ask where you're headed?"

"Thailand. It's part of a group tour."

"Oh, that should be swell."

"Me and Frank can hardly wait."

After Rita had left, Leonard Fosse sat back with a wrinkled brow. Why had he blurted out about her cancer? Why couldn't he just keep his lips zipped? Not to mention how had he known it? It was the same feeling as when he had argued with his brother about dessert.

"With your diabetes, you need to avoid sugar."

"Diabetes? I'm not diabetic." Pete had said.

"You are." Leonard had said it with confidence. Everyone around the table had been surprised, including himself.

A week later, Pete had called him. "How did you know?"

"I...I don't know. I just did."

"Lisa thought about what you said, and insisted I get a tester. She said I've been sleeping too much on weekends. Anyway, you were right – my sugar's high. I made an appointment with the doctor."

"Good."

"But still, how did you know?"

"Pete, I really don't know. This last year, I've been sensing people's health problems. I told my neighbor she should take zinc supplements. Two weeks later she thanked me, said her skin problems went away."

"Now that's really weird." Pete paused before saying, "Anyway, thanks a mil. And give Dorothy my love."

A couple of weeks after scheduling her vacation, Rita came into his office early, before Leonard had turned on his computer or finished setting up his desk.

"Morning, Rita."

She sat down and said nothing.

He looked up.

She was staring at him intensely. "How did you know?"

"Know? Know what?"

"About my cancer. How did you know?"

He looked up, and held his breath. He had almost forgotten. "Oh, yeah. My God, I'm so sorry."

"We needed vaccines to travel to Thailand, and the doctor recommended a blood test two weeks afterward to be certain they worked. The blood test indicated a problem, and the mammogram showed a small lump."

"How big is it?"

"That's the thing, Leonard. Dr. Petrie said it was barely visible. How did you know? How *could* you know?"

He looked down for several seconds, shaking his head. "Honestly, Rita, I have no idea. This last year, I began sensing these things. At first, it was only occasional, and my first thought was, 'midlife crisis.'"

She raised her eyebrows.

"Well, I'm 42, and these things do happen."

"Okay. But Leonard, how does that explain the accuracy?"

"I don't know, I don't know. The thing is, I try to keep silent, but I can't. Like with you – it just comes out."

"And I'm thankful for that. Dr. Petrie seems sure we got it very early. He says I won't need chemo."

"That's good. Actually, terrific."

"Anyway, thank you. I'll need to cancel the vacation, and schedule some sick leave."

That evening over dinner, Leonard related the incident to his wife.

"That's wonderful," Dorothy said. "She won't have to go through a two-year torment like aunt Rose. At times, she was in so much discomfort, I wanted to cry."

"I just wish I could understand it. How do I know people are sick before they do? And even diagnose it?"

"I know you don't believe in God, Leonard, but just maybe..." His frown did not surprise her. She was only an intermittent churchgoer, but her belief was solid, even if hazily defined. On the other hand, he was agnostic. As he liked to quip, his belief was, "definitively indefinite".

A month later, Leonard arrived home to find two vans parked outside his home. As he pulled into the driveway, the vehicles disgorged cameramen, guys with microphones, and other camp followers. Leonard noticed Dorothy peeking out the side of their curtains.

"Mr. Fosse, Dick Pook from ZLCH TV. Could you comment on the report about your medical psychic powers?"

"What? Psychic? What are you talking about?"

"This morning, Ms. Holly Olson tweeted that you diagnosed her illness."

"Well...yes. I did tell her she had a back condition. But I'm not psychic."

"Then how did you know before her doctors? Before even she knew she was ill?"

"Well, probably just a lucky guess, I suppose."

"Mr. Fosse, Henry Hatcher from NDDL Broadcasting. Are you aware that Ms. Olson's tweet initiated a barrage of comments from other people you've diagnosed?"

"Uh, no. Actually, I don't even have a Twitter account."

"Did you study medicine? Where did you get your medical knowledge?"

"Look guys, I don't have any special medical knowledge. I just get these feelings..."

"So, you *are* psychic," Pook said.

"No. They're just hunches. Like a gambler who gets a hunch that turns out to be a winning number."

"But Mr. Fosse," Hatcher said, "at last count, there were over 20 people you've helped. That's an awfully lot of correct hunches."

"Look, fellas. I don't know any more about this than you do. I've helped a few people, and that's a good thing. Now, excuse me."

As he walked toward his front door, the crews trailed in his wake, like froth behind a boat.

Dorothy opened the door and gave him a hug. "Hopefully they'll get tired of waiting, and just go away," she said.

***

Herman Roker reached his home in Scottsburg, Indiana at 6:17 in the evening. He opened the door of his pickup truck and laboriously slid over to the step, then strained to lower his 290-pound bulk to the ground. Entering his home, he called out, "Beth, I'm home."

She came from the kitchen and gave him a peck on the cheek. "How was the trip?"

"Oh, about the same. Made good time outbound. Boss is happy."

"That's good. I'm just starting dinner. Should be ready in 20 minutes. You go and clean yourself up."

After dinner, they watched TV, as usual. As usual, she crocheted and he drank a beer and munched on chips. At 10:00, as usual, they went to bed. As usual, sex was out of the question – had been for a decade, and not only because of his weight. She didn't believe in contraception. It was, as she liked to state it, "Against the way God intended."

Remembering the image of her 200 pounds shorn of clothes, Herman Roker did not object. As usual, he agreed with God.

***

On Monday morning, when Leonard and Dorothy went to work, the media froth reappeared. They followed Leonard to his workplace, but he found refuge inside. Eventually, they gave up. One van followed Dorothy to the Lorca & Halloway law firm, where she worked as office manager. As she exited her car, one well-primped woman approached her, a cameraman scooting after.

"Ms. Fosse, Celina Seely from BERP News. How does it feel having a psychic husband?"

"He's not psychic, for heaven's sake."

"Then how does it feel having a telepathic doctor husband?"

"Telepathic? What are you talking about?"

"Well, what would you call your husband?"

"Leonard." Dorothy turned and quickly walked to the door.

That afternoon, Leonard jumped to an internet news page. His name was the second article down, just beneath the one on an impending nuclear war between India and Pakistan. At the end of the day, two more vans were waiting for him outside his workplace.

"George Louch of TWRP news. Have you considered turning your abilities into a business?"

"Absolutely not, Mr. Louche. And why are you so focused on money? You should be concerned about your Lyme disease."

Louche stopped, speechless.

The next morning, a Saturday, Leonard and Dorothy's breakfast was interrupted by the doorbell.

He leapt out of his seat. "If that's a reporter, I'm going to punch him in the nose." Dorothy ran after to restrain him.

The man in the blue suit and silver tie said, "Mr. Fosse, I'm Howard Sullivan, one of the producers for the Sunday Gold News program." He handed Leonard a business card. "We'd like you to be a guest for an interview with Roger Stratham."

"Not interested."

"We would pay you for your time. Five-thousand dollars."

"Not interested."

Sullivan looked down, then back up. "How would 10,000 dollars sound?"

"Still not interested, but thanks."

"Alright. The station has authorized me to offer as much as 15,000 dollars."

"He's interested," Dorothy interjected.

Leonard gave her a hard look, but she returned a harder one.

Two days later, the makeup woman finished working on Leonard. "There, how's that?" she said, handing him a mirror.

He marveled at the absence of wrinkles that creeping time had made an intrinsic part of his self-image. He raised his eyebrows. "I hope my wife recognizes me."

A quarter hour later, Roger Stratham introduced him to the viewing audience. Stratham, studiously coifed and attired to appear casual, summarized to the camera the phenomenon of, "Leonard Fosse's seemingly miraculous powers." Then he turned toward Leonard.

"Would you tell our viewers what it's like to give a diagnosis? What is the inner sensation you experience?"

"It's just a feeling, Roger, rather like recognizing that your dog has to be let out to…well, you know. The only difference is that with illness, I feel compelled to say something. It's an impulse."

"Have you ever experienced any other psychic phenomena? Perhaps as a child?"

"Never. This all started about a year ago."

"Was there a trigger event?"

"None that I recall. I have no idea of the cause."

The interview continued for another quarter-hour, followed by questions from the audience.

"Mr. Fosse, I'm Sally, and I'm listless all the time now. Have been for the last year. The doctors have done test after test, but can't explain it. What is wrong with me?"

Leonard turned toward the host. "Can she come closer?"

Stratham said, "Would you come down to the stage, Sally?"

When she was about ten feet from Leonard, he said, "Stop taking Pterodax. It's affecting your upper colon."

"Miss, are you taking Pterodax?" Stratham asked.

"Yes. I am. It was prescribed by my doctor to control hives. Can you recommend an alternative, Mr. Fosse?"

"No, no. I would have no idea. Ask your doctor."

The rest of the hour was spent with similar questions from the audience. Leonard was exhausted by the time he got home.

"You gave the right answer to that woman," Dorothy said, "the one named Sally. Bob Lorca said you should avoid all medical advice."

"You're discussing this at work?"

"Well it's all over the news, and I work for a law firm, so, why not get a little free legal advice?"

"Okay, makes sense."

"Just tell them to see their doctor. He said that if any of the advice went wrong, we could be sued. And he said that whatever you do, don't accept any money from the people you help. Otherwise, you could be sued for practicing medicine without a license. Oh, and he also said you need to rephrase your advice. He saw you tell the reporter he had Lyme disease. He said you should state it as an opinion." To Leonard's expression of confusion, she said, "Tell them you 'think' they have such and such, or they 'may' have so and so."

"But I know what they have."

"Yes. But just in case any of your diagnoses should prove wrong..."

Leonard said nothing, but his indignation was evident.

"...just in case it should happen," she insisted, "we don't want to be sued for a wrong diagnosis."

The following evening, the doorbell rang.

A sunny smile lit Dorothy's face. "Why, Pastor Steele, what a lovely surprise. Please, come in." She took his coat, and introduced Leonard.

"So, this is the miracle worker I've heard so much about. How does it feel to become famous?"

"Honestly, Pastor, it's annoying. Now I understand how movie stars feel when they can't even go out for a hamburger without some stranger bothering them."

Steele hesitated before answering. "Consider this. If you have the power to help people, aren't you morally bound to do so?"

"Of course," Leonard said warily, feeling he was being pulled into a Socratic argument. Did Steele really expect to convert him?

Intuiting Leonard's reaction, Steele smiled. "As you know, we believe your power comes from God. Dorothy has already made it clear that you're not a believer, and I don't expect to change your mind, but our congregation could use your help. Would you be willing to meet with our congregation and provide whatever help you can for their health?"

"You want me to attend your Sunday service?"

"Yes, and meet with individual congregants afterwards."

"Alright," Leonard said. "I'm not a believer, but I do believe in Christian charity. So, in the interest of human kindness, I'll see some of your parishioners. But understand, I can't be inundated. Let's limit it to 20 people. I need you to make that clear to your congregation."

Steele's first reaction was disappointment, but he quickly saw an advantage in Leonard's proposal. His announcement about Leonard Fosse's presence would draw enough people to overflow his church. At only 20 diagnoses per Sunday, he could expect a large crowd every service for months.

"Whatever makes you comfortable. Shall we schedule it for a week from this coming Sunday?"

"That sound's fine."

When Leonard arrived at the church on the appointed day, the crowd was literally lined out the front door. He considered the scene. '*Like Lourdes or Compostela? Or maybe The Running of The Bulls?*'

At the end of the regular service, Steele addressed the congregation. "As all of you are aware, Leonard Fosse has agreed to help 20 of you with a diagnosis. Twenty of you have been chosen by a lottery, and I will be calling your names shortly. However, I'd like Leonard Fosse to please come up and say a few words to the congregation." Pastor Steele's clapping began a wave of applause, which quickly overcame Leonard's reticence.

Leonard slowly walked up the steps at the side of the dais and to the lectern. "I feel the need to be honest here. I'm not a member of this church. In fact, not even a believer. But I find myself in possession of a gift that can benefit humanity. As a part of humanity, I want to help any and all that I can. And so, I thank Pastor Steele for giving me this opportunity to help you."

The applause was loud and long, followed by Steele calling out the 20 names. The lucky score walked to the front of the nave where the deacon organized them into a line. Leonard met them one at a time and engaged each for about a minute. Some were relieved, some surprised, a few devastated. The audience watched, captivated by the drama as it played out person by person.

On the drive home, Dorothy said, "I'm very proud of you, Leonard. You helped a lot of people."

"Yes. I know." He paused. "You know, at times I felt like I was condemning some to painful treatments, even death." Her look was nearly one of indignation. "I know, I know," he said, "I'm just the messenger. But some of the messages are sad. Really sad. I'm glad it's over."

Except it wasn't. Steele waited until Wednesday to visit him and talk about a return engagement. He knew that a few words about the previous week's disappointed needy would tug at Leonard's conscience.

***

At Boxy's Truck Stop, Herman Roker's path once again crossed Lyle Crumpton's. The two truckers were chewing on their lunches as Faux News Network aired an interview with Dr. Wei, and Dr. Pradesh. The two archeologists were discussing a recent study of a structure that some had argued was Noah's Ark. Their study had discredited the claim.

"Ain't that disgustin'," Lyle said.

"It sure is. Easy for them outsiders to deny the Bible. If they don't like God, I say kick them back to the swamp they came from. You know, if I'm on the road into the weekend, I always find a church on Sunday. It never fails to raise my spirit."

Herman had spoken a truth fundamental to his existence. His sexless, fat, tired life of endless concrete roads would have been unbearably lonely if not for the confidence that Jesus was always with him, and not just on the crucifix that hung from the mirror. Half the time, his satellite radio was tuned to the Wholly Holy Network, whose preachers from various fundamentalist churches declaimed the faith. At night, the motel TV had Faux News Network, and though the latest events did irritate him, at least the FNN commenters provided comforting reasons why those who held views other than his own, were wrong.

Lyle brightened. "Heck, let 'em talk to that Fosse guy. That's a real prophet."

Herman tapped the table. "That's exactly what I was thinking. He claims he's not a believer, but just give him time."

"I sure hope he sees the light."

"Yeah, but what I'm sayin' is that I think Fosse's a prophet. The light is already coming through him. He's a sign of God's grace."

Lyle nodded. "Nice to know some people are on the right side."

***

At Leonard's second Sunday service, Steele told the assembled, "Although Leonard does not know the source of his power, we do. We believe his power has come from God. Why has God chosen Leonard? We cannot know. But understand this – he is to us what the prophets were to the Hebrews. Whatever his belief, I say, 'God bless Leonard."

A multitude of *amens* echoed through the church.

At first, Leonard resented Steele's bringing in the issue of belief, but then he reminded himself that it *was* a church, and, after all, Steele, as a good Christian, meant it kindly. And the weekend talk shows featured clerics of various denominations praising God for sending Leonard to humanity. Like Steele, they compared him to Ezekiel, Daniel, Malachi, and other biblical figures. All the clerics ascribed God as the source, identifying Leonard as a channel for His power, and a proof of His grace. A few visited his house, asking him to visit their churches, even offering to hold special mid-week services to accommodate his schedule. However, he politely refused. There was only so much of Leonard to go around.

One Saturday morning, as they were sipping their coffee, Dorothy said, "You seem awfully quiet this morning.

He looked at her, and after several seconds, answered. "I've been thinking. I know nothing about medicine, other than avoid too many carbs. And even doctors can't diagnose without tests and MRIs, and sometimes they still get it wrong. So how *do* I know?"

She smiled. "Well, you know my answer to that."

"The thing is, I've been thinking, maybe you're right."

She set her cup down and stared at him. "Really?"

He nodded. "Just looking at it rationally, what other explanation is there? And this stuff about the Holy Spirit...well, I finally realized that's kind of what it feels like."

She sat back, her jaw slack.

"It's just that it's not something I do. It seems to happen to me, or maybe through me. Beyond Steele's church services, I find myself talking about others' illnesses. It just comes out on its own."

As he paused, she nodded.

"I mean, I've heard about the Pentecostal speaking in tongues," he continued. "I'm not sure I would go that far, but it feels like my diagnoses come from someone else."

"Maybe we should talk to Pastor Steele about this."

She called and made an appointment for that afternoon.

Steele listened attentively, letting Leonard air his feelings, his doubts, his uncertainties, which went in both directions. Finally, he spoke. "Leonard, everyone in our congregation would warmly welcome you, but I want you to be sure."

"Pastor, I've been thinking about this for weeks. I am sure."

Steele smiled. "In that case, I'll make the announcement tomorrow. And if you have any questions concerning belief or doctrine, or about the church, don't hesitate to call me."

On the following day, just before the service, Pastor Steele announced their new member, a convert from agnosticism. The applause endured, and Leonard felt obliged to rise and, with hand on heart, acknowledge their kindness. They, in turn, rose, while continuing to applaud.

Meanwhile, the Sunday crowds grew, and the fame moved the bishop to visit their church one Sunday. After leading the service and witnessing Leonard's gift, he suggested baptism to Leonard. "If you are willing, I'd like to perform the ceremony myself."

Leonard agreed, and they set a date two months in the future. In the interim, Pastor Steele would give him instruction.

***

About two weeks later, Leonard got sick at work. He was going to drive home, but collapsed just outside his office.

They notified Dorothy, who rushed to the hospital. Leonard shifted in and out of consciousness, but he was able to talk to her during his wakeful moments.

"What's wrong?" she asked. "Where does it hurt?"

"It doesn't. I don't know. It's just..."

After a few minutes, a doctor arrived. "Mrs. Fosse, may I have a word?" He led her outside to a row of chairs. "Mrs. Fosse, I'm Dr. Morgan. We've gotten the results of the MRI. I'm afraid your husband has a tumor at the front of his brain."

"Oh my God." She felt her face flush as she teared up. "Is it cancer?"

"We won't be able to tell until we biopsy it. Fortunately, it's at the front of the brain, where we can operate using endoscopic surgery." He could see she wasn't processing his words. "It's a fairly minimally invasive method." Her expression remained half-blank. "Mrs. Fosse, I want you to take a deep breath."

She finally responded, and was surprised at how quickly her panic attack receded. "What do you recommend?"

"We should get him into the OR tomorrow. We've done this kind of surgery before. And I'll be assisting Dr. Knowles, one of the best brain surgeons I know. We'll need your approval before we go ahead."

The following morning, the surgery was performed and biopsied. Dorothy cried when she heard the tumor was benign. He remained in the hospital another three days, visited by neighbors, friends and co-workers. Church members came by with gifts, and Pastor Steele chatted with him. They prayed together.

It was all very pleasant, perhaps the main reason Leonard didn't tell Dorothy until he went home. "My gift is gone."

"Don't worry. I packed them all in the satchel before they wheeled you out of the room. Don't you remember?"

"No. You don't understand. I can't read people's health anymore."

The implications slowly grew in her. "You think it was the tumor?" she asked.

"It seems that way. I didn't want to tell the other parishioners. Or Pastor Steele."

"I don't understand."

"Of course you do. It wasn't God. It was the tumor."

"Don't say that," she pleaded.

"Dorothy, what other explanation is there?" He looked down and shook his head. "Unless God makes tumors. Or the tumor *was* God." For the first time in days, he smiled. "How would that fit into the Bible? The Book of Tumors? Tumors 12:3, 'Lo...'" He chuckled until he raised his head.

Her look cut him off. "I'm sure your power will return, just as soon as you recover," she said.

"Sorry. I'm just tired."

"We see the doctor in three days. We'll ask him about it."

But Dr. Morgan was equally puzzled. "I'm not certain I believe any of it, and I certainly can't predict the possibility of you regaining this power you say you possessed. However, what you've said makes me think of Seizure Alert Dogs. Have you heard of them?"

Dorothy and Leonard looked at each other, then at Dr. Morgan. They shook their heads.

"We pair some epileptics with dogs specially trained to detect the very subtle odors that precede attacks. It allows the epileptic to live a more normal life – to drive, for instance. And I've read of dogs that can detect cancer and diabetes in people. And traditional Chinese medicine performed diagnoses from the smell of a patient's urine."

"I'm sorry, doctor, but I'm not understanding." She said, with an edge to her voice. "What does this have to do with my husband?"

"Well, the tumor was in the area of the brain responsible with olfactory processing – odors, that is."

"I know what *olfactory* means." She paused. "I'm sorry. I'm just upset."

"Totally understandable, Mrs. Fosse. Let me say that for now, it's just speculation. I suspect the tumor enhanced Leonard's ability to detect odors associated with various medical conditions."

Leonard leaned forward. "But doctor, don't those dogs need to be specially trained?"

"Of course, because they don't by nature understand what we want from them, nor what disease is. But we humans do."

Leonard sat back, trying to digest the concept.

Dorothy said, "But as you said, it's pure speculation."

From the edge in her voice, Dr. Morgan understood that Dorothy was resistant to the idea, though he was uncertain about the reason. "And that is all it will ever be. Leonard's case is unique, at least as far as I know."

Though he wasn't able to return to work for another two weeks, Leonard was able to attend an interview by Les Moore on the *Yes and No* television program.

"Mr. Fosse, there is one question that I know is on everyone's mind. Do you still believe in God?"

"Well, I'd say there might or might not be a God. We have no way of knowing."

Moore paused, clearly surprised. "Isn't that a return to your old belief in agnosticism?"

"Actually, agnosticism isn't a belief, merely an absence of belief."

"But a couple of months ago you declared a definitive belief in God's existence."

"I did, but obviously, I've had reason to reconsider. Everyone spoke of me as a prophet, comparing me to those in the Bible, and I became convinced it was true. You might say that I had evidence for sharing their belief, and I no longer do."

"Then, can you summarize your current belief for our viewers?"

"Well, two things, really. First, I doubt I'm a prophet in the conventional sense. But second, neither were the biblical prophets. I'm forced to conclude that they too probably had aberrations in their brains – tumors, or lesions, perhaps – that enhanced their powers. To others, their abilities would have seemed miraculous."

"That's an unusual view. I don't think I've heard of anything like it before."

"I've been doing some reading these last couple of weeks, and I've discovered that extensive evidence exists linking prophets with mental conditions. Ezekiel, for instance, was epileptic, and a patient in Israel had a seizure while his brain was being monitored. He later reported that at same instant, he experienced seeing God."

As they left the studio, Dorothy was silent. And during the drive home. And after they had entered the house. His attempts to trigger conversation were futile. Finally, he stood directly in front of her. "What is the matter?"

She faced him directly. "What's the matter? Are you serious? So, now you've told the world the prophets were fake, and it's, 'What's the matter?' I never cared about our religious differences, but what about the congregation? They're going to feel insulted. What am I going to say to them?"

"But you've always known I doubted the prophets – hell, the whole Bible."

"Yes, I knew. But you've just told the whole world. You had a huge following. How many of them will lose their faith?"

"Look, we've always agreed that faith is a matter of conscience. They'll make their own choices, like they should. Besides, I've concluded that religion is a good thing."

Her mouth opened but no words came out. She stood there with her brow wrinkled, but remained speechless.

"There's a lot of brotherhood and sisterhood," he explained. "There's a strong feeling of togetherness. Maybe the part about God is wrong, but the part about human fellowship is very right. The church is a good thing, regardless of doctrine."

She smiled as she saw how right he was, how their mutual tolerance was a part of their love, and how much he valued the church's sense of sharing in God's love. She smiled. "Then you'll keep going?"

"Absolutely."

The following Sunday they entered the church 15 minutes early. They were barely through the vestibule when someone shouted, "There he is!"

Various other shouts followed, and soon all the congregants were facing them and shouting. A few threw Bibles and hymnals at them. The crowd did not settle down until Steele strode down the main aisle.

"What are you doing here?" the pastor demanded.

"We're here to join the service," Leonard said.

"After what you've said and done? Look at the attendance. It's a third smaller than it used to be, before you ever set foot in this building with your...your miracles."

Dorothy said, "Pastor Steele, you knew from the very first that Leonard was not a believer. You invited him yourself."

"That was before he announced to the world that the prophets were mentally ill." He turned to Leonard. "You probably think that Christ was just someone with a brain disorder."

"Interesting idea. I hadn't considered that."

Steele's eyes widened and his face turned red. "Get out of here. You are no longer welcome here on Sunday. Or any other day."

As Leonard turned around and began slowly walking toward the door, Steele said, "You too, Dorothy. I'm sorry to have to do this, but you'll always remind the congregation of your husband's damage to the faith."

"Pastor Steele, this is very unchristian of you. We've known each other for many years."

"I'm sorry, Dorothy. I have to protect the congregation."

For Leonard, the one good thing that came of the church encounter was that his wife was no longer angry at him. Her outrage at Steele captured all her fire. He hoped he could put the entire affair behind him.

However, on Monday morning, the operations manager was waiting in his office. "Close the door, Leonard."

It didn't matter that Paul Jorell was a man of few words. Leonard immediately intuited the purpose of his presence. "If it was up to me or Kent, we'd love to have you stay here until retirement. But the firm can't afford the bad publicity."

"Bad publicity? The issue was religion, not laser cutting."

Doesn't matter. You're all over the news. Some of our customers are likely to be offended by your characterizing biblical figures as just a bunch of crazies."

"Now wait a minute, Paul. I never..."

"Leonard, I know you didn't use those words, but that's not important. People make decisions on impressions, not facts."

"Of course. That's why they're religious."

"This isn't a debate. If we retain you in a managerial position, our name will be tarnished. Kent has already been contacted by two TV journalists. They will be here this afternoon, and you'll have to be gone before they arrive."

"Jesus, Paul, I've been here eight years. What kind of..."

"Save your breath Leonard. I hate this, and so does Kent, but we have to go up to his office now. If it helps your feelings, you should know he has a very royal severance package waiting for you."

Once he had returned home, Leonard considered his future. What other firm would have him? The stigma would follow him wherever he applied. He dreaded a worse thought. Dorothy might also arrive home early.

However, her day turned out to be normal – so normal that she was very surprised at his news. "What are you going to do?"

"I've had all day to think about that. Their hush-money severance was large enough to support us for a long time, and unemployment insurance lasts six months. By the time I have to find a new job, the whole thing will be old news. I'll just be *What's His Face*."

"Thank God," she said.

***

About three months later, Dorothy called from the TV room. "Leonard, come here quick."

He rushed in. "What's the matter, honey?"

"Have you started a business without telling me?"

"A business? No. Why?"

"Look."

The commercial for Fosse Unlimited was ending. "If you want the power to help your family, your friends, and yourself, contact us at 555-MIRACLE today, or visit us online at fosseme.com"

"What the hell...," he muttered

"I know. It's about your power." They say they can give anyone the power to diagnose health conditions. You sure you don't know...?"

"Dorothy, this is the first time I've heard of this."

"But they're using your name. They can't do that without permission. They could be sued."

"Could and will. Let's look it up, find out more about this."

They went to the computer room. She pulled a chair next to his while he tapped on the keyboard. "Fosseme.com. Okay, here it is. Let's see...." He looked around at her. "Apparently they've created artificial tumors out of a plastic. They insert it into a person's skull to replicate what happened to me."

Dorothy said nothing, though her bug-eyed stare said everything.

"I know, I know," he said. "It's got to be the whackiest idea I've heard in a while, and this has been a pretty weird year."

"You're right. But then, they're using your name. Without your permission, right?"

"For crissake, Dorothy. I've already told you. I had nothing to do with this."

"Let me talk to Bob Lorca tomorrow. I can have him write a cease and desist letter."

The thought satisfied Dorothy, but not Leonard, who decided to confront Fosse Unlimited personally. He called them, and the next day, drove to their headquarters, about an hour away. He was ushered into a large, but bare office – white walls, light grey drop-ceiling tiles, dark grey carpet, and only a calendar for wall decoration. The vertical venetian blinds – off-white, of course – completed the interior design. '*Hell, even the hospital looked less clinical than this.*'

"Mr. Fosse, it's an honor to meet you. I'm Carl Aubert."

"Nice office," Leonard said, knowing his irony would be lost on the 40-something figure before him, coatless, and sporting a slightly loosened bright orange tie.

"Yes. I wanted it to resemble one of our operating rooms, which is the core of our business, of course."

"I'll get to the point, Mr. Aubert..."

"Call me Carl," He said with a self-approving smile.

"Look, Carl. I don't care what crazy schemes you and your company concoct, but you have no right to use my name. Frankly, I could sue you and probably make a chunk of money, but I'm not interested in that. I just want the spotlight off me and this whole affair."

Without the least change in his smile, Carl said, "What makes you think we're using your name?"

"What?" Leonard quickly tried to make sense of the question. "Ah, you're going to tell me you named it after Bob Fosse, the stage director?"

For the first time, Carl's smile disappeared. "Who?"

"Never mind. Where did you get the name *Fosse*, if not from me?"

The smile returned, along with raised eyebrows. "Oh, it's the name of our co-founder, Vern Fosse."

"Vern Fosse?" Leonard compressed his lips. He was becoming irritated at Carl's frozen smile. "I'd like to meet this Vern Fosse."

"By all means. Walk this way."

Carl led him out the side door of the office, down a couple of halls, at the end of which was a small office, whose door carried the label, *Vern Fosse*. Carl opened the door. Behind a small desk sat a large fleshy man in short sleeves. His slightly disheveled hair did not proclaim 'executive', any more than his open collar and the graying tee shirt beneath it.

"Vern, I'd like you to meet Leonard."

Vern delivered a limp handshake and a wide smile. "You work here too?" Vern asked with a country drawl of undefinable geography.

"Uh, no. No, I don't. Tell me Vern, just what do you do here?"

"Do?"

"Yeah, as in, what is your function within the company?"

"Function?"

"Your job."

"Oh, I come in whenever I'm needed."

"Needed for what?"

"Whenever I'm needed."

"I think that's enough," Carl said, still smiling.

After they had returned to Carl's office, Leonard said. "You don't think I see what you're doing here? You hired that knuckle-dragger puppet just to use my name."

"Leonard...you don't mind if I call you Leonard?"

Leonard was about to object, but considered the alternative – he had the same last name as the stooge they had just left. "Not at all."

"First, Leonard, Mr. Fosse is most certainly not a puppet. He's one of our VPs, and a valuable partner in this cutting-edge enterprise. Second, it's not your name at all. It's his name. And third, our lawyers say it's all perfectly legal. Besides, if it were to happen that one or two people confused the company name with yours, what harm could there be in that? Your reputation would grow. And given the unfortunate direction it has recently taken, I would think you'd welcome that."

Leonard restrained his urge to punch the smirk off Carl's face, but instead, departed Fosse Unlimited, feeling helpless.

***

At Truck Nuts Oasis, Herman Roker sat with Nolan Kiel. They had run into each other many times along their various routes. FNN was once again discussing the "Fosse Fake Phenomenon" as John Jason referred to the new social phenomenon. His *JJ Fighting For You* show combined commentary and interviews with a lot of dubious experts. On this particular afternoon, he 'reported' that Fosse Unlimited had manipulated their own stock price, thereby cheating thousands of "hard working Americans" out of their "hard earned money."

Finally came the commercial break.

"So, how're your kids doing?" Nolan asked.

"Oh, Isaac got laid off. School budget cutbacks."

"That's too bad. I hear a lot of schools are falling apart. The buildings, that is."

"Yep. Ever since they took God out of the classroom."

Nolan nodded. "It took a long time, but we knew it was coming."

"Now we got this Fosse traitor. First he pretends he's a prophet, then it turns out he's an atheist." He shifted in his seat.

"You okay, Herman?"

"Damned constipation. It's startin' to cost me money."

Nolan downed the last of his burger and wiped his fingers. "How so?"

"I have to stop more often." Nolan looked perplexed. "Personal pit stop."

"Gotcha. My uncle had it, too. Real bad. Finally went to the doctor, got a prescription. Cleared it right up."

Herman nodded. "Yeah. Maybe I should do the same."

The television image displayed the Fosse Unlimited building.

"Ain't that disgustin'," Nolan said.

"Face it, Nolan. They want to take away our salvation. Yours and mine."

"Well, they ain't gonna get anywhere with me. My parents raised me right."

"Nor with me and Beth, but what about the unborn?"

"Whaddya mean?"

"If the country they grow up in makes bigwigs of guys like Fosse and all his sacrilegiosity, what are the chances of them getting saved?"

Nolan stared at him for several seconds with his mouth open. "Good Lord, I never thought about that." He paused, looking out the window. "How come we got so many kooks in this country?"

***

Over the following months, Fosse Unlimited's stock – symbol FU – rose quickly as patients acquired newfound abilities. In March, the NON broadcasting network began a weekly series, *Miracle on F Street*, hosted by Norman Spat. Despite their allergic reaction to the whole affair, Dorothy and Leonard could not avoid watching it.

> "For our first show in this new series, we have invited Dr. Charles Ribble, NON's medical consultant, to explain to our audience the extent of this medical miracle.

Doctor Ribble, how widespread has the Fosse procedure become?"

"It's still small, Norman, but it's growing fast. Fosse Unlimited reports that about ten thousand people have taken advantage of this medical breakthrough."

"That's impressive, doctor."

"It is. What's even more impressive are the surprising results. While some reported the expected ability to detect disease, several people's heightened olfactory powers have gotten them jobs with the TSA."

"The TSA? For what purpose?"

"The TSA told us they have hired Fosse patients as replacements for bomb-sniffing dogs."

"What's the advantage?"

"They don't have to clean up after them."

At the commercial break, Dorothy remarked, "Maybe some good is coming of this, after all." She looked at her husband. His expression spoke more than words might have. "Well, it *could*," she insisted.

"It had better. People think Fosse Unlimited is my company. What if something goes wrong? Who do you think they'll blame?"

***

Two months later Beth Roker arrived home from her job at the county gas utility. She tossed off an automatic, "Hi, honey," before noticing his expression.

He patted the couch cushion next to him. "Come sit."

"What is it?" Her voice trembled.

"I saw the doctor today. He says it's cancer."

Beth teared up. "How bad?"

He just looked at her.

She sobbed. He wrapped his arms around her.

"It's stomach cancer. He says it's spread to the intestines."

"We'll get a second opinion."

He patted her gently.

After a minute of crying, she choked out the words, "How long?"

"They can't say for certain. The doc guesses about six months."

She whimpered and pounded her leg. Then she took a breath to settle down. He'd need her support. "Can't he give you something for the pain?"

"He said he can reduce the pain a little."

"Lord. With you not working, how are we going to pay the medical bills?"

"I've been thinking about that," he said.

***

Soon after the *Miracle on F Street* show, other companies, like hyenas catching the scent of commercial carrion, had entered this new and growing business sector. By May, Glossy Unlimited had begun using a method similar to Fosse's. However, their synthetic tumors were inserted into a different area of the brain, one that controlled speech. Their intention was to bestow an enhanced linguistic ability, and their target customers were professionals seeking to enhance their career status. As their advertisements stated it,

> "People will judge you by your speech,
> your vocabulary and your ability at
> expressing your thoughts and ideas. Who
> doesn't dream of a higher station in life?
> Glossy can fulfill that dream."

However, most of the results were surprising. Only about a third of the Glossy alumni became more articulate in a professional manner. Another third became merely more poetic. Executives gave rhyming presentations to their clients, most of whom had never moved beyond the 'Hickory, dickory, dock' level of literary sophistication. The twitter crowd quickly named them *today's prophets*, which, even more quickly, was shortened to TP. Unfortunately, the last third of Glossy's patients sporadically spoke in the strangest, unidentifiable languages.

The truth came out in an interview with Barry Guey on the *Golden Flame* religion show.

"They're speaking in tongues," stated Rev. Thomas Charles as confidently as if he himself had invented the cryptic language.

Rev. Kwame Smith nodded and told Guey, "Praise Jesus! Definitely speaking in tongues. These are signs of the Lord's presence."

In other interviews, ministers and preachers noted that some of the TPs definitely sounded biblical. David Orphus. pastor of the Holy Orphus church of Glendale, Tennessee, noted the following as examples.

"Until the boy will choose to toy with the right both day and night, your land in haste will lie in waste."

"The hes and shes of yours will leave you sick and poor, bound with yards of ropes, you can't uphold the hopes among your people, you stupid dopes."

Orphus was unequivocal in his proclamation. "These are surely the words of prophets."

The Most Reverend Carlos Zapalez agreed. "These are the Isaiahs and Ezekiels of our time. We must heed them, or the Lord will punish us."

Though the media tried to get Leonard to appear for interviews concerning "this latest miracle," he steadfastly refused. Public exposure had already warped his life. However, the media had an endless supply of wannabes to fill both traditional and social media with their 'expert' opinions.

On balance, most of them agreed with Dr. Luhan Wei that, "This latest example of the Fosse method proves that the biblical prophets were probably afflicted with brain disorders."

However, Dr. Nahil Samaal cautioned that they did not know enough. "Perhaps they had one or more ischemias, rather than tumors."

The major networks created call-in multiple-choice surveys with questions like:

> The biblical prophets were probably:
>
> A) Crazy
>
> B) Deluded
>
> C) Medically handicapped

D) Dishonest

E) All of the above

***

As they exited the Fosse Unlimited driveway, the employees lowered their window for the man beside the sidewalk sign. It read "A FREE FLOWER OF THANKS."

"Hello, miss. A flower to thank you for your fine work."

"Well, thank *you*. Is this from the company?"

"No, miss, just a thankful citizen."

"Well, that's very kind of you."

This script was repeated several times, except for male drivers. "Hello, sir. A flower to thank you for your fine work. Are you Mr. Fosse?"

When Fosse reached the exit and answered, "Yes," the man pulled a gun and shot Vern Fosse dead.

Herman Roker made no attempt to escape. In fact, he was waiting for the police with hands raised and the gun on the ground.

That afternoon, he was interviewed by police detective Cesar Morales. "Mr. Roker, you're going to be charged with murder in the first degree. That means premeditated."

"Yep." Roker said.

Morales raised his eyebrows. "You're admitting it?"

"Yep."

"Would you like to tell us why you killed Mr. Fosse?"

"Sure. He was doin' Satan's work, turning the world against Christ. I'm protecting the salvation of future generations. I wanted to do one last thing for Christ before checking out."

"Checking out?"

"Yep. Got cancer. I hope the prison hospital rooms have TV."

***

Leonard and Dorothy were stunned by the evening news. They both understood that Roker had probably mistaken Vern Fosse for Leonard.

"I'm worried," Dorothy said. "What if someone else comes after you?"

Her husband smiled. "Nothing to worry about. The press has ignored me for months, and we've got volunteers from...what do they call themselves?"

"Atheist Hordes Of Liberty, or AHOL."

"Yeah, that's right. So, we have AHOLs guarding our house, and I've been canned, so they won't find me at work, and the church kicked us out, so nobody will find us there. It's perfect!"

She rolled her eyes. "You're still unemployed. We're one income short in this house."

"You know, Dorothy, I've been thinking. That idiot Vern Fosse probably got paid a hefty salary to help the company steal my name. And there wasn't a thing we could do about it. But then some other idiot comes along and kills him. I'm thinking, maybe there is a God."

She looked at him to see if he was serious.

He wasn't.

The Exceptional C Student

Gary Foster was surprised to see his brother through the small window in the classroom door. They waved to each other. Gary continued with the remaining ten minutes of his history lecture. When the bell rang and the river of students gushed out the door, he wondered for the hundredth time whether their haste should be ascribed to a boring lesson or to their youth. His brother entered and closed the door.

"Frank, what brings you to the college? Hopefully not to arrest one of my students."

"No, not today. But who knows about tomorrow?"

Gary noticed his brother wasn't smiling. That wasn't unusual. His years as a detective in the Canetown police department had increasingly molded his manner into habitual formality. Gary understood. Repeatedly dealing with criminals had cut a rut into his demeanor. In an interrogation, a wrong word or action could make the difference between a confession or the suspect lawyering up; or worse, between a conviction and a case dismissed on a technicality.

Frank closed the door. "We have a rather...unusual situation with one of your students."

"Oh? Who?"

"John Nelson. He says he's one of your students."

"Hmm. Yes, I believe he's in my Tuesday-Thursday class. Ten in the morning, as I remember. How did he come to your attention?"

"We had a rape just off campus. We questioned a few suspects matching the description – short, dark complexion, black hair. He was the only one unwilling to provide us a DNA sample. So, we take him in for questioning, and pull the old cup of water trick."

"Cup of water?"

"Yeah. If they take a sip, they leave traces of DNA. We don't insist they drink. We just place a cup of water on each side of the table. Eventually, they drink."

"Would that be admissible?"

"Absolutely, as long as he leaves the cup behind."

Gary shook his head. "Good God! I have a rapist in my class?"

"No. He isn't the rapist."

"Then, why..."

"Why am I here? Because we found something rather strange. Are you familiar with DNA?"

"No. Ask me a question about the Ming Dynasty, I'd probably have the answer. But biology? All I know is don't eat too many carbs. Oh, and dogs get fleas."

Frank's lips went into a half-smile. "Different animals have different numbers of chromosomes. Humans have 23 pairs. Male, Female, Black, White, Hispanic, Asians – always 23 pairs."

Gary nodded. "Yeah, I think I read that somewhere."

"John Nelson has 37."

Gary blinked several times, before asking, "And this means...?"

"Don't know. Neither do the people at the lab. They're sure we must have corrupted the sample – some chemical agent, they suggested. Gary, I handled that cup as carefully as possible."

"Okay. So, what do I do with that? I mean, how am I supposed to respond?"

"I just thought you should know. You might want to keep an eye on him. He's no rapist, but something weird is going on there. And obviously, you didn't get this from me."

"Okay. Got it. Thanks."

For lunch, Gary grabbed a sandwich plate in the cafeteria and took it to his office. He checked through his records. *'Nothing unusual. He's a C-student. Hmm. what's this? Now that is odd.'* He switched screens and printed out a list of John Nelson's other courses. By the time he reached his next class, he was just finishing eating his sandwich on the fly.

At the end of the day, he dismissed his class a few minutes early and walked to the biology department. Rebecca Silbert's class was still pouring out of her room.

"Rebecca, can I have a few minutes of your time?"

"Sure. What can I do for you?"

"We'll need to go to your office."

Rebecca knitted her brow. "Sure."

Once in her office, Gary said, "John Nelson is a student of yours. Have you noticed anything odd about him?"

"John Nelson...let me see." She tapped a few keys and perused the screen. "Not really. He's a C-student."

"Uh, huh. What about his individual test scores?"

"Okay. Let's take a look. Hmm. Yeah. This is a bit odd. All his test scores are exactly 75 percent, except for the 10-question quizzes. Those are all sevens and eights."

"Averaging exactly 75 percent," Gary offered.

She turned toward him. "So, why is this of interest to you?"

"I'm interested because this has to be mathematically rare. In fact, it would be interesting to calculate the odds, especially because his scores in my class are identical."

She turned back to the screen. "There's something else here," she said. On the quizzes, the scores alternate from seven to eight every time."

"Mine too."

"What are you saying, Gary?"

"That he is getting the scores on purpose." As she was trying to digest the idea, Gary continued. "It's as if he were trying very hard to maintain an exact C-average."

"Exactly in the middle of the range?"

"Yes. Exactly in the middle."

She paused before proceeding. "Why would he do that? That doesn't make sense."

"You think *that* doesn't make sense? Wait till you hear this. He has 37 pairs of chromosomes."

Rebecca laughed. "Gary, the scores are an odd thing. But 37 pairs? All humans have 23 pairs. Period. If I remember correctly, only a bear has 37 pairs, and John Nelson certainly is no bear. Where did you get this crazy idea?"

"I can't reveal the source, but I know it to be impeccable. Absolutely reliable."

"Checked by a DNA lab?"

"Yes. Checked by a DNA lab. I can't reveal anything more. Sorry"

Rebecca's smile faded. Her first impulse was to label Gary a flake, but she knew better. *'He's as down to earth as they get.'* "Okay, let's see his other classes. Here – he has physics with Daniel Longtree. Let's get to his office. He usually stays over."

Daniel Longtree encouraged his students to come to him with questions after the regular school day. His door was always half-open.

Rebecca tapped on the door. "Daniel, I'm glad we caught you."

"Hi Rebecca, Gary. What's going on?"

"You have a student in Physics 102. John Nelson?"

"Sure, Rebecca. I remember him."

"Notice anything odd about him?" Gary asked.

"You mean other than his handshake?"

"His handshake?" she asked.

"It's kind of…well, clammy isn't quite accurate. I'd say it reminds me of a leather throw pillow Wendy once bought for the house. I never liked it. 'Cowhide's okay,' I told her 'but for a throw pillow, I hate the feel of leather.' He paused as the two visitors looked at him. "Well, you know, cowhide has texture. His hand – his skin – felt like leather. It was just…odd."

"We were really wondering about his grades," Gary said.

"His grades? Sure. Give me a second here. Yeah. He's a C-Student."

"Exactly 75 percent?" suggested Gary.

"As a matter of fact…"

"What about the individual test scores?" asked Rebecca.

Daniel tapped a couple of keys. "Hmm. This *is* odd." After a few seconds, the light went on. "Why did you ask about his scores?"

Gary answered for them both. "Rebecca and I found exactly the same pattern in our classes."

"Come to think of it," Daniel said, "I remember being surprised once when he got a particular question wrong on a quiz. I forget which one now, but at the time, I remembered that he had gotten it right in class when I had called on him. At the time, I just figured he forgot or maybe choked up."

Gary decided to indulge in a bit of irony. "Oh yes. There's one other little thing. He has 37 pairs of chromosomes."

"Tell me this is a joke." Daniel looked at the serious expression on both of their faces, and his jaw dropped. "Oh Jesus! It's really happening?"

Rebecca and Gary looked at each other. She asked, "Is *what* really happening?"

"Don't you understand? If he has 37 pairs, he's an alien."

"Alien…as in, from another planet?" Gary asked.

Daniel brushed his chin beard with his palm. "More likely, from another solar system."

Gary and Rebecca both remained skeptically silent. They had been exposed to Daniel's belief in aliens' former visits to Earth.

'*What was it before – geoglyphs?*' Rebecca tried to remember Daniel's fascination – or perhaps obsession would be a more accurate word – with the giant figures etched into the plains of southern Peru, figures visible only from a vantage point high above the ground. '*But something's definitely up with John Nelson,*' she thought.

Gary was recalling *Chariots of the Gods*, Von Daniken's book, which Daniel had pestered him into reading. At the time, Gary had remained unconvinced, but now he was doubting his doubts. '*Was I hasty in my judgment? Something's definitely strange here.*'

"So, what should we do now?" Rebecca asked.

Daniel still appeared upset. "You don't understand. There are only two reasons aliens would come to Earth – either to hurt or help us."

"So, what are you saying," Gary asked. "Should we alert the authorities?"

Daniel chuckled as he shook his head. "This creature has traveled literally trillions of miles. They likely have discovered the secret of warp drive. If they're that advanced, who do you think could protect us? The police? Our military? These creatures would look on our most advanced weapons the same way we look at a cave man's club."

"Pardon my dry logic," Rebecca said, "but if he's here either to help or to harm us, and we can't defend ourselves if it's the latter, we might as well assume the former."

"Meaning..." Gary prompted.

"Meaning, there's no reason not to sit down and talk with him."

Daniel paused, then nodded. "Actually, you're right. If they were here to hurt us, they already would have. Yes. Let's open up a communication channel. There is so much we could learn from them. Just think – fusion energy, warp drive, quantum computing."

Gary leaned forward enthusiastically. "I'd be interested in their values. If they have already achieved so much technologically, and not blown themselves up, it means they conquered something more important than space. They've gotten past the barbarism, the divisions, the hatred that has plagued humanity since...well, our entire history."

"True," Daniel said, "and if they can show us how to do that, all the money we throw into military expenditures could be diverted to science and engineering."

"More important," Gary continued, "think of how it would change us culturally. We would stop thinking tribally. We would be forced to think of our world and our species within a universe of other intelligent species. That alone could encourage more cooperation."

"And medicine – it could revolutionize..."

Rebecca interrupted, "I hate to throw a few chunks of logic into the gears of your well-oiled dream machine, but I think we need to keep in mind that this is a different species. Not to mention, that even if he were *Homo sapiens*, our two cultures would have evolved along totally separate paths. Their values are certain to be far different than ours."

"So?"

"So, Daniel, their technology would be directed toward the needs of their culture and their biology, not ours. Perhaps their purpose for space travel is to find food." To Daniels perplexed expression, she explained, "As in *us*."

"That's ridiculous."

"Is it? Look, Daniel, you yourself said that our most advanced weapons would be like caveman clubs are to us. So, what do you think our species would be to them?"

"She has a point, Daniel."

Rebecca continued. And their medicine? They're a totally different species. Their devices might not work for us – might even be destructive. And Gary, I hate to pop your bubble too, but the Germans produced some of the most advanced science and philosophy, but that didn't insulate them from degenerating into Naziism."

Gary nodded. "Again, a good point. Reconsidering, I have to admit that we don't know their purpose, or for that matter, their willingness to help us. And also, how our fellow humans will react to them. History is filled with bouts of xenophobia. I may have been a bit hasty."

"Okay," Daniel said, "so, where does that leave us. What are we to do?"

Rebecca broke the several seconds of silence. "We could speculate till the Moon turns to green cheese. The only way to know his purpose for certain, and what benefits his people might bring to our planet, is to sit down with him and find out more. What do you guys think?"

Gary and Daniel both nodded.

"Let's look at his schedule," suggested Gary.

On the following day, they were waiting for him outside a lecture hall when the bell rang.

As he exited with the rest of the herd, Rebecca said, "John, we need to talk to you for a few minutes."

"Okay."

They walked to her office, and sat down on the extra chairs they had already procured.

Daniel initiated the conversation. "John, we need you to be honest with us. Who are you?"

"John Nelson."

"No, I mean, who are you really?"

"John Nelson."

Gary decided to shift their approach. "And where are you from?"

"Surrey, Wisconsin."

"Oh, let's cut through the Styrofoam, here," Daniel said. "We know you're an alien."

At this, John stiffened. He sat silent as he looked from one to the other. "Could you define what you mean by alien?"

"Not someone from another country," Gary suggested.

"Another planet," Daniel said.

"You have extra pairs of chromosomes," Rebecca said. After several seconds of silence, she said, "You're not *Homo sapiens*."

"How did you figure it out?"

Daniel spoke for the three of them. "That doesn't matter. We just want to know why you've chosen to come to this planet."

"And why this college?" added Rebecca.

John was silent for several seconds. Then he replied, "To learn."

Daniel and Rebecca looked at one another. Gary rolled his eyes. Finally, Daniel asked. "To learn? From us? What could we possibly have to teach you?"

"We have a problem in our star system."

"Just for my own curiosity," Daniel said, "which star system is that?"

"We call it Broelchin. You know it as Tau Ceti."

"Daniel searched his memory. "That's 12 light-years away."

"Yes. That's right. Our planet is called Vashon. A sister planet, Yaxtum is farther from Broelchin, and developed more slowly than ours, but now their civilization is gobbling up resources in our planetary system. Our combined rate of consumption is unsustainable, which makes them a threat to our civilization. We didn't know how to stop them."

Rebecca leaned forward. "But why would you think we Earthlings could help you? You're obviously far advanced over us. We barely made it to the Moon and back."

"But you're very good at killing."

"What? Killing?" Gary exclaimed.

"Yes. We have no experience killing. Our crops are very high in protein, so Vashonians never evolved as hunters. Only gatherers. We don't know how to kill. Especially in large numbers."

"But that's crazy!" Gary's voice was just below a shout.

Rebecca turned toward her fellow teachers. "I get it. They developed more like bonobos than chimpanzees." Then turning to John, "But why would you take biology and physics?"

"I really didn't want all those courses, but World History 2A is only open to degree programs. I had to take a minimum course load."

"And the 75 percent scores?" asked Daniel. "What was the reason for that?"

"I didn't want to stand out. I made sure my grades were average. The biology was fairly simple, and the physics at our childhood level. I did have to study your history, though. I wanted to avoid being noticed. Obviously, that part of the plan failed. But the wig part worked." At this point he removed his hairpiece, revealing a totally bald pate. "This was also to avoid attention. Plus locking the elbows."

"The elbows?"

"Yes, Professor Longtree. We have two on each arm. Mine had to be surgically fused – you understand, to keep up appearances. It makes back itches sheer torture. I don't know how your species endures it."

"Back scratchers," Daniel answered, with pride.

"So, this mission of yours – learning to kill – is why you came to me with so many after-class questions?" Before John could respond, Gary answered his own question. "Come to think of it, they were all questions about historical destruction of cities – Jerusalem, Shangdu, Troy, Nineveh, Hiroshima."

"Yes. And don't forget the Holocaust," John said. "I realize the course has not yet reached the 20th-century, but the German's program was extremely effective."

Rebecca shook her head. "Good heavens! I can't believe this is happening."

They were silent for a while.

Then John spoke. "Well? Will you help us?"

Daniel's mouth hung open. "What is it you want? For us to help you kill? To commit mass murder?"

"Yes. Exactly. Your species is especially good at it. It's true – sometimes it's only a few hundred, sometimes even less. But you also have a lot of experience at large operations. You've managed to cover the full spectrum of killing." John's voice was relaxed and friendly, as if he'd been ordering a latte with cream, mocha and a double shot of vanilla for someone else.

Daniel's lips tightened. "We certainly will not help you. What you're asking us to do is unconscionable. Commit mass murder? What kind of people do you think we are?"

"Well, as a species, a killing one. But as individuals? I don't know any of you personally, but you seem like nice people. Helpful people. I did not anticipate you would object. Perhaps you could direct me to another person? Someone more willing to share your knowledge?"

Rebecca drew back, wide eyed. "This is insane. You're insane."

"Not just him, unfortunately." Gary shook his head. "Some humans too. He's no crazier than a lot of people – leaders, ideologues, their followers."

Daniel nodded. "Good point. I was reading yesterday about the Chinese public. They still revere Mao. Hell, he starved tens of millions of them with his Great Leap Forward."

Daniel turned toward John. "We're not going to help you. And neither will anyone else in this college."

"Well, then, perhaps you could direct me to someone who would be willing. I don't mind traveling."

Daniel smirked. "Obviously." After a few seconds, he said, "No. We won't help you. Not a chance."

"But why?"

"What you're suggesting is immoral. Helping you with mass murder?"

For the first time, John appeared hesitant. "Then...why do you do it?"

They sat in silence, looking at each other. Finally, Rebecca said, "Because we are a flawed species. It's not a virtue. It's a flaw."

John hesitated. "What a strange attitude. You talk as if you cannot control your actions."

The three professors looked at each other.

"Okay," John said, "I guess I'll have to rely on books and the Internet. Unfortunately, most of their content is mere facts. They sometimes talk of motivation, but human and Vashonian psychologies are very different, and it's very difficult to understand the feelings that go with your species bloodthirsty ways. I'm especially curious about human techniques for tricking individuals as well as for slowly entrapping large populations. And most important, how to organize one's comrades to be so...I guess the word is, *systematic*."

Gary looked at the other professors, then back to the student. "Frankly, John, I hope you never understand those feelings – both for your people's sake and for the inhabitants of Yaxtum.

"I'll have to move to a different city. Obviously, I won't be able to leave a forwarding address. Anyway, thanks for your understanding."

What the Shadows Say

Dirty Work

The driver of the TYD delivery truck must have realized he was two minutes behind on his schedule. As he fast-walked away with the package, he didn't notice a man exiting the vehicle behind the truck. Nor had he noticed him at his previous delivery stop. Actually, his schedule never allowed him to relax enough to notice much besides streets and addresses. By the time he had placed the package on the porch and rung the doorbell, he could barely see the back of his truck driving away. After a couple of quick expletives, he grabbed his cell phone.

It took Ron Kirk seven minutes to reach the alley and park the truck. A half-minute later, Marty pulled up with his van, whose sides proclaimed *Church's Transport*. Marty and Jason jumped out and helped transfer as many boxes as possible, which was most of them. It was not merely because Ron and Jason were brothers that they were so efficient. The team's previous practice had turned them into a precision drill team.

Jason's watch alarm went off. "Four minutes," he announced. They all piled into the van. Jason drove away, careful to keep within the speed limit.

"How much of it did we get?" Jason asked, as he removed his gloves.

"Almost all," Marty said. "A few big boxes, but I tossed half of those. Too light."

"I think we got some jewelry or something. Small boxes," Ron said.

Marty shook his head. "Doubt it. The ones I picked up were too heavy."

"Maybe you're right," Ron said.

They pulled into an alley and stopped at the back of a blue building that fronted on Charles Street. Ron jumped out, unlocked the entrance, and opened the roll-up door. He pulled it back down immediately after the van was inside. The three unloaded the vehicle and began what had become another routine – Ron opened the boxes and extracted the contents, Jason listed them in Marty's spiral-bound notebook, and Marty separated out the obvious throwaways. Afterwards, Marty would determine the value of each item to estimate how much the fence would pay. They reloaded Marty's van with the 'keepers' and off he would go. Occasionally some of the valuables would be bulky – chairs, a kitchen table, and such – and Marty would pay them extra to follow him to his rental space and help him unload.

The Charles Street building had been a small magazine publishing house, now another victim of the digital era. The once-thriving, now vacancy-ridden part of town was perfect for their covert business activities. The ground level had a couple of large tables, a computer desk, enough open space for their truck, and window blinds kept permanently lowered. The upstairs was less spare, with living quarters and a small kitchen and bathroom. At 20, Ron was a mere two years younger than Jason, but some whispering instinct sustained the pecking order. Ron had become aware of it in his mid-teens, but he didn't mind. He and Jason got along fine. In contrast, Ron had a bad feeling about Marty from day one.

The brothers had discovered him through Brad Klepper, a coworker at Unbenders Auto Body shop. "You know, Jason, if you want cleaner work, maybe I could connect you with someone."

"Yeah? Who would that be?"

"Someone I know. I do odd jobs for him every now and then. Always pays good. Maybe he needs someone full time."

Jason kept polishing the headlight bezel. "If it's so good, Brad, what are you doing here?"

"This guy, he does things that aren't always legit. I don't mind stepping over the line now and again, but I wouldn't want to make it a regular gig. A job here, a job there, a little extra money. And if he does go down, the cops aren't going to think of me as part of his gang. Hell, I don't know who his gang is, or even if he has one. Don't want to know. Anyway, I don't mind the dirt. It's a steady paycheck."

Jason looked at him. "So, what would I be doing?"

"No idea. Don't even know if he has anything. I'll contact him, let you know if he's got a need for someone." He started to walk away, then turned. "Would your brother be interested too?"

"Yeah. I think so, if this guy of yours has room for two."

That's how the brothers had met Marty, who enlisted them in his new scheme. Both age and temperament separated Ron from him. At 28, Marty had already zigzagged long distance through an unorthodox life, as one might charitably describe it. Though Marty had always delivered, Ron couldn't shake his distrust. It wasn't just Marty's lucrative connections with those in the shadows – fences, forgers, alarm company employees. Ron realized that with this new enterprise, he had become a part of that alternate culture. And it wasn't his habitual smile. Marty never frowned, regardless of the situation. His mouth always ranged between frozen confidence and a tight-lipped display about as sincere as a starlet's rouge. No. It was just a feeling, like the one he had at age 12, just before his father abandoned the family. Only with Marty, the proof had never come. One time, Marty was late with a payment. "Listen guys, I got an investment that's runnin' late on the payoff. I'll get your money next week. Promise. Sorry for the lateness. Do you need a little cash against it to tide you over?"

Ron was certain he was going to bilk them. The following week, Jason called Marty. "Look, I got a car payment I'm already late on. I need it, like, yesterday."

"I was just about to call you. My money man just contacted me. My jackpot finally came through. Tell you what – if you're in a hurry, meet me at..."

The address in tarnished metal numbers was a ragged comic book store on 22nd Avenue. It didn't look like much. Then too, neither did the neighborhood. Their entrance was announced by a set of small jingling bells mounted on the door frame. '*Quaint*,' thought Ron.

Inside they saw a beach ball of a man sitting in a back room. He managed to roll to the front. "Help you gentlemen?"

"Our friend, Marty Porter, told us to meet him here," Jason replied.

"Ah. I take it you two are Ron and Jason?"

"Yeah. I'm Jason, and this is my brother, Ron. Where's Marty?"

"He's due here anytime now. I'm Tim. Tim Larson." After they had shaken hands, he said, "Can I get you guys anything. A Coke? Something stronger?"

Jason shook his head. "Nah, thanks. We're good. So, you sell comics?"

"Actually, we call them *graphic novels*." He chuckled. "Words that bring a higher price. But if you haven't figured it out yet, you will. It's not exactly my main source of income."

"Which would be...?" Ron asked.

"Let's just say I make sure that people who are owed get paid – without the complications of the records that banks keep. I think of myself as an in-between guy."

Ron nodded as he looked at the comic books on display. "Forty-seven dollars? Really?"

"That's a 1966 Hulk in near-mint condition. Pretty rare. Most stores, it's fifty-five dollars."

Ron looked up at him. "People in this neighborhood pay that kind of money?"

"A few. Like I said, not my main source of income."

Ron had to admire the setup. The rent must have been cheap, the front was a great cover, and it was slow enough for Tim to avoid frequent interruptions.

The bells on the door rang.

"Hey, guys. I guess you already met Tim." Marty looked at Tim. "Did you get the envelopes put together?"

"Sure did, Marty. Hang on." He disappeared into the back room. Less than a minute later he returned with three envelopes, one clearly fatter than the others. "Here you go."

He handed the envelopes to Marty, who put the fatter one in his leather messenger bag. He handed the other two to the brothers. "You'll find a bit of interest for my being late." As Jason opened his envelope, Marty quickly said, "Don't count it till you're back in the car." He pointed to the windows. "Too visible here."

Marty had kept his word, but Ron's distrust abated only slightly. Though Marty might have guessed, Ron never voiced his suspicions. For one thing, he was a couple of inches shorter and 20 pounds lighter. For another, what could he point to? Marty always paid them their cut.

Ron did speak his mind to Jason, but only once. "What's the matter with you?" Jason had yelled. "Marty's brilliant! This whole thing's working only because of him. Otherwise, we'd both be back in the body repair shop, grinding and welding and covered in dirt. Look!" He extended his hands, palms down. "See any dirt under the nails? Skin smudged with grease? And you know why they're clean? Marty. That's why." He had returned to his magazine for a few seconds, before adding, "You've always been paranoid."

Perhaps Jason was right. He had first rendered that non-professional and totally free diagnosis eight years earlier. Totally free and totally wrong. Their father had indeed left them, exactly as Ron surmised, exactly as Jason could not accept. But equally, Ron realized something about himself. His father's betrayal had probably scarred him with insecurity, a distrust of others he might never completely shake. And Jason was also right about the dirt. Growing up with a single mom and no dad narrows life's choices. But still.... "So, doesn't it bother you that we're completely dependent on him? How much do we actually know about him?"

Jason's forefinger stabbed downward. "I know he knows electronics. We don't. And everything nowadays depends on electronics."

On that count, Jason was right. Marty knew everything about subverting keyless ignition. "When a driver presses the start button," he once explained, "the vehicle sends out a signal that triggers the driver's key fob. The fob sends back a digital response code. The ignition module recognizes it and starts the car. All you need is a detector that can read and repeat the code."

Well, not all. The fob signal was weak, a range of about a dozen feet, less if you were outside the truck's metal body. Someone had to walk past the truck with the detector as the delivery drivers returned from their stops. Ron was assigned that task, as well as breaking the door window for the actual theft of the truck. Jason thought Marty's idea was brilliant. Ron's surreptitious Internet search showed it was available to anyone who dared. And Marty always dared, especially if it was somebody else driving the stolen vehicle.

A truck a day – always switching delivery companies, neighborhoods, even cities – netted them more than their auto repair jobs, and gave Ron time to study for his community college night courses. He remembered when Marty first found out about college. "Oh? What are you studying?" he asked.

"Criminal investigation."

Marty looked at him for a few seconds before breaking out in laughter. "You're serious?" Ron's look was very serious, and irritated. "You *do* realize that you're the type of person you're going be tryin' to catch?" In fact, Ron had not thought about that. Marty laughed again and shook his head. "Guess you're going to have lots of experience by the time you graduate. Sure to make captain in no time." He chuckled some more.

Ron didn't see any humor in it. "Actually, I plan to go into private investigation. Own my own office."

"So, you get your college degree and open up your own business? Not a bad gig."

That night, Ron went to bed thinking about the next day's job. But Marty was right. In an industrial espionage case, he'd be trying to nail guys like himself. But he knew he'd be good at it. He'd always had good instincts. His suspicions about his father abandoning the family was only the first of many instances of good intuitions. Ron was certain that, in time, he'd be proven correct about Marty. But was he himself imperceptibly drifting into a Marty? Then again, he was trying to escape this life. Marty wasn't. Marty would always be drawn to the shady side of any street he walked, and even more to the back alleys. He always had to test his sword of cleverness against society's norms. Ron realized it was a game one must inevitably lose. There would always be that one dare too many, that one job that went wrong. Would Ron's come before he graduated and went legit? And even then, would he abandon Jason to Marty's inevitable fate? Or back to his hated body shop job? Or could Jason find a third path? The many ifs and coulds and woulds dissolved into sleep.

The next day's job was easy. The target was a TransOT truck, and the haul looked good. Almost all the cartons had insurance stickers, which indicated something valuable within. Unfortunately, sometimes its only value was sentimental. Ron always felt bad about these. The scrapbook or heirlooms meant something important to someone. He once suggested they should sneak them back to their owners.

Though Jason was sympathetic, he quenched the idea. "What are we supposed to do? Go to every address and drop them off? What if we're spotted?"

"Maybe take them to the shipping company? Like drop them off in the middle of the night."

"And when someone else spots the boxes," Marty had retorted, "they'll grab them instead. You need to stop all this weepy stuff. It doesn't go with our particular line of business."

Ron continued unpacking and never mentioned it again.

But this day was different. Everything with an insurance sticker had value – two expensive cameras, a necklace, two top-of-the-line video game systems, some well-packed antiques; some very old stamps. Then there was the suitcase.

"Hey guys, look at this." It was a large aluminum case with a pair of unusual latching locks. "Some kind of electronic lock."

"Where'd you get that from?" Marty asked.

"It was inside this cardboard box."

"Let me see."

"Who to?" Jason asked.

Marty turned the carton over. "Seeside Shipping." He turned to Ron. "Ever hear of them?"

"Not spelled that way. Some place on Hunter Street."

Marty turned toward the case. "Well, let's see what's inside." He surveyed the latch at several angles, then said, "It's a smart lock. Probably uses a smart phone with a special app."

"Can we get the app?" Jason asked.

"Probably not. Besides, each owner puts in his own code. No, this calls for a low-tech solution." He went to his toolbox and returned with a sledge hammer and a cold chisel. He glanced at Ron. "Get a two-by-four a couple of feet long."

He lay the top of the case on the wood. With the two brothers holding the case steady, Marty placed the edge of the chisel between the case and the latch, and began pounding. After a few swings, he said, "Damn! This is tough stuff. This here chisel's vanadium steel." However, after several more whacks, the latch was split from the case. He did the same for the other latch. Persistence bred success, and success bred a smug smile.

Jason too was smiling as he opened the case. Then he furrowed his brow. "What the hell?"

"What is this?" Ron said quietly, thinking half-aloud.

They looked at Marty, who was obviously equally baffled. "Something medical maybe?"

Ron shook his head. "Why would something medical need a digital timer?" He removed the mechanism from the suitcase, and followed the wires from the timer with his fingers. He turned the mechanism over. "Uh, oh."

"What?" Jason asked.

"This is some kind of explosive device."

Marty smirked. "A bomb? Don't be ridiculous. Here, let me see." He pushed his way in closer. As he examined the device more closely, the smirk faded. "No shit."

The three of them stood around the case, staring.

Jason finally broke the silence. "Why would anyone ship a bomb via TransOT?"

"Maybe they wanted to blow up Seeside Shipping, or someone in the company."

Ron hurried around to the next table and opened his laptop. After a few minutes, he said, "No such company." After a pause he began rapidly tapping. "The address is a residence. Anyone want to pay for a Lookie Who search subscription?"

Jason looked at Marty.

"Why me?"

"'Cause you got a roll of bills in your pocket, and we don't," Jason said.

After several minutes of registering and searching, they discovered the house was a rental. The owner's information showed nothing noteworthy, and the renter, if there was one, wasn't in the data.

Ron spoke up. "Marty, you know anyone with a Geiger counter?"

"Geiger counter? What...you think it's a suitcase nuke?" He was smirking all the way up to the edge of a laugh.

Ron turned red. "Look, I don't know, you don't know and Jason doesn't know. All we know is that gray stuff along the tube appears to be C4. So, until we know more, let's not rule out anything. Now, can you get us a Geiger counter?"

It was the first time Marty was cowed by Ron, but he also recognized the commonsense logic. "I'll make a few calls. I'll find one to borrow from somewhere."

"In the meantime," Jason said, "I'd like to know who the renter is. If we have a terrorist, he needs to be stopped."

Marty nodded. "Let's take a drive."

"Wait. We'll need a cover story," Ron said. He went to the printer and inserted a label sheet. He quickly entered two addresses into the computer, and printed out their labels. "Get me one of the boxes from the previous haul. One with useless stuff. He removed the old labels, stuck on the new ones, and resealed the box. "We just tell them that it was delivered to the wrong house."

"What if they ask which house?" Marty said.

"We give them the same address, only one street over."

Marty raised his eyebrows and nodded.

A half-hour later, Ron parked the car a couple of doors from the house. Marty said, "You go, Ron."

"Why always me?"

"Because you look the most innocent. A regular babe in the woods."

Ron's face reddened slightly, but he complied. After pressing the doorbell button and knocking twice, he looked back at the car. Marty motioned him over, but Ron had another idea. He walked directly next door. An elderly lady soon answered.

"Hi, miss. We live in the next block over and they accidentally delivered this to our house. It's addressed to your neighbor," he pointed, "but I can't seem to get an answer."

"Oh, I don't really know them. They mostly keep to themselves. And you see the weeds in front? They'd be even higher if they bothered to water the lawn."

"Well, do you know when they might be home?"

"Not really. They aren't around much." She leaned closer to him and spoke more quietly. "I'm not prejudiced or anything, but I think they're Arabs or something. Not very friendly."

"Well, I hate leaving this on their front step. It might get stolen."

"I know what you mean. Why, when I moved into this neighborhood 25 years ago, it was..."

When he got back to the car, he summed up the conversation. "She says they looked like Arabs. I'd vote for terrorism."

"Let's call the FBI," Jason said.

Marty held up his hand. "Lemme do it, Jason. I got a lot of burner phones, so they won't be able to trace it. I also know which office to call."

The next day, after their usual job, Marty dragged out the Geiger counter. The two brothers waited while Marty figured out how to operate the device. As he brought the sensor close to the suitcase, it began clicking more and more rapidly, until it sounded like a continuous buzz. It was touching the tube the C4 was strapped to. The three said nothing as they looked at each other. Finally, Marty summed up what they were all thinking: "Shit!"

"Jesus!" Jason said. "If this goes off, this whole city is toast."

Ron shook his head. "The timer's not turned on. Besides, it's not an explosive bomb. It's a dirty bomb."

Jason turned toward him. "And you know this how?"

"Suitcase bombs are heavier, and don't use regular explosives."

"So, now you're an expert on nuclear bombs?"

Marty's sideways grin nettled Ron. "No. It's called the *Internet*."

Marty strode over to confront Ron, who backed up a couple of short steps. By the time Marty had almost reached him, Jason was between them. Marty paused, stopped by Jason's eyes. Though the two were the same height, and Marty heavier, Jason had the bigger attitude.

"Cool it, Marty."

And Marty did cool it. "Okay, okay. You sure it's a dirty bomb, Ron?"

"Yeah. Remember the news reports about terrorists getting hold of nuclear material? I figured it was another exaggerated threat, so I looked it up on the internet. Dirty bombs use chemical explosives, like this C4." He looked at the case and its cold metal mechanism. "I guess not so exaggerated, after all."

As he wandered around the floor, Marty appeared to think aloud. "So, we have a dirty bomb shipped to a rental home. So, what do we do with it?"

"It's obvious we can't sell it," Jason said. "I don't even want your fence to know we have it."

Marty looked at him, then shook his head. "No, he wouldn't want any part of it. No way."

"Did you call the FBI?"

Marty shook his head. "No, I did not. I thought more about it. Callin' them without evidence is pretty useless. They'd need the suitcase. Tell me how we're supposed to turn it over to them. Drop by their local office and say, 'Hey guys, look what we found'?"

"And we can't just leave it at the front door of a police station," Jason remarked. "We might get caught with it."

Marty shook his head. "Any public place – museums, city hall – they all have surveillance cameras."

Jason said, "And dropping it in a public park? Anyone might pick it up and start fiddling with the timer buttons."

Marty said, "Good point, Jason. I guess we'd have to leave it someplace where the police will show up quickly, but somewhere with no surveillance cameras and not too public."

They became silent, contemplating the situation.

Finally, Marty spoke. "Say, I've got an idea. What if we bust a window in a store?" The brothers looked at him, obviously confused. He continued, slowly and deliberately. "In the rundown neighborhoods, the small stores have old alarm systems and no surveillance. We find one with a glass door, break it, say, after midnight, to set off the alarm. Then we toss the suitcase inside. The alarm will bring the police, and bingo! They find the suitcase."

The brothers slowly nodded. "Yeah. We let *them* call the FBI," Jason said. "That's brilliant."

Ron nodded. "Yeah, that would work. But we'll have to duct-tape the case closed. Keep it from opening up and dumping the contents when we toss it."

"Better we use metal strapping," Marty said. "The cops can open it with tin snips."

Jason said, "We'll have to wipe off our prints."

"More than prints," Marty said. "We'll need to get rid of any DNA we might have gotten in there."

"How do we do that?" Jason asked.

"Vacuum for hairs, then rub it down with bleach, inside and out. One more thing. After it's cleaned, we wear caps until we dump it."

Ron said, "Which is where?"

"Lemme see. I know a store that sells backpacks, light campin' stuff. We'll go tonight."

"Who's going to bust the glass door?"

Jason looked at Ron.

"Why do I always get the dirty work?" Ron said with anger.

Marty chuckled. "Okay, okay. I'll do it."

The brothers looked at him. Marty had never done the front-line work.

"Well, Ron's right. He's always our point guy. This time, I'll do it. Besides, that way I can make sure it gets done right."

Ron chafed at the last remark, but kept silent. Marty was merely irritating, but the suitcase was the real problem.

And once again, Marty delivered. The job went exactly as planned.

The next morning, Ron searched online for local police reports.

"Jason, take a look at this."

"Hmm. Yeah, so?"

"It says a broken door, and several items stolen. And nothing about a suitcase."

"Well, they probably just don't want to talk about it. A dirty bomb would scare the bejeezus out of everyone. The FBI probably told them to keep it hush hush."

"But the stolen goods? We never did that."

"Hmm. Don't know. Maybe part of the cover up of the bomb. Or the owner trying to pad his insurance claim. What difference does it make? It's off our hands. Let the FBI handle it."

The threesome continued their 'business enterprise' for another few weeks, netting some pretty good hauls. But one day, the job went wrong. They had just parked a TYD truck at their prearranged transfer point, when they heard sirens. Coincidence? They looked at each other and jumped into their van. They made it out of the side street a few seconds before the first red and blue lights turned into view some two blocks away, coming toward them at high speed. After the police cars passed them, Marty pulled into a parking space. They all got out, looking as casual as they could. That's when they heard the helicopter.

Ron froze, and Jason's eyes opened wide. "You think they spotted us?"

Marty spoke slowly. "No, or they wouldn't be travelin' away from us."

"But how did they react so fast?" Ron asked.

"Did you make sure you weren't followed?"

"Of course. Same as usual."

Marty was silent for a minute. Then he said, "Let's go."

It was a silent ride back to the shop. Marty stood at the center of the floor, silent, and finally nodded. "Well, that's it."

The brothers looked at each other. Then Jason said, "That's what?"

Marty wrinkled his brow. "The end of our enterprise."

"What exactly happened back there?" Ron asked.

"There's only one explanation. You weren't followed, yet they knew exactly where to go to find the truck."

"You mean, GPS?"

Marty nodded. "They never put trackers on their trucks before. I guess they got tired of gettin' robbed."

Jason shook his head. "So, what do we do now?"

"I finish offloadin' the merchandise and pay you guys your cut. Then I guess you'll be findin' yourselves regular jobs."

"Shit!" Jason began stomping tight circles. "Shit!"

"Look at the bright side," Marty said. "We had a pretty good run. A gig like this...well, it always has an endpoint. The endpoint isn't prison, so...hey, we made ourselves some green."

"What do you plan to do?" asked Ron.

"Me? I got an offer for work last week."

"Yeah? Where?"

"In Newark."

Jason brightened. "Doing what?"

"Various odd jobs. I'm afraid it's just me."

As Jason's enthusiasm faded, Ron asked, "Who for?"

"Tony Petrelli."

"The mafia guy?" Ron smirked. "You're going to work for the mafia? Really?"

"The money's good, which is good enough for me."

Ron nodded. "Okay. But just remember – you get too close to the flame, you'll get burned."

Marty smiled and turned around. As he walked away, he said, "I'll contact you guys next week to settle up what I owe you."

"Yeah," Ron muttered, "sure you will." He turned to Jason. "Don't hold your breath waiting for the money."

"Look, I don't know what your problem is, but Marty's okay. If he says he'll pay, he'll pay."

Ron wondered at his older brother's naivety. But the following week, Marty did return – not with just their cut, but an extra ten percent.

"What's that for?" Jason asked.

"You guys been great to work with. Besides, I'm going to be rollin' in the stuff soon. Think of it as a goodbye gift."

After he had left, Jason turned to his brother. "See, I told you he was alright."

Ron was surprised and embarrassed. *'Maybe I pegged him wrong.'* The next day, he remarked, "You know, Jason, since we're out of the business now, we should think about renting an apartment."

"Why? The rent's cheap here, and we've got lots of space on the first floor."

"It's not like a home. It feels hollow." During their time with Marty, he had hated the "lots of space," especially on weekends. The reverberation of their footsteps made him uncomfortable, as if the lonely sound might seep into him. He could not account for it, but it goaded him to spend both days upstairs, a refugee from the echoey emptiness. Monday's haul would bring boxes and contents that dampened the feeling of a dead-end destination, made it seem livable.

Jason had looked down on Ron's 'sensitivity,' as he often called it with a heavy dose of sarcasm. But now, he had a solution. "We'll bring my large TV down here, buy a cheap couch, a little furniture. It'll be our living room."

Ron nodded. With Jason on board, he was optimistic. "Okay. With a little paint, a few padded chairs...maybe a coffeemaker and toaster at the sink...yeah. That would work." Together, they would make it into a real home.

The brothers began their job search with Unbenders, but the shop had no openings. Jason eventually found employment at Jim's Auto Body Shop, but Ron was luckier. He went to work at an auto parts store that sold both retail and wholesale. It paid less, but the work was relatively clean, and left him less tired in the evenings. He hated falling asleep over his college homework. Besides, he wanted to find his own kind of work. Working together in their own business had made his brother's shadow less comforting, even annoying. He loved Jason – certainly appreciated the passion of his protectiveness – but they were unalike. Ron realized their paths had diverged several years back. It was only a slight angular difference, but over time the distance had grown. Perhaps Jason understood – perhaps not – but he too needed for Ron to have his separate existence.

A couple of months after Marty left, all television and radio stations interrupted their regular programs. There had been a small explosion in the Holland Tunnel. Radiation had spread throughout the tunnel, shutting down all transport between New Jersey and Lower Manhattan. Everyone at Jim's Auto Body shop stopped work and watched as the stations relayed the trickle of information.

By the weekend, the police had reported the discovery of the remains of a metal suitcase a half-mile beyond the tunnel. The FBI spokesman stated they believed the suitcase had been used to carry the tunnel bomb. "We ran chemical and radioactive analysis of the inside of the case. There were minute traces of C4 compounds, and the case itself had signs of exposure to radiation."

Ron turned from the television to face his brother. "I feel guilty. We should have called the FBI, told them about the place on Hunter Street."

Jason nodded. "Yeah. I never thought about it, that someday they'd make another bomb."

The following weekend, Ron was in the college library when his attention was arrested by the cover of a magazine. He made a copy, brought it home and showed it to Jason. "You see it? Both latches missing?"

Jason looked at it. "So? They probably blew off when the C4 exploded."

Ron shook his head. "Look closer. The chisel marks. Both sides."

Jason squinted. "What the..." He looked up at Ron. "Shit. Same case." His voice had gone quiet. "But how...? We saw Marty break the window and toss it in."

"And we heard the alarm go off," Ron added.

"Jesus! Someone else must have picked it up. We don't know how long before the police got there."

"That would explain why other things were stolen from the store," Ron said. "But how did they get it to the terrorists?"

"Maybe they didn't," Jason said "You know, we've always assumed there was only one terrorist group. A lot of Muslims live in Philadelphia."

"Not just Muslims. A lot of right- and left-wingnuts too. Tons of grievance groups."

"What the hell do we do now?" Jason said, almost to himself.

After several seconds, Ron said, "Nothing. We can't unbreak the egg."

Jason grabbed his phone. "I'm going to call Marty, see what he thinks." The phone buzzed for several seconds before it was picked up. But it was someone else, someone who didn't know anyone named Marty. Ron said, "I guess he had to change numbers when he went to work for Petrelli."

"Why don't we visit him? It's not that far. Besides, I saw that Petrelli guy on TV. He was red hot over the bombing. They had to bleep out half the words he used talking about the terrorists."

"I don't think we should mention our connection with the suitcase. He might not understand."

Jason nodded. "Hey, is our Lookie Who subscription still active?"

Ron jumped to his feet. "Great idea. Let's find where he lives." The brothers couldn't find Petrelli's home address, but a half-hour's search spit out three of his business addresses in New Jersey. They were on the road in ten minutes. Petrelli wasn't at the first two, but when they inquired at the *Suits for Suitors* store in Rutherford, the manager told them to wait. Fifteen minutes later, Petrelli's men, which included two refrigerator-sized gents, escorted them to a back room. It was a well-lit office, quite unlike the movie settings where some guy gets 'worked over.' It took only a few seconds for Ron to realize that reality ignores movie clichés.

"My name's Paul Casselleti. I work for Mr. Petrelli. I understand you two have been making certain indiscreet inquiries about my boss. Maybe you should explain why." While not as big as the other two, Casselleti would be the image that would pop into your head if someone said 'bouncer'. Combined with his dark complexion and thick hair, he conveyed an impression of someone much more vital than his 50 years. Even without his two associates, he could have intimidated the brothers physically.

Jason said, "Look, our friend Marty went to work for your boss. Suddenly, we can't contact him. He left no forwarding address. I guess that's our fault – we never asked. But now, his phone number's been assigned to someone else. We're just worried about him. Plus, we wanted to say 'Hi.'"

"Look, kid. Mr. Petrelli's an important businessman. You don't just drop in without an appointment. Capish?"

Ron nodded. "Okay. I see what you're saying. Sorry."

"This Marty got a last name?"

"Porter. Marty Porter."

"Never heard of him."

Jason looked at Ron, then asked, "Well maybe he works in a different county?"

Casselleti and the two Mr. Refrigerators broke out in laughter. "County? That's rich. Look kid, I'm Mr. Petrelli's number two. I know everyone – literally everyone – in our organization, which just happens to be a little larger than the county – as in the whole east coast. And there isn't any Marty Porter in it."

Jason reached into his wallet and pulled out a photo. "This here's Marty."

Casselleti shook his head. "Never saw him. And I don't forget faces. Which you should take to mean, I'll remember yours. Now do yourselves a gigantic favor and don't be coming around asking for Mr. Petrelli." He paused before adding, "Or me. Unless you want an extended conversation with my two associates." He stood and buttoned his blazer. "Understood?"

"Yessir." Ron said. "Sorry to have bothered you."

As they drove home, Jason was obviously dejected, but Ron felt happy about their day together. He'd never want to be in business again with his brother, but working together on this small adventure had brought them closer. In their attempt to contact Marty, they were equal partners. It was a good feeling.

The brothers returned home and resumed their normal lives, Jason working in the body shop, and Ron in the auto parts store and attending college at night.

One day Brad Klepper came into the parts store. "Ron, how are you? You working here now?"

"Yeah, the last couple of months. How are you doing?"

"Doing good. Just need parts for some weekend work on my car." After a few minutes in the aisles, Brad brought the parts to the counter. "Say, you still working with Marty?"

Ron began to scan the items. "No. That kind of ended." He paused the scanning and looked at Brad. "You hear anything from him?"

"Nope. Not since April. It was a weird job."

"Weird how?"

"He had me get a briefcase from a store."

Ron stopped moving. Also stopped breathing. "Briefcase?"

"Yeah. He told me this store in the Ventura district would have it waiting for me at a specific time. I arrived a few minutes early, but the store was closed."

"Uh, huh."

"You know what was even weirder? This car pulls up right on time, and who do I see get out? Marty. He walks up to the door, which is glass, and breaks it! Just like that, and throws the case inside. Then he turns around and gets back in the car. You believe that?"

"And what was in the case?"

"No idea. He gave me strict instructions not to look inside. Besides, it was strapped with metal. I delivered it to him the next day. Easiest 200 dollars I ever made. Got a couple of extras from the store, too."

Ron nodded, took a deep breath, as he curbed his facial expression. But at lunchtime, between his anger and nausea, he couldn't eat. And he didn't tell Jason of his conversation until evening the next day.

Jason turned red. "Jesus! He must have sold the case back to the terrorists. The Petrelli job was a lie."

Ron nodded. "Yep. A cover story to explain his disappearing act."

"If I see him again, I'm gonna kill him. I swear it."

"First we have to find him," Ron said. "I've been thinking. Maybe Tim Larson knows."

"The money man? Hmm. Only how do we get him to tell us?"

"I've got a plan."

The next day at lunchtime, they both drove to the comic book store. The bells jingled as before, and Tim came to the counter. "Hi, gentlemen. Long time no see."

"Nice to see you too," Ron said, as they shook hands.

"We were wondering. We were straightening out our shop, and came across some of Marty's tools. They're electronic, probably valuable. But he didn't leave a forwarding address."

"Not for me either. He hasn't called, and when I tried to phone him, some stranger answered. Said he didn't know any Marty Porter."

Ron tried to consider his options, but none came to mind. "Yeah, we did the same."

"Look, I'll call you when I see him. He's bound to show. I've got some money waiting for him."

Ron nodded. "Ah, from his fence, I suppose."

Tim furrowed his brow. "His fence?" He smiled. "He didn't use a fence. He was his own fence."

The two brothers looked at each other.

Tim wrinkled his brow. "He didn't tell you he had a fence, did he?"

Ron quickly recovered. "Uh, no. We just assumed."

"Hell, he's dealt in..." At this point he gestured with air quotes, "questionably acquired goods...for years. He was the fence for other pinchers besides yourselves."

Ron decided to end the conversation before Jason lost his cool. "Well, we have to be getting back. Let us know if you hear from him."

"No problem. Nice to see you again. And if you ever need a go-between..."

When they got to the car, Jason's face was red. "Bastard! He said he had to give the fence 20 percent before the split."

"Yeah, his Three Musketeers talk was all bullshit. One-third plus twenty percent is half."

"No wonder he seemed so generous," Jason said. "He could add a little extra now and then, and still screw us."

Ron tilted his head. "And who decided the value?"

Jason's eyes slowly widened, then he exhaled. "Oh, shit."

"We need to look up the items when we get home. You remember some of them?"

That evening, after they had returned from work, Ron sat tapping the keyboard while Jason read off the list he had written down from memory.

"Two-hundred-fifty?" Ron bellowed. "Shit, he called it two-hundred. I remember thinking the price had come down a hundred bucks in a year's time."

Ron tapped some more. "Here's the set of Riteford crystal glasses. Four, wasn't it? Two-hundred."

"He said a hundred, didn't he?"

Ron just nodded.

Jason lowered his head. "Jesus. You were right. He's a cheat. And it's all my fault."

"No, my fault too. With all my suspicions, I never thought to check the prices. I mean, it would have been so simple. I just figured he'd leave one day without paying our cut."

Jason's face lit up. "What about the rental space? Maybe they know something."

After work the next evening, Jason's drove them to the rental space facility. He exceeded the speed limit most of the way.

The office man wore a tag marked *Arthur* and a paunch that said he sat around too much. Jason admired his clean hands. "No. No Marty Porter in our records."

"He's got to be there," Jason said. He's in space 217. We helped him move stuff there." His voice was strained.

Arthur could see Jason's state of mind. "Look, I'm not supposed to be giving out names, but the guy renting 217 is not a Marty Porter. It's somebody named Walsh, and we haven't heard from him. Wish we had. His credit card's bouncing and he's almost three months behind on his rent. Two more weeks and we deactivate his code and open the space for rent."

"About six-feet, late twenties, curly hair…"

"Look, mister, I don't know who looks like what. We have over four-hundred spaces. I can't even remember what the sexy women customers look like – at least, not their faces." He snickered at his own cleverness. "Far as I know, the other clerk might have signed him up."

Ron put his hand on his brother's shoulder. "Come on. Let's go." He turned to Arthur. "Thanks for trying."

When they reached the car, Ron said, "He must have used a fake ID. Hell, for all we know, maybe Marty was an alias. Probably not that hard to find a forger who can make a license good enough for Arthur." He was silent for several seconds. "I'd bet my last dollar he's planning to leave the country.

"Planning? If he's got a fortune, he probably left weeks ago."

"Hopefully, he hasn't gone yet. He'll probably need a forged passport, other IDs good enough to pass TSA. Or maybe waiting for Homeland Security to lower the alert, or maybe having trouble moving the money offshore."

"Or maybe long gone," Jason insisted. He was silent for a half-minute. "So, what now?"

"I don't know. Let me think."

When they reached home, Ron started searching the web. Afterward, he went to his room upstairs, and lay on his bed. A half-hour later, he returned downstairs. Jason was watching a movie. Ron sat on the couch and looked at him. "I've got a plan."

Jason muted the television. "Okay. So, how are we going to get what he owes us?"

"Forget about the money. It's gone. Besides, I've got something better. Much better."

After discussing it, Ron called *Suits for Suitors*, gave his name, and left a message. Less than an hour later, Casselleti called him. "I hope you're not wasting my time."

"Definitely not. I have some information for your boss."

"Is that so? What kind of information?"

"Information he is definitely interested in. Best not to talk about it on the phone. When you hear it, you'll understand."

"Tell you what. You drive up tomorrow. Meet me at the same place as before. But it best not be for nothin'."

The next morning, as the brothers drove to New Jersey, Jason listened as Ron described the story he had concocted. When Casselleti arrived, Ron did most of the talking. "I saw Mr. Petrelli on television after the tunnel bombing. He was angry. Very angry, and swore revenge if he could find the perpetrators."

Casselleti, sitting on the edge of a desk, tilted his head back. "Go on."

"We have some information concerning the attack."

"And you're not going to the police because..."

"Well, the police might assume we were connected to the bombing. Besides, their level of proof would be higher than Mr. Petrelli's, and this person is very good at covering his tracks.

Casselleti pouted his lips as he nodded for several seconds. "Go on."

Ron reached into his messenger bag. "This here's a photo of the briefcase the police recovered." He handed it to Casselleti. "About a mile from the tunnel. The thing is, we'd seen that case before."

"And you did nothing?"

"Because we only saw Marty with the closed case. We had no idea it was a bomb."

As Ron continued spinning his fairy tale, Jason nodded.

"So, you're saying Marty set off the bomb?"

"I don't think so," Ron replied. "I think he sold it to terrorists."

"And how is it he came into possession of this suitcase?"

"He claimed it was in a truckload of stolen goods."

"And how do you know it's the same suitcase?"

"See the edge where the latches are supposed to be? See the chisel marks? When we asked, Marty said he had chiseled them off. The chisel marks in the photo are identical. And when we asked about the contents, he said it was just some junk inside. But he was clutching it awfully close for junk. And what are the chances of two cases exactly alike, both with similar chisel marks?"

"And where does this Marty live?"

"That's the difficult part. We don't know, but I know you and Mr. Petrelli have the resources to find out. Here's a couple of photos of Marty Porter. At least, that's the name he told us, though apparently, he also went by the name of Walsh, and who knows how many other names? The thing is, if he wants to leave the country, he'll need an ID that will pass TSA inspectors. They use an ultraviolet light to detect..."

"Sonny, I know what the TSA uses, and I get your meaning. He'll need a forger with special equipment and skills. So, you want that we should put out the word and find him. Is that it?"

"Yeah. I mean, we're like Mr. Petrelli – pissed that this guy helped terrorists attack our country. And probably made a lot of dough in the process."

"Okay, here's the deal, Ron and Jason. I'm going to inquire very carefully into this. If what you say checks out, I have a feeling Mr. Petrelli will be grateful. If not, if this is a red herring to get us to hurt some competitor of yours...well, let's not talk of unpleasantries."

"Mr. Casselleti, we have nothing personal to gain by any of this. We're not in any business – just two people working at jobs for a living. This guy helped terrorists attack this country."

***

On the following weekend, they continued their redecorating project downstairs, inching it closer to hominess. They had completed painting the walls a week earlier, and spent the morning replacing the roll-up shades with venetian blinds – a process extended in duration by their anorexic wallets, which limited them to two blinds per week. They had almost finished installing one, when they heard a knock at the door.

The strangers displayed their IDs. "Good morning. I'm Detective Pete Truman of the Philadelphia Police Department, and this is my partner, Detective Robin Fletcher. We have a few questions we'd like to ask."

"Yeah? About what?" Jason asked.

"Could we come inside?"

Jason paused, then said, "Sure," and stood aside.

Ron heard the introduction and walked over to the other three. The detectives sat on the chairs, Jason on the couch.

"Get you some coffee?" Ron said, trying to make the conversation as convivial as possible, though he was unsurprised at their refusal. He sat next to his brother.

"You may have heard about a string of delivery van robberies last year," Truman said.

Ron nodded. "Yeah. It was on the news."

"What bothered us is the traffic cams picked up a black van in the vicinity of a number of these robberies and at about the same time. We think this may be more than a coincidence." He paused, looking at them intently.

Jason shifted on the couch a bit, but Ron kept himself as relaxed as he could. "Okay, and what brought you here?" he asked.

Truman stared at Ron. Ron stared back.

Truman looked directly at Jason. "The thing is, during yesterday's briefing, the captain showed some traffic-cam photos involving our case – the stolen vans – and a detective working a crash case remembered seeing you at Jim's Auto Body Shop. The owner identified you."

"Yeah, I've worked there about a year. So what?"

"So, we thought you might be able to assist us." He rose and walked to Jason and handed him a photo. It showed the black van from the front, with Marty and Jason clearly visible through the windshield. "And this." Truman passed a similar photo to Ron, taken at another intersection. "Unfortunately, the van doesn't have a front plate."

Almost instantly, Ron saw the detective's entire case, knew how they would proceed. His college studies might pay off far sooner than he had ever anticipated. "Yeah, that's Marty. We worked for him for a couple of years."

Jason quickly swiveled his head toward Ron, but kept silent.

"Doing what?"

"Moving stuff. Helping him make deliveries."

Truman nodded to himself, then said, "Did it pay well?"

This time, Jason became creative. "Not as well as body work, but it's a lot cleaner."

The two detectives looked at each other. For the first time, Fletcher spoke. "Do you have a last name for this Marty?"

"Sure. Marty Porter," Ron said, with a *Leave It to Beaver* eagerness.

"And an address?"

Jason and Ron looked at each other. This time, Ron didn't need to pretend. "Well, we never went to his house. I have no idea."

"So, how did you do your work for Mr. Porter? Did he come here with the van already loaded?"

Ron saw the trap. If Marty loaded the van by himself, why would he need the brothers to unload it? "No. We were the loaders and unloaders. We'd drive to his storage space, load up the van, and he'd drive us to his various customers."

Jason looked at his brother, but said nothing.

"And do you remember where the storage space was?"

"Sure," Ron said, and recited the address. "We were there a few days ago, but the office guy said they had no record of Marty Porter. He claimed the man renting the space was someone named Walsh." Ron understood how the detectives would proceed. The more of Ron's statements they could verify, the more credible he would appear.

"Which office guy?" she asked.

"Someone named Arthur. His tag didn't give his last name."

Do you remember the space number?" Truman asked.

"Yeah. 217."

"I'm curious," Fletcher said. "Why did you go to the rental place a few days ago?"

"We just wanted to look him up, say 'Hi', and all that. We hadn't heard from him, and thought the storage place might have a forwarding address."

"And why did you stop working for him?" she asked.

Jason said, "He got some job offer. I guess a good-paying one."

"Do you have any of the addresses where you dropped off Marty's merchandise?" Truman asked.

"The addresses?" Ron's mind raced to find a way out of the trap. The slit was narrow, but he dove through. "He had the list of addresses, but we never bothered with it. I mean, he did the driving."

Jason caught the lie and ran with it. "Yeah, he always did the driving. We just unloaded the stuff and took it into the buildings."

"What kind of merchandise?" Fletcher asked.

"Various items," Ron said. "Some furniture, some TVs. Other merchandise was in boxes without labels."

"So, you don't remember any one of the customer addresses." Fletcher's voice was saturated with skepticism.

Ron knew he and Jason had to stick to their guns. "No. It was never important to us. I never paid attention."

The detectives were silent for several seconds.

"Okay," Truman said. "We'll follow up the information you've given us. We appreciate your help." The two detectives rose and walked to the front door. Truman opened it, but turned around for several seconds. Ron expected him to deliver the cliché about not leaving town, and perhaps that was his intent, but he merely turned back and left with Fletcher.

Five seconds passed.

"WHOA!" Jason shouted. "That was pants-shittin' stuff!" He exhaled a few deep breaths. "Hooya!"

Ron breathed deep. "Yeah...they didn't buy the unnoticed addresses bit."

"It's worse than that," Jason said. "If they do catch Marty, he won't know our version. If our stories don't match, we could be in deep shit."

"Stories don't match? Jason, he's a cheat and a slimeball. Even if he knew our story, do you think he'd help us? Shit, he'll do everything he can to lay the blame on us. Especially since he's got to know we figured out he sold the case back to the terrorists."

Jason turned pale, and rubbed his face. "Oh, crap. This isn't just a stolen goods rap. This is terrorist shit, man."

"Yeah. And it'll bring in Homeland Security on our asses." As he considered the problem, Ron could feel his heart pounding.

Jason said, "We have to hope to God that Petrelli finds him first. I never wished anyone's death before, but this guy's more than a slimeball. He can hang us."

Ron gazed at Jason, his mouth hanging open. "Yeah…literally."

"Besides, the piece of shit aided terrorists. That's three strikes, as far as I'm concerned."

Ron was thinking, thinking hard. Finally, he said, "Petrelli has his network, but the police have traffic cams, facial recognition software, all sorts of tools. On the other hand, Petrelli's guys have a week head start, and I'll bet they know every forger on the east coast."

"Fuckin' horserace, man…and the jockeys are everyone but us." Jason kept bouncing his right foot on his toe, an unconscious habit whenever he was stressed. They sat for a couple of minutes.

Ron had gone limp. Finally, he shook his head. "I can't think of any way to tilt this in our favor. We can't let Casselleti know about the police. He might speed up his search, or he might think we called them."

"That's a fire we're *not* going to touch," Jason said. After a long pause, he looked at Ron. "Shit. What if Casselleti's guys find out about the police on their own?

The mafia's got to have cops on their payroll." He looked away from his brother. "Shit!"

Ron's mouth opened, but at first, no words came out. "There's a dozen ways he might find out. The police will be questioning other people. Maybe a lot of other people. Casselleti's not going to like this."

How would it feel to wait your doom while watching an avalanche slowly plunge toward you? What does the accused man feel as the jury slowly walks in, the forewoman carrying the rest of his life scratched on a single piece of paper? *Dread* is more than a word, more than a feeling. It's a state of mind, one that enveloped the brothers for several days. They did not speak of it, but it engulfed them each like noxious smoke from half-burned buildings. It floated disquiet into their days and seeped into their restless dreams. It slowed their movements and smudged their thoughts, tainted their food with the taste of clay. On more evenings than usual, Ron joined his brother in the back alley for Jason's romance with weed.

And then there were the cars. Ron was certain he was being followed. He'd make extra turns to see if the car behind echoed his course. Sometimes it did – somewhat. However, after a couple of days of that circus, he realized the cops could always track his phone. But what if the tails were Casselleti's?

Every night, Ron scoured the internet with various search words, both hoping and fearing news about Marty, or whatever his name was. Most unusual, Jason joined him, dragging a second chair to the desk. Each night, the search ended with both disappointment and relief at another failed attempt.

But one Sunday three weeks later, a stranger showed up at their door. "Hi, I'm Mr. Smith."

'*Sure you are,*' thought Ron.

"I work for Mr. Casselleti. He said I should deliver this to you." He handed Ron a small cardboard box, about the size of a cracker box.

"What's this?"

"Mr. Casselleti says, 'Thanks,' and wants you to know that the guy you mentioned to him wasn't the guy you mentioned to him. And he had a safety deposit box with unusual contents – contents, I might add, that he could not explain to Mr. Casselleti's satisfaction." He started to turn, then stopped. "Oh, and one more thing. You do not want to deposit this, except in small amounts."

Ron slowly nodded. "I see. Tell Mr. Casselleti, 'Thanks,'" He didn't know what else to say.

Without an additional word, the faux Mr. Smith, turned and walked away. Ron went inside, flopped down onto the couch. Weeks of tension suddenly left through every pore of his body. He almost cried. Finally, he opened the box. He tightened his lower lip and nodded. As with his childhood Christmas morning presents, he was not surprised at the money, though the amount – two banded packages of hundred-dollar bills – was unexpected.

Jason came down a few minutes later. "Jesus! I had a lousy night's sleep. Think I'll just watch the game today."

"Maybe this will cheer you up."

Charon's Business

As usual, Diane Morton arrived a few minutes early with a sunrise smile.

As she entered her office in the Julianville coroner's department, Kirk looked up and said, "Busy day ahead."

"How busy?"

"Four on the floor."

Her smile evaporated. She looked at her assistant with her mouth open. "Four? What happened?"

"Crash out on 37. Happened around 10:00 last night."

She sighed. As Chief Medical Examiner, she'd was facing a very long shift. "Well, better not waste time. Let's get started."

"Which one?"

"Flip a coin. Actually, flip two coins."

***

Ten miles away, her brother, Stephen Morton was waiting for the meeting to start. Paul Jovus entered the room five minutes after the sales staff had sat down. He always arrived at the monthly meeting five minutes after everyone else. "Okay, tigers and tigresses, we have last month's sales figures, and I'm disappointed. Our sales were off two percent for the month. And I have info on where the sales went." He paused, looked around the room, then back at his clipboard. "MT Coffin gained that two percent."

A groan echoed from one person to the next, along with a few murmurs of, "MT again," and, "Jesus."

"Now, I know a lot of you are tired of hearing me harp about MT, but now you see why. We have to get that two percent back..." he lowered his tone, "any way we can."

Like everyone else in the room, Stephen understood his meaning. The lowest producer would be axed. That was the way things worked at Coffins R Us. They drove their sales force hard, but they were fair – the compensation was excellent. As top in sales, he wasn't worried, but then, he realized he might improve his numbers by learning more about MT. How did they keep their sales consistently high?

His internet searches revealed that MT Coffin Co. was owned by Larry Mosier and Gary Tucker. Their biggest customer? That turned out to be TM Funerals, LLC. The corporate filings showed it was owned by...Tucker and Mosier. *'No wonder their sales consistently beat ours. They can sell to themselves.'*

He had once suggested to Paul that Coffins R Us should expand into the funeral home business, but Paul couldn't see it. "Vertical integration? Too complicated." But apparently not for Tucker and Mosier. Stephen didn't waste time feeling vindicated. He decided to explore TM personally. Their website referred to their locations as *Passage Parlors*. Stephen had to admire their inventiveness. It was an interesting PR term, as if people didn't die, they just passed. *'Like last night's dinner,'* he mused, remembering the takeout tacos he and Maureen had eaten the night before.

It took 45 minutes to reach TM's nearest location. He parked a half-block away. He wasn't paranoid; he too had occasionally run a plate to investigate a sales target. All part of being thorough. Nor was he curious about the personnel. They only came in two flavors –

unctuous or haughty as a baron's butler. No, he wondered about their operation – what they sold, how they marketed, their unique spin.

A few seconds after entering, a Mr. Unctuous entered the vestibule. "Welcome to the Lawton Passage Parlor. I'm Marvin. How may I serve you?" He handed Stephen a business card.

Stephen read the card, then said, "My name is Les Knightly. My uncle is dying, and I'm looking for a someone to handle the arrangements. I was thinking of Knowles Funeral Home, but then I thought I should consider alternatives."

"A wise caution," Marvin replied. "Our methods are unique, cheaper, and most important, more accommodating."

"Accommodating?"

"Mr. Knightly, people are of two minds about religion. Some believe, some don't.

"And which half does TM serve?"

"Actually, we cater to both. Given that no one has ever returned from the dead to inform us of the truth, TM offers the chance to cover both bases."

Stephen raised his head. "Like betting red and black on the roulette wheel."

Marvin smiled, then simpered uncomfortably.

"So, tell me, what are the two choices?"

For believers, there's always the traditional choices of casket or cremation urn. But for skeptics, the only option until recently has been cremation. We now can offer them something new."

Stephen was impatient with the prompt, but he understood that theatrics were the essence of funerals. "And what would that be?"

"Glass." After a few seconds, Marvin recognized that Stephen wasn't going to bite twice. "We offer coffin covers of glass – bulletproof, a half-inch thick, and with a non-reflective coating. And Mr. Knightly, though the coffins are a bit more expensive, the burials cost less."

"Oh? Why is that?"

"The plots are only 18 inches deep, keeping the glass slightly above ground level. This allows families and friends to view their beloved anytime in perpetuity. We call it, the Eternal Viewing Option."

"But it would add the cost of embalming, wouldn't it?"

"Not necessarily. We offer a Basic No-Frills package. And all display coffins are filled with nitrogen to prevent decomposition, though without embalming, your loved one could become discolored over the years. Does your uncle have life insurance?"

***

Stephen didn't drive directly back to work. He stopped by his brother's place. As he parked in front of the administration offices of Pleasant Dreams Cemetery and Funeral Services, he considered Charlie's success. He had purchased an inexpensive stretch of ground a dozen years earlier and turned it into a thriving money machine. Everyone thought it was crazy, including Stephen. "But who would want their loved one buried next to a freight train line? And literally on the wrong side of the tracks. It's at the edge of a slum, for crissake!"

"Stephen, you got to think different. Not, 'Freight trains are a bad place for a cemetery,' but, 'How do I turn limeys into limeade?'"

"I think you mean lemons into lemonade."

"Whatever. Anyway, I'm gonna turn the train from a minus to a plus. Gotta think positive. Like the slum neighborhood. It makes the land cheap."

What Charlie lacked in literary sophistication, he more than balanced with entrepreneurial creativity. He built a giant wall two blocks long and a dozen feet high between the property and the tracks. Then he approached Darnell Curtis, leader of the Ravens. "You have any good artists in your gang?"

"Uhh. First, like, don't call us no gang. We a neighborhood association."

"Sorry. No offense intended."

"None taken. You just unfamiliar with the terminology. Second, 'course we got artists. Best graffiti specialists around. But whatchur needs?"

"I need real pictures, not graffiti."

"We can cover that."

Charlie led Darnell outside. "See that wall? I need pictures of heaven-bound trains from one end to the next. Say ten of them."

"And what's our end?"

"Free burials for each artist for when they get shot."

"What about the ones who don't get shot?"

"Hmm." After a few seconds, Charlie nodded. "Okay, even if they survive till old age. Ten reserved places for them."

"Maybe if you added a little green to the deal."

"Look, Darnell, I'm just starting up. Money's tight. Best I can do is throw in free markers for the gravesites. Something with pictures of roses."

"I can go with that."

"I'll need sketches of each gan...artist's drawing. I have to approve before they begin."

"Like you some kinda art critic? Especially street art?"

"Just so there's no misunderstandings," Charlie said. "No paintings I gotta paint over."

"That's true. Misunderstandin's can be bad. We have them from time to time. Can get messy." He nodded silently. "Tell ya what. I'll go ya one better. I'll throw in that each of the artists will come by every few years to touch up. You know, for weather and fadin's and such. Also, to know no one's been messin' with their art. But you gotta let them sign their work."

"Sounds fair, gettin' credit for their artwork. Sure, they can come anytime, for as long as they live."

They shook hands as a freight train's horn sounded.

The paintings turned out beautiful, though one looked a bit strange. The initial artist earned a gravesite halfway through, and the work was completed by a different guy in his individual style. Unfortunately, he was in his blue period. Afterward, Charlie had to deal with the sound of the freight train horns. His first idea was to play Handel's *Messiah* at very high volume, but the neighbors complained about the noise. He finally hit upon a salesman's approach. He directed his staff to announce to customers, each time a train horn blasted, "That there's another one on their way to

Heaven." He even installed smoke generators along the base of the wall for the final flourish of each burial service. It was as if the decedent's spirit was on its way skyward. Charlie had thought of everything.

Stephen found his way to his brother's office. "Charlie, I've found another idea to improve your operation." He related the results of his undercover efforts at TM.

"Damn!" Charlie said. "Wish I had thought of it first. Especially the bulletproof part. That would be a hit with the 'neighborhood association' people. Hmm. Maybe have to add an anti-graffiti coating."

***

One of Charlie's competitors was a mere three miles distant. Every time he drove by the Jannah Hills Cemetery, they seemed to be busy. He found this odd, given that they were an Islamic cemetery. He had no idea there were that many Muslims living in Julianville, or even in the county.

There weren't.

The three owners had a side business – no, not really a business. More like a second career. Truthfully – which they were not – the cemetery was a front, whose sole purpose was to hide terrorists from the law.

Their method was ingenious. For instance, about a month earlier, they had hidden Mohammed Kanaan and Adam Khouri, sought by the FBI for trying to purchase rocket launchers from an army logistics officer. Ahmed Atiyeh, Mahmud Haddad, and Omar Safar greeted Kanaan and Khouri warmly, but curtly.

"Welcome brothers, but we have no time to waste," said Haddad.

"Our Muslim brother is correct," Atiyeh said. "Quickly, now. You must get in these coffins."

Kanaan opened his mouth, but it was several seconds before he could say, "What? A coffin? What do you think you're doing?"

"Hiding you," Safar said. "That's our duty. And yours."

"You're intending to bury us?" Khouri asked, astonished.

"This is how it's done. We have done this many, many times. Please. Hurry."

The two terrorists stood silently, looking from the coffins to the three owners.

Haddad spoke for his partners. "It's perfectly safe. You get in, we inject you with a drug that slows your bodily processes. Then we put the coffin in a concrete vault. You'll be totally protected, brother."

The terrorists looked at each other.

"It is called retarded animation," Safar explained. "It slows down the body. And we install a tank to slowly seep oxygen into the space. It's good for four months. We've done this before. You'll be fine."

"How do we wake up?" Khouri asked.

"We dig out the coffin, inject you with a stimulant, and you wake up. That's all. Within an hour, you'll be back to normal."

Atiyeh dealt a sharp slap to the side of one of the coffins. "Come. In the name of Allah, you must hurry. Even as we speak, the authorities search for you."

***

Charlie's phone buzzed. "Hi, Diane."

"Hi, Charlie. Just wanted to check. How's the knee."

"It's recovering. The doc thinks it won't need surgery."

"That's good. And how's the cemetery doing?"

"Going smooth. The new manager seems to know the business. Maybe I can semi-retire soon."

"Well, I handle the permanently retired. They brought in four just last night."

"Four? What, another gan...I mean, neighborhood association shooting?"

"A what association?"

"Never mind. Was it gang related?"

"No, no. Some 22-year-old on drugs ran his car off the road, took out a van as well. They went into the gorge off highway 37."

"Wow. You're right. Guess we should all consider ourselves lucky."

"I've got to go, Charlie. Business."

"Okay. Pasta la visa."

Kirk, who had signaled her, said, "They're here."

Diane left her office to meet the parents of Sammy Lemmon. "We've already completed identification. You don't have to view the body if you would prefer not to."

"I'd like to see my son," Sandra Lemmon said.

Diane led her into the viewing area. Kirk pulled the sheet down from the head. Sandra cried, then nodded. She turned away and cried some more.

"We can hold him here until you make arrangements. Did you have a funeral home you want him sent to?"

"No. We're from out of state, and we never made arrangements. He was only 22." She burst into tears again.

"We're not allowed to recommend any particular funeral home, though there is one at the end of Knowles street on the south side of town. I can't remember the name, though I've heard some good things about it. Here. Let me give you the number of our office." She wrote it on the back of one of the *Pleasant Dreams* business cards. "When you make a decision, let us know, and we'll arrange for the transportation."

After Sandra Plummer had left, Diane picked up her phone. "Charlie, I've got a cold one for you."

***

Stephen knocked on Paul Jovus' door. "Paul, on the way home last night, I got an idea that might boost our sales."

"Great. Let's hear it."

"Instead of promoting mostly coffins, emphasize crematories."

"Well, you know the problem there. All our customers already have crematories, and they last a long time."

"Of course, but how many have the Flame Pipe Organ III? They're a hard sell because of the price. However, I was thinking of some music upgrades. The vets from the Second Iranian war are starting to die off. That's a whole market segment just waiting to be stacked away. We could reprogram the flame pipes to play the national anthem, or *America The Beautiful.*"

"Huh! Interesting idea."

"The only problem I see is the flame pipes currently have a limited range – only 9 full notes. That's fine for *Frere Jacques,* but the national anthem needs an octave and a half. Any reason the techies can't change that?"

"I'm sure they can. Adding a few extra pipes should be cheap enough."

"And the other thought that occurred to me is we could put them on a subscription service. Say the deceased person had a favorite song. For a small monthly fee, we could offer a flame pipe programming service that would suit every family."

Paul slapped the desk. "Yes! Just like FM music stations that take requests." He sat back and nodded. After a few seconds of thought, he said, "Actually, that could bring in a good hunk of change. The funeral home would just pass it on to the customer. Great idea, Stephen." He extended a fist into the air and exclaimed, "Yes, excellent!"

Leaving Paul's office, Stephen pondered whether he acted the same way after sex.

Stephen's suggestions were, of course, his way of impressing Paul – or, as a few of his colleagues expressed it, "kissing ass." Paul probably knew it too, but the ideas were useful. Each one had added small, but significant amounts to each month's profit.

Stephen's only competition was Cynthia Porter, and she was right on his heels. The previous month, she had hit a home run.

"Paul, I was watching TV last night when I realized we have a whole sector of opportunity just waiting for us."

"Oh?" he said.

"Yes. The show *Underground Around The World* had an episode about Embalmers Without Borders."

"You're talking about the international charity that operates in third-world countries?"

She nodded. "Exactly. They offer free embalming services to hundreds of towns and villages too impoverished to pay for them. They showed one of the burials taking place, and I realized they were just putting the body in the ground – no coffin, and certainly no vault."

Paul put his fingertips together as he rocked his chair forward and back. "So, how do we get their organization to put out money for coffins?"

"You pay their embalmers to spread rumors in the village that without coffins, the deceased's soul will escape the soil to haunt them."

Paul pursed his lips for several seconds. "Do you think the embalmers will go along with it?"

"If they get a commission on each purchase, absolutely."

"Cynthia, that's an incredible idea. Yes! By all means." He pumped a fist into the air. "Let's do it!"

As she left his office, she thought, *'Guess he hasn't been laid in a while.'*

***

Two days later, Diane called Charlie. "We ID'd the other three victims of the Highway 37 accident."

"Well, that's good."

"Could be. Do you recognize these names – Ahmed Atiyeh, Mahmud Haddad, and Omar Safar?"

"No. Should I? Sounds like Muslims."

"It turns out they're the owners of Jannah Hills."

"No shit? Wow. And they were doing so well."

"How so?"

"Heck, every time I drive by, they're digging somewhere in the cemetery. Always moving caskets and vaults around. Never realized they had so many Muslims in the county."

"It looks like they're going to have three more to bury. Sorry I couldn't send them your way."

"So, who's taking over for them?"

"No one knows. I talked to the wives, and they know nothing about the business. And there were no other managers."

"It's like we tell our potential customers. 'Buy ahead of time. You never expect the unexpected.'"

Which, of course, was true – certainly for Mohammed Kanaan and Adam Khouri, whose oxygen ran out three months later, as it did even sooner for Youssef Said, Hamza Rahal, Yasin Sabbag, and Ali Nazar – all sought by the FBI, well-hidden beneath the ground of Jannah Hills. Forever.

What We Did

Randall Dyer sat down in front of the desk. "Thanks for seeing me so soon, Ms. Yates."

"Not a problem, Mr. Dyer. And call me Kelly. You mentioned something about a problem with the police?"

"Yes. They seized my car, claiming I'm a drug runner. I'm not."

"I'm sorry about your car, but what is it you think I can do for you?"

"What can you...well, let me think. You're a lawyer. How about getting it back?"

Yates didn't mind the sarcasm. In truth, nature had inclined her similarly, a tendency she often repressed when dealing with clients who mentally drove in the slow lane, if not on the shoulder. But Randall seemed sharper than most. Still, she paused before answering, as if at a fork in the road. Finally, she decided. "Okay. Why don't you give me the details?"

"I was driving along Route 72 when I get pulled over for a cracked taillight. I mean, it wasn't actually broken, just a cracked lens – no piece missing, and I had checked it: The light itself worked fine."

Yates nodded.

"So, then he insists on opening the trunk."

"Did you give him permission?"

"Well, he said he'd find it suspicious if I didn't, and would have his department get a judge to issue a search warrant. And I'd have to wait there the whole time – probably a couple of hours. So, I agreed."

"That was your first mistake," Yates commented.

"Well, actually my second. I knew the taillight lens was cracked. I just figured it was unimportant."

"It was, but please, tell me the rest."

Randall was confused by her response, but continued. "So, the officer sees my pharma case and insists..."

"Your *what* case?"

"My pharmaceutical case. I'm a field rep for Geo Pharmaceuticals, and I always carry a lot of supplies to show doctors, clinics and hospitals. And we also dole out free samples. Anyway, he declares me to be, in his formal police-ese, 'carrying amounts of prescription drugs indicative of a dealer involved in the illegal trafficking of same'. I explained my employment and showed him my business card, but he didn't care. I got arrested and jailed till morning. Then they let me go with nothing but the clothes on my back and the stuff in my pockets. They kept the drugs and my car."

"Do you have the court paperwork?"

Randall pulled a batch papers from a small briefcase.

Yates looked them over, nodding as she flipped each page. "Well, you might have a better-than-average case here."

"Well, I would hope so. I mean, this has got to be illegal from start to finish."

Yates casually tossed the papers on her desk "Unfortunately, it's not. It's called civil forfeiture, and it's mostly legal."

Randall's mouth hung open for a few seconds. "You mean, they can seize a person's possessions without cause? For gosh sakes, what about the First Amendment?"

"Actually, it's the Fourth Amendment, and that right was curtailed by laws passed to fight the so-called War on Drugs. What happened to you is perfectly legal."

"Sounds more like a war on citizens. Can't we take this to the courts?"

"It's been argued all the way to the Supreme Court, and it was declared constitutional."

Randall tried to say something, but could think of nothing useful.

Yates leaned forward. "I know, I know. I get these cases all the time. This county is especially abusive, in particular to lone drivers. They use the assets to fund a good chunk of the police department's budget. That way, they can keep taxes low and the PD still has their toys. You should see their coffeemaker – at least $1,000, I'd guess. That's the reason I said giving permission to search was your first mistake, not your second. Even if you had fixed the taillight, they could have found another excuse to pull you over."

Randall straightened his back. "You're saying there's no way I can get my own car back?"

"Oh, sure there is, Mr. Yates. All you have to do is file a case. That would run you a minimum of $20,000 and would probably end up closer to $50,000. How much were the drugs worth?"

Randall shook his head. "That's the thing. Geo put in a call to the police and they returned the drugs to them. But not my car."

"Figures," Yates said. "Geo probably has an entire department of lawyers. The police know the company could easily afford to take it to court, whereas you can't. How much do you estimate is the value of the car?"

"I checked online. The blue book is $18,000."

"Well, it looks like you've learned an expensive lesson, Mr. Dyer – avoid Rankland, Missouri. And, I'm sorry to say, tell your friends, relatives and acquaintances."

Randall sat for a half minute, thinking deeply to himself. Finally, he spoke slowly. "I don't think they know who the hell they're dealing with."

It was as if a different person had appeared. Yates looked at him intently, trying to comprehend the change.

Randall broke the silence. "You say others have experienced this...forfeiture?"

"I've had three others in just the past couple of months."

"I'd like to contact them." He saw Yates' suspicious reaction. "There's strength in numbers."

"From a legal standpoint, I'd have to say that I doubt it. Besides, I can't give out their private information." She could see she had not dissuaded him. "I'll tell you what, Mr. Dyer: You give me your contact information, and I'll communicate your request to each of them. It'll be up to them to get in touch with you, if they wish."

"Much appreciated, and call me Randall. I have a feeling we're going to become rather well acquainted before this is over."

"You're actually going to fight this thing?"

He smiled. "Oh yeah."

What the Shadows Say

***

Randall arrived early, took a booth in the corner, and ordered coffee. About fifteen minutes later, a stout, muscular man arrived, looked around, and approached Randall with a rolling stride. "Excuse me, are you Randall Dyer?"

"I am. And you are...?"

"Dave Harmon. I'm the one who lost some tools and my truck." The rough skin of his handshake confirmed Randall's guess that Dave was a manual laborer.

"Dave, I hope you don't mind me asking, but I'm curious: What kind of tools were they?"

"Professional quality. Very expensive – probably $2,500 worth. I only buy top quality tools."

"What did they stop you for?"

"My front bumper was damaged. They said it made the car unsafe, but heck, it was just a large dent. It's not like the bumper was barely hanging on. And you?"

"Cracked taillight. Yates said it could have been anything."

"Luckily, my job pays pretty good, so I was able to buy some new wheels, but I'm out my truck, and I missed a couple of days work."

"What is it you do?"

"Maintenance work at a plastics factory. They make the granules that end up as plastic bottles, other plastic stuff. I maintain the machines, fix them when they go down."

"What's the name of the company?"

"Right now, it's Bracco Plastics. Two months ago, they bought it from Madon International, who bought it a year earlier. And who knows next year?"

"Wow. Doesn't sound like very reliable employment."

"Oh, it's reliable. The world needs plastic, and I'll always have work – I just don't know for who. And I've decided it doesn't matter. Lots of motivational posters in the locker room; just not much motivation when the company you're supposed to be oh-so-proud-of can change next week. So, I just keep on keepin' on. What's your line of work?""

"I'm a field rep for Geo Pharmaceuticals."

"Sounds nice. Guess you get to travel a lot."

"Dave, the grass always looks greener in the next guy's weed lot. It isn't. I don't *get* to travel. I *have* to travel. Trust me. It gets old. Plus, I'm blamed if the clinics and hospitals aren't enraptured by the latest Geo drug. If my visits aren't followed by significant orders, it's all my fault."

"Well, yeah. That's got to be tough. At least if I fix a machine, I can be pretty sure it's going to run right."

Someone else approached their table. He was around forty-five, with a trim build and only the slightest suggestion of a paunch. His hair was swarthy black, though Randall thought it looked tinted. "Would you be Mr. Dyer?" he said in well-articulated syllables.

"I would. And you are...?"

"Keller. Sean Keller. I'm the one who lost the three grand plus my $40,000 Volvo."

Dave's eyebrows rose. "Forty-thousand? Wow. Mine was only worth about seventeen. What was the three grand for?"

"I snagged a good deal on some lighting equipment. I'm a stage producer. I was headed to Kansas City for a new play."

"I can see why they'd want the Volvo, but why the lighting equipment?"

"They used the lights as the pretext. They claimed they were marijuana grow lights, which makes them drug paraphernalia. Yates explained it all to me."

Dave shook his head. "Hell, they got more tricks than a country whorehouse."

"Gentlemen, the law was not made for us," Randall declared. "It was made for them."

"Well, Sean, it sounds like *you* at least have an exciting career," Dave observed. "Randall and I were just singin' the blues about ours."

"Exciting? I suppose you could call it that. But I'll tell you, it's a damned hard way to make a living. People go to movies, not live theater."

"Then, how do you make money?" Randall asked.

"Sometimes we don't. You have to be careful what plays you put on. *My Fair Lady* always brings them in. An Ibsen play is a break-even, if you're lucky."

Dave raised his eyebrows. "So, you do it for the love of art, I guess."

"You have to. Productions are at the mercy of temperamental actors, overly creative directors, and incompetent promoters. Other than that, it's a breeze."

About this time, a Black man of medium build approached. His cowboy hat matched his boots, not to mention his drawl. "Mr. Dyer?" He scanned the group.

Randall stuck out his hand. "You must be Mr. Norman."

"Just *Tim* will do, thanks."

Randall introduced everyone, then said, "So, as I understand it, you're the only one who sued."

Tim nodded. "Yup. Matter of principle, mainly. Ms. Yates told me the suit could cost way more than the $2,000 I lost. What she never mentioned was the possibility of the case not even getting' past the startin' gate."

"So, what happened?" Dave asked.

"The biggest loss was my car, but Ms. Yates told me that was a lost cause. But I was also carrying some pricey tattoo parlor equipment. My brother's opening his own business, and it was his money I used to buy it from a supplier in my state. But the court said I lacked 'standing'. I guess I should be grateful. Her bill came to a lot less than it might've."

Sean spoke up. "So, by 'standing', they were saying you didn't have the right to sue?"

"That's exactly right. It was my brother's money, so only he could sue, but he's not as bullheaded as me. So, that's that."

"Perhaps not," Randall commented.

All heads turned toward him, but Sean spoke first. "So, Randall, what is the purpose of this meeting? A class action suit?"

"If that were possible, I might consider it," Randall replied. "However, I've researched this, and Yates is spot on. It's already gone to the Supreme Court, and what the police are doing is legal."

"Legal?" Dave exclaimed. "How can it be legal to just grab our cars and money without having to prove anything in court?"

"Yeah. What happened to 'innocent until proven guilty'?" Sean added.

Randall paused to make certain he had everyone's attention. Finally, he spoke slowly. "None of us is going to get our cars back. That's that."

"Then what are we all doin' here?" Tim asked.

"Well, like you said, it's a matter of principle. For me, the relevant principle might be a bit different." He looked directly at each before continuing. "My principle is to punish when punishment is called for. And considering how much they've robbed us, I'd say punishment is definitely called for."

Sean put his drink on the table and leaned back. "Could you be more specific? Because, it sounds like you're talking about breaking the law."

Randall smiled. "Well, it appears we already have, Sean. My math comes in at around a hundred grand we've lost collectively. Apparently, we must have already broken the law big time, though I can't remember doing anything wrong. Can you?" He paused and looked each one of them in the eye. "The question is, are each of you going to accept being victimized?"

"Specifically," Sean insisted.

"Okay, here's my idea…"

***

The next day, the four of them rolled into Rankland, drove around the police station, but could see no car lot nearby. Randall parked at a market and Tim went in to make some inquiries.

He came out a few minutes later. "The gentleman inside said the impound lot's about a mile thataway."

They drove to the lot, which was at an intersection a block off the main drag. "This is good," Dave remarked. "No police station around and no residences."

"The sign says dogs. That might be a problem." Randall said.

"And a camera on the corner of the building," Tim observed. "We'll have to take a closer look later. Probably a camera on the other corner of the building too."

"We'll need to take some photos. This is a lot like scouting locations for a movie," Sean remarked.

"Our cell phones," Randall suggested.

"They're turned off. Remember?" Sean reminded him. "To avoid tracking?"

"Not enough pixels, anyway" Tim said. "We need to see details. I've got a camera at home with a telephoto lens."

"What is it you do, Tim? A photographer?" Dave asked

"No, I'm an inventory tracker for a grain storage company. Sometimes I need to physically inspect the silos. It's easier to take pictures from 30 feet away than climb all over ladders and conveyors to get up close."

"So, at least you're not stuck in an office all day."

"You ever been in a silo, Dave?"

"Can't say I have."

"Well, it's 120 degrees, which would make anyone sweat like a pig. And most of the year it's filled with grain dust, which means you have to wear a respirator, which makes you sweat like two pigs. I probably lose five pounds everytime I have to do an inspection. And forget about keeping your clothes clean and dry."

Dave shook his head. "Wow. Seems like nowadays every job sucks."

"Okay. So, it sounds like we have a plan," Randall said. "We meet tomorrow in the library parking lot. Tim, you'll have your camera. Anyone got a friend? Someone the police have never seen?"

"For what?" asked Dave.

"We'll need someone to physically walk around the impound lot, right next to the fence. They might spot something not visible from the street, especially at driving speed. And it has to be someone the Rankland police won't recognize."

Sean spoke up. "I have the perfect person."

"Keep in mind it also needs to be someone we can trust to keep quiet."

"Oh, she will," Sean said.

The next day, everyone arrived in Randall's van, except Sean, who showed up with his friend. "Gentlemen, this is Jessica Byrne."

"A midget?" Tim said, in disbelief.

"Actually, Mr. Cowboy, we prefer 'little person'. Strongly prefer. 'Midget' is rather offensive to us little people."

"Shucks, miss, no offense intended. Just not what I expected. And the name's Tim." He stuck out his hand.

She shook it with a lively grip. "Call me Jessie." Her voice sounded sharp, despite the Oklahoma drawl.

Sean introduced Randall and Dave.

"O…kay," Randall said slowly. "Sean, how much have you told your friend?"

Byrne answered for him. "Enough for me to know you don't like cops, which fits my hat just fine. I'm not terribly fond of them myself, though I'd rather not go into historical details. And Sean mentioned some time ago how he got screwed over. According to him, all your situations were similar. Have I got that about right?"

"You haven't missed a beat yet," Randall replied.

"Good. Now just let me get in the back and get myself ready." She crawled to the back of the van and removed her pants and shirt, revealing a whole second set of clothes underneath. She put on a baseball cap before returning. "How's this work for you?" she asked Randall.

Everyone laughed. "Well, I'll be knocked over with a feather," Dave remarked. "You look just like a kid – I'd say, eight or nine years old."

"Jessie's one of our regulars in the theater," Sean explained. "She's extremely versatile."

"Great choice," Randall said. "Nobody suspects a kid."

Byrne nodded. "Well, then, what are you waitin' for, Randy boy? The sun'll be settin' in eight hours."

They dropped her off a half block away from the impound lot, then drove to it and parked on the other side of the street. Tim sat on the side opposite the open window, and took several photos. "Okay, Randall, pull out and take it slow to the stop sign. Wait there 10 seconds, and when you take off, go slow some more. I'll be snappin' the whole time."

Randall drove to the next corner, turned right, and found a parking space a half-block up the street. Byrne reached them 10 minutes later and got in the rear seat.

"I don't know the details of what you're planning, but there's one nasty mongrel in that lot. Practically ate the chain-link fence trying to get a piece of me."

"That's something we didn't consider," Tim remarked.

"We'll think of something," Randall said. "How about we just throw him a piece of raw meat."

Byrne spoke up. "I suspect that would end up being you. This beast didn't have that kind of disposition."

"What kind is that?" Dave asked.

"The kind that, when faced with a choice of one pound of beef or 180 pounds of tasty *homo sapiens*, would choose the smaller morsel. I'm just sayin'."

Sean rubbed his chin. "You know, one of our actresses plays with her dog using something called a flirt pole. Have any of you ever heard of them?"

Dave turned on his tablet. After a couple of minutes, he said. "Hmm. Well we could probably make one, but they're less than $30. How about we stop at a pet store on the way out?"

"Here's a better idea," Randall said. "How about we stop in another town where we won't be recognized later?"

Tim nodded. "Sounds like a plan within a plan."

***

At precisely 8:00 pm, everyone put on their earmuffs, and Dave slid the side door open six inches. Tim steadied the rifle on the back of the adjoining seat. He put the scope's crosshairs on the camera mount and squeezed off a shot. The camera dropped and dangled from its electrical cable. He repeated the shot for the camera at the far end of the building. Next came the floodlights. The impound lot went black. Dave closed the door and Randall drove around the block, dropping Sean and Tim off a half-block from the impound lot. Tim carried the briefcase. Randall drove to the lot, parking on the sidewalk a mere inch from the fence. Dave opened the sliding door and extended the bolt cutters to begin snipping the wires of the chain-link fence in two vertical lines about a yard apart. The dog was at the fence in a few seconds, barking and snarling. Randall worried about the noise attracting attention, though the van was too close to the fence for anyone to see what was happening. Dave left the bottom cuts for last. As soon as he cut the first, the dog began pushing against the loosened portion, but the van's running board kept it in place. After the second cut, Dave withdrew the cutters and slid the door closed.

Randall slowly pulled away while Dave switched positions. He opened the rear door about 10 inches, limited by a wire secured to the cargo area. He extended the flirt pole four feet out. As the dog began to chase it, Dave called out to Randall: "A little faster…okay, too much, slow it down a bit…that's good, hold it there…"

Meanwhile, Sean and Tim walked to the cut section of the fence, and raised it for each other to duck through one at a time. They pulled it back down so it would appear normal, and walked swiftly toward their pre-arranged locations among the cars. Neither man spoke a word. Tim opened the briefcase and handed Sean one of the portable drills. They each proceeded to drop beside the rear tires of the cars and drill holes through the tanks. It proved easier than Sean had expected. He had not realized most were made of plastic. As they moved from car to car, the fumes became more and more noxious. By the time they had finished, Sean was coughing. He ran to the fence and waited for Tim, who carefully pulled from his coat pocket one of the fuses he had extracted from some fireworks. He lay it on the ground, half of it in one of the pools of gasoline that had collected on the uneven lot. He signaled to Sean, who looked around, then turned back and nodded. Tim lit the fuse, and rushed to the fence, which by this time Sean had raised. They both walked back the way they came as Sean made a call on the phone he had borrowed from Byrne.

When the call came, Randall sped up, leaving the dog far behind. Dave withdrew the flirt pole and closed the rear door. By the time they picked up their teammates nearly a block from what had been the impound lot, they could see the conflagration's glow against the nighttime sky.

"Hey! That's a hell of a job you guys did," Dave said.

"Let's celebrate a job well done." Tim suggested. "How about we go to the next town and toss down a few brews."

"Not tonight," Randall said. "We haven't even seen each other tonight."

"Okay. How about Thursday instead? And two towns away?"

***

249

The Sassafras Garden was crowded and loud. "I've passed by this place before, but never stopped in," Byrne said.

"You'll love the food. Drinks are a bit pricey, but this is a special occasion," Tim said.

Dave agreed. "Yep. I think we showed the cops that crime don't pay."

Randall nodded. "What we did was spectacular. Everything went off without a hitch. But I'll bet dollars to donut holes they'll be back on the road tomorrow, stopping cars, intimidating drivers, threatening detainment for search warrants, and so on and so on."

"On the other hand, "Dave said, "it does feel good not being just a victim. Even if we didn't change the world, at least we proved we aren't helpless."

Byrne spoke up. "That's true. You're not ducks in a shooting gallery. Not even bothersome flies. More like wasps. You've got a sting. I didn't get fleeced by the Rankland PD, but as a little person, I feel like I've grown a foot just being a part of this. Admittedly a small part."

They all chuckled. "I'll drink to that," Tim said.

Randall spoke up. "I've been thinking. Thinking hard. Most police departments try to do the right thing. But this forfeiture law is a temptation. With tight budgets at all levels of government, police departments all over the country have got to feel temptation to cross the line."

"Using forfeiture as a standard funding source," Sean observed. "Good point. I know the feeling. Theater producers are always scrambling for cash."

"As a part-time actor," Byrne said, "I can attest to that. By the way, Sean, how about a raise?"

Sean smiled. "My God, Jessie! You haven't even finished your first drink, and already you're drunk."

Randall's phone rang. "Hi, Kelly. How are you? Uh huh. Sure, they're here with me. Hang on a second." He looked at his dinner mates. "You guys free tomorrow around 11:00?" They all nodded. "Sure Kelly, we can all be there."

After Randall hung up, Tim asked, "What does she want with us?"

"Don't know, but I'm not too concerned. At least it wasn't the Rockland PD."

"More important," Tim remarked, "how did she know we were all together?"

Randall stopped smiling. Suddenly he *was* concerned. And so were his companions.

*****

The next morning, Yates said, "It appears you boys have been rather busy."

"Why, whatever do you mean?" Sean replied with excessive innocence.

Yates apparently got the irony, but wasn't smiling. Randall wondered why. Was legal action hanging over their heads? '*No,*' he thought, '*if the PD knew who we were, they wouldn't call Yates. They'd just arrest us.*' Then he identified her expression: Sadness. "So, what did you want to see us about?"

"Late yesterday afternoon the state court announced a ruling that Rankland's seizures violated state standards and were also constitutionally indefensible."

She paused for several seconds. The four men were silent, waiting for her to continue. "What that means is that all your cars would be returned to you, along with any equipment you lost. However, the cars all burned up in a very mysterious fire."

"So, you're saying, if the cars hadn't burned, we could have gotten them back?"

Yates nodded. "Did any of you gents happen to keep up your insurance policies?"

The four looked at each other, but all of them shook their heads.

"I kind of figured that – the reason I waited several hours before calling you. I hate to be the bearer of sad tidings. For all the limitations and shortcomings of the law," she said, "sometimes it works better just to follow it."

***

As they slowly walked toward their cars, Sean said, "Well, at least we might get some of the equipment back. It's not a complete loss."

They were silent for several more steps. Then Tim spoke up. "You know, for all the loss, it felt good." Everyone stopped and stared at him. He wondered if they thought he was crazy.

Instead, Dave said, "You're damned right, Tim. Still does."

"Yeah," Randall said. "For a few hours there, we weren't helpless."

Sean nodded. "I guess I have to agree. It was almost like a vacation – a rather expensive one, but I'll remember what we did for the rest of my life."

Randall raised his chin. "And not regret it for a moment."

Everyone else nodded in agreement. Then they shook hands, got in their cars and went their separate ways.

And for the rest of their lives, they remembered their marvelous time together.

Robert's Rules of Disorder

<u>John</u>

I nodded toward Leonard. "The chair recognizes Leonard Gammond."

"Mr. Chairman, I move that we discuss Proposition 17."

Jerry Winger raised his hand. "Point of order, Mr. Chairman. KED does not take positions on public ballot issues."

"What are we here for, anyway?" Leonard said. "If I wanted to just sit around and discuss political theory, I could have gone down to the bar."

Jerry stood. "Mr. Chairman, I have raised a point of order. Under Robert's Rules of Order, we should address my objection first."

I inhaled and masked my reaction as well as I could. I'd had enough experience to understand the situation – yet another discussion at the edge of another slide down to another verbal slugfest. "You are right, Jerry, and my ruling on the point of order is that it is invalid. There is a difference between internal debate and the organization taking a position. The Kinship of Enlightened Democracy was founded on the principle of open discussion. That means KED members can debate and discuss any issue, regardless of its political status. Is there a second to the motion to discuss Proposition 17?"

Bob raised his hand. "I second."

"Bob seconds the motion," I said.

Jerry stared darts at him. He should have known Bob would support me. He always does. Our camaraderie goes back to the second Iraq war, where we had each other's backs more times than I can remember. It's also where we bore witness to the kind of life the Iraqis had endured under Saddam. That experience increased our appreciation of freedom and democracy. I returned feeling that public discussions were vital to maintain our values – American values – really, Western values, the fruit of the Enlightenment. Unlike most Americans, I no longer take those ideals for granted. In Iraq, I had been Bob's second louie, but that was only a temporary rank, one I lost when I declined officer school. I had decided I could benefit my country more as a civilian – not through my executive career, but by fostering community engagement. And that's what led me to form KED. The church community room was very suitable for our purposes, with plenty of space for membership growth. Only the pictures on the wall – some circus posters – detracted from the stately character of our meetings.

At the beginning, I had wanted Bob to join the board, but he declined. "Look, John, I'm a supporter, not a leader." I knew he was right, but if he had wanted the position, I'd have arranged it for the initial leadership team. After that, he'd have to earn reelection, like everyone else. I dislike the practice of favoritism, despite our personal history.

The debate over state Proposition 17 was civil, long, and in depth. I was pleased as the members expressed their views. After five months, the KED meetings were developing the kind of culture I had envisioned.

At our sixth meeting, Heather Jensen stood. "Point of order, Mr. Chairman. Pete, I have to say that your remark about transgender persons was offensive. Under our bylaws, we are supposed to be an inclusive organization, and that means we cannot tolerate bigotry."

Pete Weinberg turned red. "Heather, board members are allowed to express their opinions. If you don't agree, so what? I want an apology."

Heather raised her head. "Apology? For what?"

"For calling me a bigot. Members are not allowed is to call each other names."

"I did not call you a bigot. I said that your *opinion* was bigotry."

Marsha Bickel, also a board member, said, "I fail to see the difference."

Sally Batteau stood. "A bigot is one who regularly practices bigotry. Heather only cited a statement, not a general outlook. I think Heather would agree that Pete doesn't have such a general outlook." Sally was always the organization's package deal – a one-person almanac, dictionary and thesaurus. She sat down, her back perfectly erect.

"It's still name-calling," Pete said, "which, as I remember is expressly forbidden by KED's charter. Am I correct, John?"

I smiled. "Well, you just called me *John*." A few of the audience chuckled, but I quickly realized my mistake. It's impolitic to ridicule anybody. "Seriously, Pete, she didn't call you a name. She characterized only the opinion. Heather and you obviously have a different reaction to transgender people. Can we let it go at that?"

"Just as soon as she apologizes."

I inhaled. "Look, Pete, maybe she did push the limit a bit, and maybe you did too, but..."

"I did not," declared Pete.

"*I* most certainly did not," said Heather.

I liked Heather, especially because she had traveled so far from her tempestuous youth. She was once a member of the Fawkes 50, the group of anti-corporate radicals. Their protests had often degenerated into riots, and their array of other outrageous actions had disrupted operations of several large corporations. I asked her once if it was her year in jail that had reformed her.

"Reformed me? Naw. I still have the same ideals and still hate corporations. I just saw that our actions were turning the people against us, getting them to sympathize with their own exploiters. I learned it was just a matter of patience and better tactics."

After serving her time, she returned to college, became a nurse, and now directs her energy in constructive ways. In her disagreement with Pete, I could see her comments were not unjustified, but still, I checked my urge to tell Pete to shut the hell up – as well as the urge to strangle him. KED was meant to bring together people with disparate views for reasoned discussion, but his opinions were always strident. My mind raced to arrive at a diplomatic solution. Pete burned that bridge before the first beam could be laid.

"If she will not apologize, I move that we expel Heather Jensen from the Kinship of Enlightened Democracy."

"And I second the motion," said Marsha. Her statement was followed by murmurs from the audience.

Gary Vacks said, "Okay, but remember a 60 percent vote is required."

I looked at him in disbelief. Bob, Gary, and I had always stood together, favoring more open-minded tolerance of differences. Talking to him later, I learned that Gary had been more observant than I. From his board seat, he had observed the audience and noticed that most heads were moving sideways. He was right. Of the 20 people present, only seven voted for the motion.

Pete reddened and pursed his lips, but said nothing. As far as I knew, the kerfuffle was over.

At the next meeting, our numbers swelled. Ten new members arrived. New members were always a pleasant surprise, but ten? I was delighted. Only Gary was suspicious, but he said nothing.

I talked to him a few months later. "Of course, I wasn't suspicious," I said. "I had nothing I could point to. Heck, I was pleased that word of our group had spread."

Before the next election, eight more members had joined. At that election, one of them, Brenda Pinkton, was elected to the board, replacing Gary. And still, we didn't get it.

At the very next meeting, Pete spoke up and said, "Mr. Chairman, I move that we expel Heather Jensen from the Kinship of Enlightened Democracy."

I was stunned. "On what grounds?"

"For violating section D17 of our bylaws."

"Name calling? Pete, we've been over this before. It's already been rejected."

"Under the bylaws, a previously rejected motion can be reintroduced provided it has a majority approval by the board."

Now it became clear. With 18 new members, all recruited by Pete and Marsha, they had captured control of the board and 60 percent of the floor. Heather lost the vote, and silently left. Bob nicknamed the new group of 18, *Pete's Shills*, or *PSers*, for short. He was always clever at quips. The PSers quickly introduced other rules, including a ban on new members. That meant I would never be able wrest back control of KED. They modified other bylaws as well, but the real stab in the heart came when Pete made an end-of-the meeting announcement.

"I think it's time for our organization to play a greater role in the politics of our time. It is my intention for KED to do more than provide a setting for polite conversations on political ideas. We are in a position to actually affect the politics of our era." The room was silent as he paused for dramatic effect. "I move that KED become an advocacy group, pushing our government to adopt policies and take actions we think will benefit our nation."

Someone seconded the motion.

As the only non-Pser on the board, I felt it was my duty to pose the most obvious objection. "Pete, where are we going to find the kind of money lobbying requires?"

"Who said anything about lobbying?"

Brenda, newly elected to the board, suddenly became the voice of experience. "It's called networking."

"The thing you don't understand," Pete said, "is that money does talk, but social media talks louder, especially if 10 or 15 organizations can link together to post jointly. Also, all of them can organize demonstrations to attract attention from traditional media. Together, this army of organizations can actually get things done, not just talk."

"Pete, what kind of advocacy are we talking about here?" I said. "What kind of legislation are we seeking?"

He shrugged. "Well, I guess that would depend on the members' preferences." His pretense at humility wouldn't have convinced a baby. "Does anyone have any suggestions?" he asked the members.

"How about spreading democracy?" Jerry said. Several audience members grunted in agreement. I noted they were all PSers.

"And how do you intend to do that?" Bob asked.

"Any way we can," Pete answered.

I finally said, "Meaning?"

"It's called intervention," Brenda said.

"Dictators need to be overthrown," Marsha said, "either by their own people or by us."

Tom, one of our charter members, spoke up. "You *do* know that's been tried before, and it didn't turn out well."

Pete nodded. "We learned a lot from our mistakes. We'll be better at it in the future."

I looked at Bob. I was surprised he didn't roll his eyes, or shake his head, or even look sideways. He just sat there, stone faced.

But I was flabbergasted. My own organization had been stolen from me. Its entire purpose, my entire ideal, had slipped away from me. They would keep me on the board, but I knew I had become a mere figurehead, easily outvoted by the PSers.

Gary, Bob, and I lunched together the next day.

"What are you going to do?" Bob asked.

I slowly shook my head. "I don't know. I can't think of any way out of this."

"Everything's gone," Gary said. "The kinship, the enlightenment values, the democracy."

I tried being philosophical. "Just when things were easing up at home. Melissa got accepted at Ohio State and Kevin is finally settling down, becoming an adult. I thought that life was becoming what it's supposed to be. You do everything right and the road is supposed to run straight, but now we have this washout."

"More like a sink hole," Gary remarked.

"Maybe we can start another group," I said.

Bob shook his head. "What's to stop the same thing from happening again? I mean, come on. No matter how many rules you set, no matter how thick you make the bylaws, there's always a guy like Pete who'll figure out a way to play heil Hitler."

Gary slapped the table as he rose. "Well, I know what I'm going to do. I'm dropping my membership."

After Gary had departed, I said, "I'm not ready to follow him, Bob, and I hope you won't either. Their ridiculous plan to move the politicians with social media and demonstrations is bound to fail. Eventually, they'll realize their strategy is futile, and we'll get back to sanity." I quickly reflected on what I had said. "I don't know. Maybe I'm just fantasizing. Maybe I'm too attached to the group, or perhaps too idealistic, but I just can't surrender to dictatorship."

Bob nodded. "Whatever, John. If you're staying, then I am too."

At the end of the next monthly meeting, just as we were getting into our cars, a commotion was taking place around Pete. I got out and wandered over.

"Somebody slashed my rear tires."

"You need help changing it?" someone asked.

"They slashed both of them."

I went around to the other side. It was flat too. He wanted to call the tow truck right away, but Cal suggested he do it the next day, when it was light. Finally, Pete accepted the suggestion, along with a ride home.

What bothered me most was that several members kept side-glancing Bob and me. No one said anything. Discussion had become irrelevant.

***

The following month, during the usual chitchat before the start of the meeting, Pete was in the middle of a considerable crowd. I sauntered over to Bob, who was also observing them. "Looks like he's Mr. Popular, tonight," I said.

"Not really. Notice who they are?"

I observed more closely. "Aren't they the PSers?"

Bob nodded. "What do you think they're planning now?"

"Don't know, but I'm going to find out." I walked over to them. "Bill, what's going on?"

Bill turned, facing me directly. He was silent.

"What? What?"

"Do you know anything about the vandalism?"

"What vandalism?"

"Like the tires on Pete's car?"

"Oh, yeah. Last month."

"I remember Bob coming back from break after everyone else."

"So what?"

"Look, John. I know you and him are tight, but I need to ask you a direct question, and I'd like you to be straight with me."

I was perplexed. "Of course. Why wouldn't I be?"

"Did he slash Pete's tires?"

I was shocked. "Of course not. So, he had a phone call that ran past the break. Why would that make him suspect? For heaven's sake, Bill, his hobby is reading history."

He just looked at me.

"What's this all about, anyway?" I asked.

"It seems that over the last couple of weeks," he nodded toward the crowd around them, "these people here have been the victims of more vandalism."

"Vandalism? Who?"

"All of them. All 19. And not just slashed tires. I'm talking broken windows on cars and houses, a house partially burned, a car set on fire."

I was shocked. "Bill, do these things sound like something I'd be a part of? You know I reject violence. If I knew anything about this, you could be certain I'd tell you. Hell, I'd just call the police. It's entirely unacceptable."

"No shit, John. How about your buddy?" He lifted his chin toward Bob.

"Bob? Impossible. Even if he wanted to, how could he vandalize 19 people?"

"Maybe he had help." To my look of confusion, he suggested, "Gary?"

I shook my head in disgust. "For crissake, Bill." Somehow, we were suspects. Later, I learned the authorities had questioned Bob.

I turned and I walked over to Bob. "Do you know anything about the vandalism?"

"The tires on Pete's car? Sure, but that was a month ago."

"They remember you coming back from break after everyone else."

"Yeah. I was on the phone. So what?"

"Look, Bob. We're friends, but I need to know. Did you slash Pete's tires?" I hated asking the question, but I needed to be absolutely certain. I might have to go to the mat for him.

"Of course not. Like I said, the phone call ran past the break. Why would I slash his tires?"

That was an odd question. We both knew he was upset at the PSer takeover.

Then he said, "Heck, you'd have more reason than me to vandalize his car. He took the chairmanship from you – hell, your whole organization."

That was stranger still. Technically, he was correct, but he knew it would be completely against my nature. On the other hand, I knew him well enough to recognize his sincerity.

"What's this all about, anyway?" he asked.

"It seems that over the last week, the PSers have been the victims of vandalism."

"Really? Who?"

"All of them."

"ALL?" He was genuinely surprised. "What kind of vandalism?"

"Broken car windows, house windows, one house partially burned, a few…"

"Burned? JESUS!" His voice had risen. Heads turned our way.

Yes, his surprise was genuine. He could never have become an actor. In Iraq, I could always tell when he fudged the truth, even just a hair's width. "I'm relieved that you had nothing to do with it," I said.

"No. This is the first time I heard about it."

The discussions that night were subdued. I noticed Bob leave during the break, and a couple of the PSers amble outside for a smoke. I knew they were deliberately keeping an eye on him. Through the door, I could see Bob on the phone, but only for about a minute. After that he paced around a little, then returned inside. The PSers returned shortly after. When I first imagined KED, this wasn't at all what I had in mind. Mutual suspicion, distrust? Exactly the opposite of bringing people together. It was depressing.

At the next meeting, there was another commotion. It seems more vandalism had occurred, and to the same 19, including Pete. I also noted that the PSers had shrunk to 12. Obviously, there was no way to exclude the subject from discussion.

Ron stood, instead of merely raising his hand. "Mr. Chairman, we need to discuss the vandalism."

"Damned right," said Mark. "Where was Bob on the 12th, when my gazebo was burned to the ground?"

"Yeah," said Hank, "and the 17th when all four tires on my truck were slashed?"

Bob stood. "Well I'd have to look on my calendar about the 17th, but on the week of the 12th, I was in Ohio on company business. You can check with my company, or I could show you the ticket reservations."

"Then maybe Gary," Pete interjected.

"Can't say nothing about Gary," Bob said. "Haven't talked with him for a couple of months."

"Mr. Chairman, I move that we inform the police that Gary is a possible suspect."

Before Pete could answer, I said, "You should know, that I've talked to Gary. He called me a couple of weeks ago, and apparently, some of you Sherlocks, in your infinite cleverness, already contacted the police. They investigated, and he too had alibis for a number of the nights in question."

"What about Heather?" Pete said, "She's the one who got kicked out. And don't forget her past."

Some of the PSers mumbled and murmured their herd concurrence.

"For God's sake, Pete!" I was disgusted. "Mr. Chairman, you can pursue it with a police complaint, if you wish, but I suggest you not waste our meeting time with your obsessions. According to our bylaws, we are not supposed to use our time in pursuance of personal matters."

The rest of the meeting progressed normally with a discussion about the effect of Turkey's declining economy, and the possibility of overthrowing its president. The break was uneventful. Earlier that day, I had phoned Bob and asked him to spend break time inside.

But later, I considered, '*What about Heather?*' I'm a sufficiently good judge of character to know she had traveled far from her rebellious youth. But still, *someone* was targeting the PSers. Had the injustice angered someone else? Perhaps a few? Noland? Ricardo? I soon saw how easily suspicion could consume relationships. I shook off the paranoia, and concentrated on KED's purpose.

As the months passed, the vandalism continued and the number of PSers waned, until only Pete himself remained. That's when I called Gary.

"How would you like to take your place on the board again?"

"I wouldn't."

"There's an empty seat, and I need you to fill it."

"Have you forgotten? I quit KED, and they don't allow new members."

"No, you didn't."

"Huh?"

"You never quit, Gary. I kept you on the list and paid your dues."

"What? Why would you do that?"

"Call it hope, call it stubbornness. I just couldn't accept your quitting. All the PSers are gone except Pete, and now I need you present to get a 60 percent majority, and you on the board to allow a motion to change the rules and then expel Pete."

There was a pause. "Jesus, John. You had this all planned out?"

"More like all hoped out, actually. But opportunity has dropped from the tree, and I'm ready to catch it."

"Okay, buddy. I'll be there. We'll get you back your group."

And that's the whole story of how we preserved our little corner of civilization.

Bob

It all started when Pete made some jerkoff comment about transsexuals. Heather called the comment bigoted, which could have applied to his whole self, though she didn't actually say that. Anyway, he tries to get her expelled, but can't get the 60 percent vote required. Not even close. Over the next few meetings, we get a lot of new members. While that delighted John, founder of the group and my best buddy, it left both of us puzzled.

John and I had done an Army tour together in Iraq, and remained in contact after our return. In fact, he's the one who convinced me to move to Joliet, telling me about the good job market. That and my divorce, shortly after I found out my wife's 'overtime' was actually some guy's time spent over her in bed. Anyway, John was right. I landed a good position in the corporate purchasing division of Hank's Toy Stores Inc. So, when he decided to form this group we call KED – that's the Kinship of Enlightened Democracy – I became member number two. Truthfully, I didn't find the name inspiring, but it contained everything he considered important about its purpose. Gary joined soon after, and the three of us became a clique, though John insisted we vote our conscience, not our personal relationships. Whatever.

I helped him with the monthly fee for the St. Anselm Church community room. The space wasn't at all elaborate like the main hall, but it was in good condition, had padded chairs, and adequate space for growth. Some tasteful soul had hung prints along the walls to relieve the hospital-white color – mostly cirque-de-soleil posters. Perhaps the same person had been responsible for placing the large indoor potted plants in each corner. Either way, bless them. Altogether, it was pleasant, though frankly, I don't think John thought much about interior decoration. He was a political idealist with little regard for esthetics, more concerned with things like our membership ethnicity – mostly white, like us. He thought it might be hypocritical. I thought he worried too much.

What we should have worried about were the new members we gained in the meetings following the Pete-Heather nonsense. At the third meeting, we had elections, and Gary got replaced by Brenda. Then Pete called again for Heather's expulsion, and all 18 new members voted in favor. Only then did we get it. The 18 were Pete's shills – PSers, I named them. Then they proceeded to change our bylaws to close off entry to new members, as well as other measures that basically turned KED into a mini-dictatorship. But the kicker was when Pete announced that KED was changing directions, becoming an advocacy group to push for change. What kind of change? 'Promoting democracy,' he called it. What he meant was cramming it down other country's throats. My time in Iraq showed me the results of pushing our ways onto other countries. A lot of corpses.

They left John on the board, but we both knew he'd only have a speck of influence, not actual power.

I was raised in a pretty conventional household. I never heard my dad tell a dirty joke, and my mother required us to follow the rules. I was about 10 when I finally realized that she actually stepped out of bounds plenty of times – not very far, but still…. Maybe I inherited her fudge-the-line gene.

It took a couple of weeks for me to concoct a plan. The problem was the need for accomplices. My family and relatives were a few states away. I had some friends and co-workers, but I doubted their willingness to do what had to be done. Immersed in their comfortable lives, they wouldn't have the necessary motivation. Who would? Then it hit me. People with commitment.

***

The letters above the entrance weren't as big as I'd expected. Women Against Misogyny had always impressed me as kickass, assertive, but the WAM letters were only a foot tall and a dull green. The entry led to the left down a hall created by an interior wall. At the end sat a receptionist. The rest of the office was busier than I had expected, even for a Saturday. Except for the entry hall and a few offices at the back, the layout was entirely open. "Excuse, me. I'm looking for Shirley Geste?"

"Do you have an appointment?" asked the polite, but unsmiling woman. Her tag said *Leona*, her bobbed hair said 'strictly business', and the tattoo on her forearm said, "W.A.M."

"No. I just need to see her for about fifteen minutes."

"Why?" she demanded, squinting about a hundred pounds of suspicion.

"Oh, there she is." I recognized her from her picture in the papers. I started to move away from Leona, but before I had taken two steps, she reached under the desk – as I later surmised, to press a panic button. I achieved only two more steps before I found myself redirected against a wall by a tall Black woman who looked like she could arm-wrestle most guys to embarrassment. A second woman quickly patted me down and checked my ID. The Black woman turned me around.

"What are you doing here, cupcake?"

"I'm here to see Shirley Geste."

"Uh huh. And you think you can just dance your way in?"

Her belittling was annoying, almost as much as having to crane my neck to face her. At six-three, she was five inches taller than me. "Look, I didn't know I needed an appointment. I figured if someone had a problem with misogyny, they could bring it to WAM, and you guys...gals...women would want to do something about it."

By this time, Shirley had walked over. "What problem would *you* have with misogyny?"

"Can we discuss it?" I asked. "Like, in your office?"

She hesitated. "Sure. Why don't you join me Sam? You too, Vi."

Sam was the Black woman who had manhandled me...actually, woman-handled me. Vi was an Asian-

American gal – not the kind you just pictured in your head – not five-foot-six and 100 pounds. More like six-feet even, though her attitude added another few inches. And she was wiry strong.

In Shirley's office, the two bodyguards sat on either side of me. "Okay, Mr. Smith, what's your misogyny problem?" Her voice carried a tinge of sarcasm.

"Call me Bob. And the problem's in an organization I belong to, the Kinship of Enlightened Democracy – KED, for short. We had a woman – a charter member, mind you, kicked out only because she's a woman."

Okay, okay. So, I stretched the truth a bit. Or maybe a lot. Exaggerated, but for a good cause – righting a wrong. Not the wrong of misogyny, but still, a wrong. Besides, I kind of figured that these female warriors would find the actual details unimpressive.

"The procedure is for her to come in and make a complaint," Shirley said. "Once she's filled out the paperwork, we'll follow up on it."

"That would be your normal procedure. I doubt it would get results. All they have to do is claim something about her behavior and demonstrate they followed the rules. Of course, they went to unusual lengths to change the rules, just so they could expel Heather. So, I was thinking of...abnormal procedures."

Shirley said nothing, but ever so slightly pursed her lips. "Am I misunderstanding, or are you suggesting something illegal."

"It might edge over the line a bit."

She stood. "I'm sorry Mr. Smith. We're not interested."

"Wait a minute," I said. "Wasn't it WAM who firebombed the Golum Pro-Life office last year? And what about your counter-demonstration that turned into a riot a couple of months ago?"

"If you had done your homework, Mr. Smith, you would have found that Golum is in Missouri, outside our district. WAM's mandate is clear – we oppose violence. As for the riot, we didn't start that, nor do we approve of our members' involvement. I've made that clear to them, as I'm making it clear to you right now."

With that, she walked out. Vi and Sam rose. Sam said, "This way, please."

However, they didn't lead me to the exit. Instead, they escorted me to another office. Vi extracted a device from the desk drawer and began moving it all around me, a few inches from my body. It was when she scanned my chest that I first noticed something odd about her. She was a he. It just proves they *don't* all look alike. (Sorry, that joke might never come around again.) Anyway, I'm usually more observant, but in the heat of the action and my attempt to convince Shirley, I hadn't paid close attention.

"He's clear," she said. "No bugs."

Sam stood in front of me, her head slightly tilted. "Why don't we go outside?"

An ominous suggestion, but given her height and muscles, not as scary as refusing.

Once outside, we began walking slowly, me in the middle. "Okay, cupcake," Sam said, "Here's the thing. We volunteer for WAM part-time, but we also have our other interests. For instance, ever hear of Group Boudicca?"

"Uh, no. No, I don't believe I have."

"On the web, it's called a pantheist group. As usual, the web portrays it a tad incorrectly. You know, nature, wiccan, that sort of PR."

"So, you run it?"

She chuckled. "Run it? Oh, sweet cream, isn't anybody runs it. No manager or director stuff. We're all equal. And what do you think we call ourselves?"

I was completely in the dark, including where the whole conversation was going. "Boudicists?"

She glared for a few seconds, then realized I wasn't scoffing at her. She chuckled. "No, my little angel cake. We're all called *mistress warriors*. All equal. However, some of us take the title more seriously than others."

"Oh, Boudicca," I exclaimed, "usually known as Boadicea, the queen-warrior of the Iceni tribe. The one who almost defeated the Romans around 60 AD, but her army completely lacked discipline. *That* Boudicca."

Sam furrowed her brow. "Who wound you up?"

I shrugged. "I read history. Kind of a hobby." I turned to Vi. "Are you with the Boudiccas too?"

"No, no. I used to be in another group, but right now I'm just an affiliate."

I waited for her to fill in the blank.

"It's a motorcycle club...for special women."

I silently nodded.

"Chicks Sorta," she added.

"I understand. But what's the name of the group?"

"Chicks Sorta *is* the name of the group."

"Oh, sorry."

"You have to understand," she continued, "that any actions we take on behalf of Heather and this KED group would be off the books. Purely personal, no connection to WAM."

Finally, light. "Absolutely."

Sam said, "Me and Vi need to talk this over, then we'll meet again. A coffee shop, I think. Give us your info."

Afterward I drove home, thinking I had accomplished quite a lot. However, I've always had a cautious streak, a tendency to look for the loose bolt in any plan...or person. I checked online for Group Boudicca and Chicks Sorta. They were for real. Sam had been spot-on. Boudicca was listed as a pantheist group, and Chicks Sorta was indeed a motorcycle club. It had been created five years earlier for transgender and transvestite women. Vi was a welder for some company that made power systems.

Four days later, Sam called and we met the following Saturday. They were already seated at a corner table when I walked into Slurpy's Diner. The décor could be designated *Woodsy OCD*. The tables and chairs were plain glossy-coated wood, though thankfully, their seats were padded. The counter had about 10 stools, also wood, and the walls were painted in various wood tones. I figured the owner really liked wood. The mono-theme was partly relieved by the wall prints, thankfully not pictures of forests. I sat down on a chair opposite the two women.

"I assume you checked up on us," Sam said.

"And I assume you did the same," I replied.

Sam nodded. "So, let's finish getting acquainted, shall we? I'm Samantha Oakes. Sam for short."

"And I'm Vi Hu, short for Vivian."

I nodded.

"Formerly, Vincent, if you're wondering."

I was. "No, not at all."

Vi said, "We need you to tell us the details of this misogyny thing you mentioned."

I had decided to come clean. I figured I'd have to eventually, and I preferred they heard it from me instead of someone else, like John or Heather or some other member. I told them the truth.

They looked at one another. "And how is this an act of misogyny?" Sam asked.

"First, she never called him a name. She accused him of hypocrisy, really. Second, they would never have expelled a guy. I've seen plenty of arguments where guys accused other people – including Pete – of worse things, and not one ever got expelled. Never even a suggestion of banishment. And third, Pete's views are definitely retro."

"The problem," Vi began, "is that the outcome isn't someone losing their job or their property."

"There's no serious issue here," added Sam.

"Isn't there?" I asked. "Are you certain of that?"

Sam lifted her chin. "Okay, angel cake, what's the serious issue?"

"You know, Hitler never broke the law. He lawfully became chancellor and then changed the laws to turn a democracy into a dictatorship. Look at today's prime minister of Hungary, formerly a true democracy. His party captured a large enough majority to change their constitution. Today, he controls the courts, the newspapers, the civil service – all perfectly legal. He never broke the rules. He just changed them, and technically, the country's still called a democracy. And Poland's the same – basically, a dictatorship created by legally changing the laws. Do you see what I'm saying? Democracy, freedom can be destroyed anywhere if any side gets enough power to change the rules. That's what Pete's done." I suppose I'd become a bit too enthusiastic.

The women were silent for several seconds. Then Vi said, "But what does this have to do with misogyny?"

I quietly said, "Pete kicked Heather out because she's a woman. He couldn't get enough votes the first time around, because the majority understood that Heather hadn't done anything wrong. So, he gamed the system by flooding the membership with his buddies – people just like himself. Then he changed the rules so we can't ever put things back as they were. It's like state legislatures became majority Republican. What did they do? They used their majority to redraw voting districts to ensure they stay a majority forever. That's why abortion has become all but outlawed in several states. That's misogyny. And they've used their permanent majorities to pack the courts. What do you think is going to happen to abortion rights nationally?"

They were silent again, but I could see I had moved them.

Finally, Sam said, "At the university, I'm a professor of Black Studies. I know all about Jim Crow laws. They were constitutional because of the manner in which the Constitution was interpreted. So, I can relate." She nodded for a few seconds. "So, what is it you're suggesting to alleviate your situation – the action you described as 'a bit over the edge?'"

I felt I had to tie it all together better. "My little situation is a reflection of the big situations I just mentioned. They use the letter of the law to subvert the spirit of the law. If we can't stop them at the 'little' scale, how are we going to stop them at the big scale?"

"Yes. I get it. But how do we do that?" Sam persisted.

"Make them understand that they are vulnerable, that continuing their legalistic dictatorship will cost them."

"Specifically."

Damn! This gal couldn't be detoured. But then, I thought, that could also be a good thing. If I could get them started, they would stay on course until the job was done. I cleared my throat. "Well, they changed the KED rules, so we change society's rules. A few slashed tires, a few broken windows — no injuries or anything physical. Just a campaign of pain, so to speak."

Her eyebrows practically rolled over to the back of her head. "*That's* what you mean by 'edge over the line...a bit?'"

Vi smirked. "Campaign of Pain. C-O-P. Kind of ironic." She turned toward Sam. "I like that."

Sam stared at her, open-mouthed. "You're on board with this?"

Vi looked at her. "You know why I cut some distance between me and Chicks Sorta? The new leadership wanted to ride to rallies and fairs and do touristy things, instead of supporting protests and demonstrations. They were turning us into a social club. It rankled several of us, but the rest remained. I made up a story about working overtime, and backed halfway out."

I looked down at the table, then back at them. "Okay, look, I haven't been totally up front with you. There's something else." I recounted the PSers' new direction for KED, then laid out my feelings. "They're going to push for another Iraq or Afghanistan. That upset me even more than the misogyny. Your idea of war changes when you see your buddy loaded on a stretcher with one of his feet missing. Pete never even wore a uniform. What's worse, he's apparently making connections with other groups, trying to start some kind of a movement. If he succeeds, a lot of people are going to die. John thinks they won't succeed. But what if he's wrong? A lot of people could to die in some far away place."

Sam seemed to sag. "No, you haven't been straight with us. Misogyny wasn't your real reason, after all."

"The misogyny's real," I replied, "but getting people killed is realer."

She straightened a bit. "You should have been more honest at the beginning."

"If I'd gone to WAM with the problem of more wars, Shirley would have shined me on. WAM is about women's issues. I thought about veterans' organizations, but a lot of their members are still into the rah-rah mindset. One of them would have talked. Look, I'm sorry for not being up front, but I'm trying to keep body bags from coming home."

"Okay, okay. I get your passion," Sam said, "and I agree – the last thing we need is another war, but your approach – vandalism, destroying property, I don't know…"

Vi looked at her. "Ah, you *do* call yourselves *mistress warriors*, do you not? And Sam, he's right. This isn't your nice civilized classroom. This battlefield's in the real world. The bad guys are in charge – inside his group, and outside, too."

Sam pointed her fingertips toward me. "Then why doesn't sweet cheeks here do it himself?"

They both turned toward me.

"I'd be near the top of their suspect list. After the first couple of hits, they'd have eyes on me. Look, I went through plenty of fighting in Iraq and Afghanistan. I'd have no problem getting back in the game. But we've got to do it smart."

Sam looked at Vi, then back at me. "Excuse us."

They both walked outside. I watched them as they moved hands and pointed fingers, but I couldn't tell which way the seesaw was tilting. After a few minutes, they returned.

"Okay, cupcake," Sam said, "we're inclined to agree, with a half-dozen provisos, as the lawyers like to say."

Vi counted off on her fingers. "First, you got to have skin in the game, too. That means, you do the first one. Second, we have to see you doing that first one. Third, no injuries. No one gets physically hurt. Fourth, if any of us get caught, they do not – do not ever – involve the others' names. They declare they acted alone."

Sam nodded. "Even if it means slammer time."

"Fifth, if you do involve us or WAM, we get to break your ass."

"Right into the hospital," Sam added helpfully.

They paused as they looked at me. Stared, actually.

"And sixth?" I asked.

"I only got five fingers on my counting hand," Vi said. "The other one I use to flip people off. Five's enough."

I nodded. "Deal. Our next meeting is on the 25th. Here's the address." I wrote it down on a napkin. "I'll be slashing a couple of tires on Pete's car during break — around 7:30. Just park across the street."

Vi said, "You can use this if you want." She reached down and pulled a knife from a concealed ankle holster. It's various hooks and serrations were more intimidating than its main cutting edge. "If this is more than you can handle, I have a bowie knife."

"Thanks, but I have my own."

That afternoon I went out and bought a small stiletto.

***

The evening after the next KED meeting, the three of us met at Slurpy's.

"Okay, you passed the test," Sam said. "We'll need a list of all their meeting dates and all 18 members."

"Actually, 19, including Pete. I already copied them from John's list." I handed them the sheet of paper.

They looked at it. Vi nodded. "They're all fairly local. Shouldn't be a problem." Her smile seemed a trifle too confident. Sam's too. What was bothering me?

I spent the next few weeks with my usual routine — work, a few evenings at the gym, other evenings wrapped in my favorite chair with a book.

At the next meeting, I watched a crowd that had gathered around Pete. John joined me. "Looks like he's Mr. Popular, tonight."

"Not really. Notice who they are?"

He looked again, and saw they were the PSers. Showing his usual leadership, he immediately walked to them and made some inquiries. After a surprisingly long conversation, he returned. "Do you know anything about the vandalism?"

"Like the tires on Pete's car? Sure, we were both there."

"They remember you coming back from break after everyone else."

"Yeah. I was on the phone. So what?" I might have sounded a little too indignant. Pretending is not one of my natural talents. A thousand hours of drama school would be wasted on me.

"Look, Bob. We're friends, but I need to know. Did you slash Pete's tires?" Of course, he would ask. They don't make them any straighter and narrower than John.

"Of course not. Like I said, the phone call ran past the break. Why would I slash his tires?"

He just looked at me. I realized my question was silly. He certainly knew I was miffed at Pete. But then, my creative cells kicked in. "Heck, you'd have more reason than me. He took the chairmanship from you – hell, your whole organization." He remained silent. "What's this all about, anyway?" My question was sincere. I wanted to know what the PSers had told him.

"It seems that over the last week, the PSers have been the victims of vandalism."

"Really? Who?" My method acting was improving.

"All of them."

"All?" Suddenly, I no longer needed acting lessons. I had become a 'natural', my voice rising all by itself. I leaned in and spoke quietly. "What kind of vandalism?"

"Broken car windows, house windows, one house partially burned, a few..."

"BURNED? Jesus!" A few heads turned toward us.

"Yeah, and a couple of cars." He tilted his head. "You didn't have anything to do with this?"

"No, John. Nothing. This is the first time I've heard about it."

Okay, so it wasn't entirely true. But it was mostly true. I mean, maybe if it had been a couple of broken windows, or a few slashed tires, then yeah, that would be a complete lie. But all 19? And burning down houses? Setting cars on fire? Those were all new to me.

The PSers were glancing at us sideways. For the first time, I became aware of a piece missing from my plan. I too could become a target. I could be vandalized. Did any of them know my address? Of course. The PSers had three board members, all with full access to the membership list.

I decided it would be a good idea to spend the break outside. I could watch my car and appear casual while making a call.

"What the fuck did you guys do?" I whispered.

"Do? Why, sugar cube, I have no idea what you're talking about." It felt a little better that Sam was a worse actor than I, but then I realized she wasn't even trying.

"Look, I..."

"You know, I'm in the middle of something. Why don't we meet for dinner, say at six tomorrow? Slurpy's okay for you?"

"First I want..."

"SLURPY'S OKAY WITH YOU?"

I took a breath. "Yeah. Slurpy's sounds great."

She hung up, but I pretended to engage in conversation for another minute to keep an eye on my car. However, only a couple of PSers were outside, both at the entrance side-glancing me until I finally returned inside.

***

We had to wait about 10 minutes for a table, but I figured that was a good thing. The noise of the crowd would mask our conversation, just in case someone had put a private investigator on me. Was I paranoid? Perhaps not, but I was learning. Once the ritual was done – seats, drinks, food orders – I leaned in and began to say, "What the..."

"Cupcake, don't ever, ever, talk about our special business over the phone."

Vi nodded. "Somewhere between dumb and stupid. Maybe closer to stupid."

I nodded once. "Okay. Sorry about that. But still, what the hell were you two thinking?"

"Angel cake, you wanted us to do a job. We did it. And now you're complaining because...?"

Her obtuseness pushed me over the edge. "Well, miss chocolate, I mentioned slashed tires and broken windows, not burning down houses." I was curious how she liked nicknames slapped back at her.

Her eyebrows arched and the corners of her mouth smiled ever so slightly. "First, it was only one house."

Vi nodded. "One teeny little house. That's all."

"What about the two cars? What if their gas tanks had caught fire?"

They looked at each other, then back at me. "Of course the tanks caught fire," Vi said, eyebrows arched. "That was the idea. You *do* know they're filled with gas, I hope."

"Oh, and gas burns," Sam added casually.

I ignored the sarcasm to regain my composure. "Someone could have been killed. Remember we agreed – no deaths or injuries?"

Vi sipped on her coffee. "And no one got hurt. Our buddies carefully scouted out the targets. Sounds to me like 'mission accomplished'."

"As promised," Sam added. "But maybe I shouldn't call you *sugar cube* anymore. Sugar cubes are hard. How about *marshmallow*?"

"As in soft?" Vi asked her.

Sam nodded. "Uh, huh."

I was starting to feel like a straight man in an annoying comedy. "How about just using my name?"

Sam wrinkled her brow. "Bob? Too vanilla."

Vi shook her head as she reached for her coffee. "Especially with the "Smith" part. Way too vanilla."

My calmness floated away. "Maybe it is vanilla, but then I won't have to start calling you *Ding Dong*."

"Ouch!" Sam said, with a slight smile.

Vi looked at her, eyebrows raised. "Ouch, indeed. This marshmallow's got teeth."

Sam said, "Okay, BOB. So, what's the problem?"

"Look, the idea was to slowly turn up the heat. Let them realize the punishment could increase forever. Now you've gone all in at the start. You've..."

"Shot our wads?" Sam suggested.

"Yeah...pretty much."

"First, sug...Bob, we still have a lot of wad left. Second, if we slowly escalated, they would adapt – emotionally and practically. They'd get accustomed to the battle, and they'd start installing all sorts of surveillance devices. Maybe guards."

"And maybe John and I are going to need guards."

Vi arched her eyebrows as she looked down at her plate. "Already covered." When she looked at me, she noticed my confusion. "Chicks Sorta?"

"Relieved by the Boudiccans every other shift," Sam added.

My mouth must have fallen open for several seconds. "Wait. You have guards watching us?"

Sam nodded. "Uh, huh. You're high maintenance, Bobby boy."

Vi looked at her. "Definitely high maintenance."

Then they both cracked up.

"Seriously," Sam said, "retaliation is nothing new. We have a few surveillance people, but no, not nearly 24-7. So yeah, watch your back. We had some on your cars for a few nights. But honest, you wanted to take action..." She looked at Vi. "What did he call it?"

"'Abnormal procedures,' if I remember."

"Yeah. Abnormal procedures. And you didn't expect an abnormal risk?"

"I have to admit, I didn't think that far ahead."

Vi said, "Just so you understand, you need to be on your guard. And this first wave probably won't take us across the finish line. We'll likely need a couple more."

Sam leaned forward with an intense look. "You say you read a lot of history. Well, we Boudiccans have read about warriors, and we've learned one important thing. Don't start a fight without a total commitment. Otherwise, you strengthen the enemy."

Vi looked at me. "She means, like, 'What doesn't kill them makes them stronger.'"

Sam nodded. "Exactly like."

***

A few days later, I had a visit from detectives Carl Newton and Danielle Flynn. I had just gotten home from work, and I invited them inside. I offered them coffee, then tea, which they refused. It was difficult to determine if they were suspicious or just routinely pursuing names the PSers had provided. I had little trouble convincing them that defeat in a private discussion group would hardly be motivation for criminality. Also, it was my good luck to have been traveling for work on one of the evenings in question.

At the next meeting, a half dozen of the PSers were gone. I met my confederates the following week, and gave them the names of the dropouts. We had all agreed on the importance of PSers realizing that jumping ship would bring them relief. Two meetings later, all were gone except Pete. In a way, I had to admire his tenacity.

Then Gary showed up. He'd been gone six months, but it turned out that John had kept him on the rolls. Even paid his dues. That's loyalty for you.

Had I been loyal to John? That question still bothers me. I mean, I did lie to him, and committed acts that I knew he would never accept. On the other hand, I also got him back his organization, which is so important to him. So maybe it's a wash. And I'm proud that I did my part in possibly preventing some future war. There's no price tag big enough to cover that.

***

We celebrated at Horse and Dog, an upscale nightclub in the heart of the city. Thankfully, the three-piece band wore street clothes. I hate the phony bow-tie formality of most fancy nightclubs. Our round table was sized for four, which was perfect. Vi had invited her good friend, Keegan, who, we were told, was a sound mixer.

"What's a sound mixer?" I asked.

"Did you see *The One Against the Few*?"

"You mean the Sandra Cameron movie? No, I'm not into karate films. Too much fakery."

Keegan took another sip of her beer. She shrugged. "Fakery pays my rent. Anyway, someone has to decide how loud to make the karate chops."

The four-piece band began a smooth number.

I looked at Sam. "Let's not let the music go to waste."

She looked at me as I stood, then rose and walked with me to the dance area. Like most nightclubs, the dance floor was better lit than the eating area. Years earlier I had formulated the 'Bob principle' – the higher the prices, the dimmer the lighting. Most of the dance floor light emanated from the stage, which formed the flat part of the horseshoe-shaped area, the remainder surrounded by dining tables.

Despite her height, I found myself staring into Sam's eyes as both of us effortlessly moved in harmony. Her whole face seemed to glow.

"I love this sung in Italian," she said.

"Which singer?"

"Why, Bocelli, of course."

"Bocelli is great, but I prefer Josh Grobin. But, why are they playing *Time to Say Goodbye*, anyway?"

"Good point." She grinned. "Maybe they're getting ready to kick us out of here."

When the tempo went upbeat, we separated and our movements continued to complement each other's. That's when I first realized how well we got along, both on and off the dance floor – even when we were gibing at each other.

When we returned to the table, she said, "Surprise! Bob here can dance."

"So can you."

She wrinkled her brow and touched her breastbone with her fingers. "Well, of course. I'm Black."

The other two gals chuckled.

I shook my head. "You're something else, Sam."

She smiled. "Seriously, where did you learn to move so well?"

"Maybe I'm a natural. Or maybe it's from years of jiu-jitsu."

"Wait," Vi said. "You know jiu-jitsu?"

"Yeah. Japanese style. Been studying it for 11 years."

"Then how come we were able to pin you up against a wall at the WAM center?"

"Because I let you." To her skeptical expression, I replied, "Well, I didn't go to WAM for a fight. I wanted your help." I looked at Sam. "Besides, I kind of enjoyed it." I hesitated before saying, "We should do it again sometime."

She stared at me. Finally, she said, "I'm still getting over that HookEm guy."

Keegan said, "You're on HookEm? The dating site?"

"Uh, huh. Professor, my ass."

Vi laughed. "Is that what he said?"

"What was he, really?" Keegan asked.

"Unemployed."

We all chuckled.

I decided to ask. "They're having a Tulip festival next weekend at International Park. You want to go?"

She looked at me for several seconds. "You suggesting a date?"

"Or two."

She casually took another bite of her salad. Without looking at me, she said, "You say you read a lot of history?"

"I do."

She turned her head and, appearing casual, said, "How much you know about Black History?"

Oops. She had me there. "Not much. History is as long and wide as the entire human story. Nobody can explore it all." It might have come out a bit like excuse-making.

"Then, let's make a deal. You enroll in one of my classes at the university, and we can date."

"A student dating his teacher? Heck, I haven't done that since high school."

Her eyes widened. Then she saw Vi and Keegan laughing. She shook her head, and took another bite of her salad. She looked back at me, her head tilted slightly. "You know what I admire about you?"

"My height?"

She suppressed a grin, which just made her even more attractive. "No, that would be number two. You have a good sense of humor. You like to gibe others, but you also enjoy getting it back."

"You know what I admire about you. Samantha Oakes?"

She smiled, enjoying the game. "My height?"

"And just about everything else." I looked at her and nodded. "I think I'm going to enjoy your class."

What the Shadows Say